Praise for Morning Shade Mystery #3:
A Case of Nosy Neighbors

"Lori Copeland's books are a true gift. Her wonderfully drawn characters shine a light on the often neglected aspects of God's character—His joy, hope, optimism, and humor. God wants His children to laugh, and Lori helps us do just that. Her books touch our hearts and encourage our spirits. Bless her!"
—***Catherine Palmer,*** author of *Wild Heather*

Praise for Morning Shade Mystery #2:
A Case of Crooked Letters

"Curl up in your favorite chair and settle back for another visit to Morning Shade, where Maude, Stella, and CeeCee have stumbled across another entertaining and heartwarming adventure. If you like Lori Copeland, you'll love this peek into a small-town writer's life and heart!"
—***Angela Hunt,*** author of *The Debt*

"Lori Copeland's unique voice: humorous, warm, friendly, and sometimes even a little sarcastic, shines to its fullest in *Crooked Letters.* I can always count on Lori to keep me turning pages. The characters inhabiting the town of Morning Shade and in particular, the home of struggling, aging novelist Maude Diamond, are truly people you'll want to revisit again and again. . . . Another winner from this terrific author's pen."
—***Lisa Samson,*** author of *The Church Ladies* and *The Living End*

"Lori Copeland has been one of my favorite authors for a long time, and her new book is Copeland at her best with the rich characterization she's always been known for as well as being laugh-out-loud funny. Copeland's new tale proves the only way to get through some of the complexities of family relationships is with a generous dollop of wry humor. If there's such a thing as grandma lit, this is it."
—***Colleen Coble,*** author of *Without a Trace*

"From the opening scene I was hooked by the refreshing humor and delightful characters in Lori Copeland's funny, cozy *A Case of Crooked Letters.* Readers will laugh at the townspeople and their idiosyncrasies in a don't-want-to-put-it-down novel."
—***Gail Gaymer Martin,*** author of *Loving Care*

Praise for Morning Shade Mystery #1: *A Case of Bad Taste*

"A delightful tale of simple life in a small town—with a surprise ending. . . . *A Case of Bad Taste* is a fun read with a sweet reminder of God's call on believers' lives."
—Laurie Copeland, *Christian Retailing*

A Case of Nosy Neighbors

LORI * COPELAND

Author of Brides of the West

Tyndale House Publishers, Inc.
Wheaton, Illinois

Visit Tyndale's exciting Web site at www.tyndale.com

Edited by Kathryn S. Olson

Designed by Alyssa Force

Series designed by Julie Chen

Published in association with the literary agency of Alive Communications, Inc., 7680 Goddard Street, Suite 200, Colorado Springs, CO 80920.

Library of Congress Cataloging-in-Publication Data

Copeland, Lori.
A case of nosy neighbors / Lori Copeland.
p. cm — (Morning shade mysteries ; #3)
ISBN 0-8423-7117-6 (sc)
I. Title.
PS3553.O6336C378 2004
813'.54—dc22 2004004787

Printed in the United States of America

10 09 08 07 06 05 04
9 8 7 6 5 4 3 2 1

January in Morning Shade was as cold as a pawnbroker's smile. It was just a fact; too bad I couldn't say the same for City Hall. Edgar Burlow had the thermostat cranked so high tonight you could boil coffee on Mayor Thurvis Throckmorton's forehead. Thurvis was a gentleman of the Old South, a Colonel Sanders without the fried chicken. Now his mane of white hair was wilting in the heat, and his mustache and goatee drooped with the insufferable temperature.

I could identify with that. At sixty—coming up on sixty-one, I often have my own 'personal summers.' As an author I'd created many a miserable condition in my mystery novels, but none topped tonight.

Thurvis tried to bring order to the overcrowded room. "People! People!" He pounded a gavel on the wooden podium. "Majority rules!"

"But, your honor!" Ralph Henderson sounded agitated. *"No* smoking? In Morning Shade—anywhere—anytime?" He shook his head. "Brutal."

"It'll save your life," Midge Grainer predicted.

I fanned myself with a folded agenda, wishing that Midge

would sit down and we could get on with the meeting. Thurvis was right: majority rules. Like it or lump it.

"Can't say that I'm overly fond of the law myself," the mayor grumbled.

It was a well-known fact Thurvis enjoyed his imported Montecristo Cuban cigars, and far be it from me to point out that every man, woman, and teenager in this room would benefit from a no-smoking ordinance, but I knew the new rule would be about as popular in Morning Shade as a porcupine at a balloon festival.

Stella, my mother-in-law, shifted in her folding chair. "Just get on with it, Thurvis. I'm burning up."

Mopping his brow, Thurvis sent a pleading look in Edgar's direction. "Can you do something about that thermostat?"

Edgar got up and shuffled to the opposite wall. Seconds later the fan clicked off. I for one was only too happy for a breath of air. I was half cooked myself.

Thurvis glanced at his notes. "Effective January 15 there will be no smoking in Morning Shade's city limits. Any person or persons found violating the city ordinance will be fined two hundred and fifty dollars." He whacked the gavel on the podium. "Meeting adjourned!"

"Such an uproar," Stella complained when we filed out of the overheated building. Bitter cold temperatures stung my face, and I quickly drew my coat collar up closer. Unless I missed my guess, this winter would break all records.

"Evening, Maude."

I giggled then caught my adolescent behavior and nodded at Sherman Winters. What *was* it about the town doctor that sent my pulse into overdrive?

Maude Diamond! Herb was barely cold in his grave—

Well, that wasn't entirely true. Herb had been dead nineteen months. If he wasn't cold yet something was dreadfully wrong.

I paused on the bottom step of City Hall and let Stella move ahead of me. I knew I was inviting a few minutes alone with the handsome doctor, but I also knew that I didn't want to be that apparent about my attraction—not that there was an attraction, but there could have been twenty years ago. Now I was way past girlish infatuations.

Sherman approached, hat in hand. My gaze skimmed his cashmere, caramel-colored overcoat, and I thought how much I appreciated a man with style. Herb had been neat, but not particularly fashionable. My husband had preferred down jackets to cashmere overcoats, and if I had ever seen him wearing anything other than a ball cap on his head, I couldn't recall the instance.

We stood on the bottom step, cold air sweeping around us. Both of us seemed to be stalling for time. I racked my brain for anything clever to say but what came out was anything but clever. "Hot in there, wasn't it?"

Sherm smiled. "Temperature-wise, or subject-wise?"

We both laughed, breaking the strained state. I didn't understand why our conversation would be forced. We'd known each other for years—I'd been close friends with Sherm's wife, Cheryl, before she died. "The smoking ban isn't going to be the most popular law on the books," I conceded.

"I'll be interested to see who keeps it. Wouldn't be surprised if Thurvis Throckmorton won't turn out to be the biggest offender of the bunch."

"Oh, Hilda will keep him in line," I predicted. The wind stung my cheeks; from the way the tip of my nose felt I knew it was as red as a cherry. My breath rose in vapory trails. Stella had reached my Buick, and she'd be leaning on the horn if she could get inside.

"How's the wrist?"

I lifted my gloved hand and stared at the object of discussion. For weeks now my left wrist had hurt, and my thumb and first two fingers on the hand had gone numb. When I'd called Sherm and told him that I thought I might be having a heart attack, he took my concerns seriously, but after preliminary tests he'd diagnosed the problem as carpal tunnel syndrome.

"Surprised you lasted this long," he'd teased. "All that typing you do." He went on to explain that the problem resulted when fluid or tight tendons press on the nerve within the carpal tunnel of the wrist. Repetitive motion causes the condition. Surgery usually alleviates the condition.

I'd smiled, but I wasn't too happy about the prospect of an operation.

"Unless it gets a lot worse I don't want to have surgery," I'd told him.

"It will get worse," he'd promised. "Some carpal tunnel cases can be treated with therapy, but your case is much too advanced."

Sherm's baritone drew me back to the present. "Looks like Stella's ready to go."

I nodded, spotting my eighty-seven-year-old mother-in-law huddled against the wind. I could imagine what was going on in her mind right now. Herb was her son, and I'm certain she wouldn't approve of this innocent conversation. "Yes—she's bored these days. No mystery to work on."

"She loves to solve crime, doesn't she?"

Morning Shade had such little crime that when something unexpected came up, Stella was in her element.

"She looks like she's getting impatient. I'd better be going."

We smiled and parted company. I had the oddest feeling Sherm would have lingered longer, and I wondered why I hadn't simply handed Stella the car keys earlier and bought myself a little time.

No fool like an old fool. The uninvited thought popped into mind while I carefully picked my way along the slippery walk. Icy patches littered the flagstones. I couldn't wait to get into the car and jack up the heat.

I drove home automatically, barely listening to Stella complaining about Hilda Throckmorton and how the mayor's wife should never wear orange. Personally, I didn't think any woman should wear orange, but that's just my preference. I knew Stella and Hilda had a long-running personality clash. But I did silently admit that tonight Hilda had strongly resembled an overripe tangerine in that unmerciful getup she was wearing.

What *was* the woman thinking?

* * *

"Mom—" CeeCee Tamaris, my daughter, peered over the rim of her cup when I attempted to pick up a piece of toast the next morning and failed—"you can't just ignore carpal tunnel. Your condition isn't going to get any better until you have the surgery."

I gave up on the toast, pushing the plate aside. "I can't just have surgery, Cee." Sometimes my daughter could be downright impractical. When her husband, Jake, died, she'd moved in with me and Stella, and I couldn't say she'd changed much in the past two years. She could be both sweet and overdramatic at times. "Do you know how long I'd be out of commission?"

CeeCee didn't understand the implications of my being incapacitated for four to six weeks. I'd get so far behind in my writing that I'd never see light at the end of the tunnel.

She drained her coffee cup and set it on the table. "Whatever, but I predict you're not going to have a choice before long." She stood and dropped a kiss on the crown of my head. "Gotta run. Have a nice day."

Usually I'm still in bed when CeeCee leaves for work. I don't keep postal hours. But this morning the numbness and tingling in my thumb and forefinger had wakened me around three. I hadn't been able to go back to sleep. I knew Cee was right; the condition wasn't going to go away until I did something about it.

When Stella came downstairs around eight-thirty, I was dressed and had already called Sherm's office. The receptionist said they could see me at nine o'clock.

"Want me to drop you off at the Citgo on my way?" I picked up my purse and tucked in a couple of fresh tissues, thinking that Sherm could surely give me something for relief until I finished my work-in-progress.

"Nope, I'm gonna walk this morning."

"It's seventeen degrees out there," I warned.

"So? These old lungs can't get any worse; besides, exercise is good for me."

"Breaking a leg—or worse—at eighty-seven isn't good for you."

Stella slipped her arms into her heavy coat. "How long do you think I'm going to last?"

"Much longer than you do," I bantered. My mother-in-law was certain she was on her last leg. "One foot on an ice cube, the other on a banana peel," she'd often quip. I was thankful that Stella's health far surpassed her expectations.

I heard the front door close and Stella shout at one of the neighbor's dogs. The spotted terrier was always dragging up something dead and depositing the carcass on our front porch. It wasn't so bad in the winter, but it could be real irritating to clean up the mess in the summer.

Apparently the canine had dropped a dead skunk on the porch and Stella was putting up more stink than the victim.

Shaking my head, I slipped into my coat and picked up the car keys from the hall table. A moment later I opened the back door and went down like a rifle shot.

Dazed, I listened to my body hitting every wooden step—count them: one-two-three. I landed at the bottom, spread-eagle, staring up into a slate-colored sky. My ankle ached like blue blazes.

The back door flew open and Stella stuck her head out. "Maude?"

"Here," I answered feebly. "I thought you'd gone." I groaned, trying to rock upright.

"I came back to get the dustpan—there's a dead skunk on the front porch." She watched my vain struggles to get to my feet. "Are you hurt?"

"Yes I'm *hurt,*" I snapped. Surely she didn't think I could fall down three steps and still be grinning. I peered at my boot, wondering if a bone was poking through. I could feel the flesh starting to swell. "Don't come down!" I warned when I saw Stella about to risk the stairs. "There's black ice on the top step."

I rocked a couple of times and managed to get upright, wondering if I'd broken a bone. Or two. I ripped off my left glove with my teeth and probed my tender, leather-encased right foot. *Ow!*

"I'll get help," Stella said.

"Call an ambulance." I knew without even looking something was broken or at least severely sprained. Both wrists throbbed from my attempts to arrest the fall. Stella wouldn't be able to help me, and Maury Peacock was the nearest neighbor.

"9-1-1?" Stella queried.

"Whatever." I groaned. "Tell them to hurry." If I didn't die from pain, hypothermia was sure to finish me off.

* * *

Within the hour, paramedics burst through Shiloh General Hospital's double emergency-room doors with me strapped to a gurney. Stella briskly followed behind the cart.

"I'll phone CeeCee. Don't you worry—does it hurt?"

"Don't bother Cee." I bit back excruciating pain. "It's just a sprain." At least that's what I was praying for. My whole left hand had gone numb, and my right foot felt like someone had doused it with gas and lit a match to it.

By the time they wheeled me into a cubicle and the boot was off, I knew I was in big trouble. Throbbing flesh—now the size of a tennis ball, spilled over my anklet.

"Bet that's painful," the nurse soothed.

You think?

It seemed like no time at all before Sherm pulled back the curtain, concern etched on his handsome features. "Maude?" His eyes caught my swelling ankle. "What's going on?"

I was just plain humiliated. "I feel so stupid." I managed to meet his concerned gaze, silhouetted against the harsh overhead light. "Stepped out the back door and hit black ice and down I went."

By now he was examining the ankle, gently probing the tender flesh. "That hurt?"

My wolf howl sufficed.

He nodded at the nurse. "Get some pictures."

In the time I took to mentally reject this whole idea, I had been wheeled away and stuck beneath an X-ray machine. The man wearing a lead apron left the room, and I heard the machine whirl. It bothered me that he'd left—and I was still in the room.

Later, back in the emergency-room cubicle, Sherm walked in, grim faced. "You've broken the metatarsal of your right foot."

That sounded serious though I didn't have the faintest notion what it meant. I shut my eyes, fighting off despair. "Exactly what does that mean in laymen's terms? Surgery?"

CeeCee came in about the time I got the news. "Mom?" She made a beeline for the gurney and engulfed me in a zealous hug.

"I'm fine." I feebly patted my daughter's arm. "Really. I can barely feel it."

"I knew I should have salted those steps last night, but I fell asleep—"

"No one's to blame," I soothed. "I should have thought of it, but by the time I got home from the town meeting I was too tired to go out to the garage and get the salt." Those wooden back steps froze over with the slightest mist.

"I'm going to put you in a cast," Sherm said. "You're not to put any weight on the injured foot. The only exception is the shower. They'll be taking you to surgery in a few minutes."

Great. I'd look like a one-legged flamingo. "How long?" I whispered, dreading the answer.

"Any minute—"

Stella leaned closer. "Sherman, how long will it take for the broken bones to heal?"

"That's hard to say, but I wouldn't count on anything less than eight to nine weeks."

"Look at this way, Maude," Stella piped up. "You must not have osteoporosis or you'd have broken every bone in your body."

Thank God for small comforts.

"Don't worry, Mom." CeeCee hovered overhead. "I'll help any way I can."

"What about the community service? Who's going to drive Stella to Shiloh every morning?"

Because of the last Morning Shade mystery—folly—I, along with Stella, Hargus Conley, Simon Bench, and Duella Denson, had been implicated and volunteered for twenty hours of hospital community service every week. I closed my eyes and took a deep breath, realizing how ungrateful I sounded. Agony can do that to a person, and I'm sure the judge would make a special dispensation in this case. "I'm sorry. I know it could be worse. I could have broken my wrists. At least I can still work."

"Says who?"

I opened my eyes to meet Sherm's. "What's that supposed to mean?"

"That carpal tunnel surgery is going to keep you incapacitated about the same length of time as this break."

I suddenly remembered today's nine o'clock doctor's appointment in Sherm's office. "I was hoping you'd be able to give me something for the pain."

"The only thing I can offer is the name of a good bone-and-joint surgeon."

I didn't like the no-nonsense expression on his face.

When he bent closer, I got a whiff of aftershave, something manly and musky. "May I make a suggestion as your friend and doctor?"

"Which would be?" I knew what he was going to say: have the surgery.

"Since you're going to be out of commission for a few weeks anyway, why not have the carpal tunnel surgery now?"

"You can't be serious."

"I am. Kill two birds with one stone."

"Why not, Mom?" CeeCee hovered over me. "Me and Grandma will help; won't we, Grandma?"

Why not indeed? I thought. *Because of the pain!*

Stella edged closer to the gurney. "I'll do anything you ask. It's winter—not much going on. I'm not working on a case right now."

"I don't know—I can't imagine being so helpless."

"We're all helpless, Maude." Sherm patted my hand. "But with God we can do all things."

I believe in God, but I wondered if I could survive both carpal tunnel surgery *and* a broken bone.

CeeCee clasped my hand. "Honest, Mom. We can do this. You can dictate your work, and I'll type it into the computer every night. I promise I won't let you get behind in your writing schedule."

"I'll cook and take care of the house," Stella offered. "I'm not helpless."

"I'll talk to the surgeon and see if we can't get this all done and over quickly," Sherm promised.

Easy for you three to say; I'll be the invalid.

The curtains parted and two attendants appeared to whisk me off. I caught a brief glimpse of the large, overhead, emergency-room clock and marveled that not an hour and a half ago my world had been perfectly normal. The two male attendants smiled. One tucked the blanket around me more securely. "Ready to go?"

"Ready as I'll get," I admitted, still wary of the plan.

Could I make it through nine weeks with my left hand swathed in gauze and a cast on my right foot?

I sighed, and my eyes silently assured Stella and Cee that I would be fine.

Face it, Maude. You're officially out of commission.

CeeCee exited the emergency room, holding tight to Stella's arm. The last thing they needed was another casualty.

"Don't worry, Grandma. We'll figure out how to get you to Shiloh three times a week."

"Oh, that's all right. I'll drive myself." She wiggled out of CeeCee's hold.

CeeCee stopped dead still. "I . . . don't think that's a good idea."

"Why not?" Stella paused at the exit and buttoned her coat. "I'm not helpless."

"I know you're not, but you haven't driven in a long time, and I'm sure Mom wouldn't want—"

"Want, schmant. Maude's in no condition to worry about me." She sniffed. "*What* is that revolting smell?"

"I don't know." CeeCee winced. "It's in all hospitals, but I've never been able to identify it."

"Smells like death."

"Now how would you know what death smells like?" CeeCee took hold of her arm again and led her out the double doors. Cold wind whipped skiffs of snow across the parking lot. "Careful, Grandma. It might be slick."

"I'm not helpless."

"I know you're not."

"I can drive to Shiloh. I'm not a baby, you know. And I can take Duella and Simon with me."

"I know. We'll talk about it later."

"You're thinking Hargus will drive us, but Hargus has already said he plans to stay overnight the days he does community service. He's got some worthless friends there. Stock-car buddies, you know."

"We'll see what Mom says."

"She'll say no, but I'm going to anyway. I'm not helpless."

They were still arguing when CeeCee pulled out of the parking lot.

Captain nuzzled me awake later that week. That cat has an internal alarm when it comes to feeding, and it's never one millisecond off. I don't even have to look at the clock to check the time. I know what time it is: six-thirty in the morning and time to feed the cat.

I hauled my aging frame, which is feeling older every day, from the sack and pulled on last year's fleece robe. Too bad Santa hadn't seen fit to bring me a new one. That's probably the only way I'll get a replacement.

It wasn't easy getting around with a cast on my foot and a bandaged left wrist. CeeCee wanted to fix me a bed downstairs, but I'm too stubborn for my own good. I managed to hop downstairs and to the kitchen without breaking anything else. Walking on a level surface was easier, although I didn't think I'd ever get used to manuevering on the crutches Sherm had given me.

I fed the cat and started the coffee before clumping out to get the morning paper. Stella would have a snit fit if she didn't have the daily obituary column to brighten her day. Why she gets so much fun out of reading about area deaths is beyond me. You'd think at her age that's the last thing she would be interested in. Maybe she's just relieved to find her name not listed. The paper was on the porch for a wonder, and I managed to pick it up without falling.

By the time I had slices of smoky ham sizzling in the skillet and biscuits browning in the oven, Stella was downstairs with her hair sticking out every which way and minus her lower plate. I'd had trouble getting the can of biscuits open, but it's amazing what a determined woman in a bad temper can accomplish.

She sat down at the table and reached for the paper. "Is that ham I smell?"

"Afraid so."

"That's not a healthy breakfast."

"Why do you care? You're always saying it's too late for you to eat healthy. I'd think you'd enjoy a nice slice of fried ham. It's lean."

"I would enjoy ham if I could find my teeth, but I'm thinking of you and CeeCee. You're young yet. Should be eating heart smart."

"I eat heart smart most of the time, thank you, but this morning I'm hungry." You only get one ride on the merry-go-round. Might as well enjoy it where food is concerned.

"Well, something's going to get us in the long run." Stella shook out the paper. "Pansy's on that grapefruit diet. Frances says she hasn't lost any weight, but all that acid has gone to her tongue. I say if you had Hargus for a son you could be forgiven for being a little outspoken sometimes."

"That would do it," I agreed. Although when it came to being outspoken, no one could beat Stella. She'd been known to throw a few verbal punches.

"Seems like diets are the in thing these days," Stella said. "Even Hilda Throckmorton is on one."

"What diet is Hilda trying?" I'd have to admit she had a few surplus pounds it wouldn't hurt to lose.

"Don't believe I've heard her say. Pansy says she's probably on two diets 'cause one wouldn't give her enough to eat."

"Stella! That's mean."

"That's what I said, but Pansy said truth is truth and we could take it or leave it."

"It sounds like Pansy *is* getting a little astringent," I said.

"She is, but she'll get over it. I think she's mad that Hargus went off to Florida, to one of those races this weekend, instead of taking her out to dinner, but shoot, you know that boy doesn't have any sense when there's a race car involved. Don't have *much* anytime." Stella grinned. "I'm on a seafood diet myself; if I see it, I eat it."

I took the biscuits out of the oven, which wasn't all that easy using one hand, and reached in the refrigerator for the butter and plum jelly.

Stella looked up from the paper. "You know, that no-smoking ordinance the city council passed isn't going over well. Particularly with the men. They're taking it real hard."

"How so?"

"Well, Vinny Trueblood, Hubert Mills, and Walt Richards all staged a smoke-in on Main Street at high noon yesterday. Hargus arrested all three. They got slapped with hefty fines, and they sure are angry."

"I'd think so." A smoke-in? And at high noon on Main Street? Shades of Gary Cooper, and the Old West.

"You know the ban was Hilda's idea. She thinks we have to keep up with big-city ideas. Ash Flat passed a no-smoking ordinance last month, so we have to have one too."

"Well, smoking is bad for you. Brings about all kinds of physical ailments."

"I *know* that, but I'll tell you what. I'm all for obeying the law, and since I don't smoke, this one won't bother me; but does it seem to you that whenever you find something you enjoy doing, someone is trying to pass a law to keep you from doing it?"

"That's life, Stella."

"No, that's what comes from people needing to get a life. Do you know Bill Rickets?"

"Can't say that I do." I poured juice and hopped around Captain. CeeCee's poodles were sitting beside their dishes, waiting to be fed, and the macaws were beginning to stir. The red one scratched absently, keeping an eye on the cat.

"Ninety-three. Arrested him over in Ash Flat for robbing the bank."

"He did *what?*"

"Handed the teller an envelope and told her to fill 'er up."

"My stars. They arrested him?"

"Yep. At the stoplight. He rode away on his lawn mower. Said he was bored. Thought he'd stir up some excitement and pick up a little extra cash at the same time. He's not hitting on all cylinders, you know. Hasn't been for years."

I shook my head. "I don't know what this world is coming to."

CeeCee walked into the kitchen and dumped food in the poodles' dishes. Captain, who had finished his breakfast, growled, so she dribbled a handful for him. He hunkered over his bowl, shoulders hunched and eyes narrowed to a slit, as if he thought we might want a bite.

"Guess what," CeeCee chirped. "There's a new kennel in

town. I've not met the owner yet, but I've seen him, and he is one good-looking dude. His name's Rick Materi. And he's on my mail route. Talk about luck."

I perked up. A new man in town? Cee needed a new interest in her life right now. She was finally getting over the death of her husband, Jake Tamaris, football hero and number-one jerk. I hoped this Rick person would be someone she might be interested in. The man owned a kennel.

My daughter brought home every animal she could find. This could be a match made in heaven.

CeeCee drove her route, conscious of a growing anticipation as she approached Rick Materi's rural box. With a smidgeon of luck, he would be out in the yard. She checked his mail. *Dogs' Life* magazine. Ditto on *Cat Fancy.* Well, you could expect those for a kennel.

A Lands' End catalog and an Edward Hamilton's bargain books catalog. So was he a reader? Interesting. She wondered what he read. At least she'd have a starting point to begin a conversation.

She thumbed through his stack. Nothing to suggest a woman lived there. One good thing about delivering mail: you could learn a lot about the people on your route by the sort of items filling their mailboxes.

She was in luck. Rick was not only in his yard but leaning on the mailbox waiting for her. She pulled to a stop and lowered the window to hand him his mail.

He reached for it, smiling. "Hello, there, pretty lady."

CeeCee grinned. "Hello to you, too. How's the kennel coming along?"

"It's coming. Stop by sometime and I'll give you a guided tour." A charming dimple winked in his right cheek.

"I'll look forward to that." Boy, would she ever!

"It's a date then."

Her grin widened. "It's a date."

She drove away, feeling like singing. He was even better-looking up close than he was from a distance, and nice to boot. The dimple was a killer. She had a hunch this was the start of something that had been missing in her life for a long time. She hadn't wanted another man after Jake. Feeling betrayed, she had withdrawn into a shell where men were concerned, which hadn't been all that difficult, since Gary Hendricks was the only man in town who had shown any interest in her, and she wouldn't accompany that jokester to a dogfight.

When she stopped at Hubert Mills's box, she noticed she couldn't stop grinning. Things were definitely looking up.

* * *

Stella walked into the Living Truth Community Hall for her kitchen-committee meeting. How had she allowed herself to get talked into serving on another committee? After chairing the spaghetti dinner she had sworn off committees. She was particularly leery of anything that Hilda Throckmorton was a member of, which pretty well ruled out anything going on in the church or town. Hilda cut a wide swath.

Pansy Conley had saved Stella a seat next to her. Frances, on the other side, removed her handbag from the empty seat and Stella slid into it, running a practiced eye over the women perched on metal folding chairs like blackbirds on telephone poles. Hilda, naturally, stood behind the speaker's stand. Her rightful place. When she got to heaven, St. Peter had better have the podium ready, because Hilda would expect to hold committee meetings on the best way to polish the pearly gates.

"Meeting come to order," Hilda chirped. "We have some very important topics to discuss today. First I want to suggest that we buy a new coffeepot. The old thing we're using is a disgrace. Now, I have priced new ones, and I'd like to suggest a Krups AromaControl coffeemaker with thermal carafe."

Stella held up her hand. "I think a KitchenAid would be better."

Hilda frowned. "Really, Stella, I use a Krups, and the mayor and I find it extremely satisfactory. Next on the agenda: do we or don't we want to hold a ladies' tea next month? Now, I think a tea is very genteel. We could prepare miniature sandwiches and petit fours. I've already written down the menu and thought about a theme; perhaps we could call it the Ladies' Garden Tea."

Stella spoke up again. "What garden's it going to be in?"

Hilda pressed her lips into a thin line. "Well, not in a *real* garden, of course, although that would be lovely. But it's a bit early for outdoor activities. It's just that I think the Ladies' Garden Tea is a suitable name."

"About as suitable as A Night under the Stars for a spaghetti supper in midwinter," Stella muttered, but her remark didn't carry enough to be overheard. No use to object. Hilda would bust a gusset if anyone interfered with her plans. The remainder of the meeting passed without further interruptions, and Hilda sailed triumphantly along, getting her own way on everything.

As usual.

The women adjourned for cookies and punch, made from Hilda's grandmother's recipe, of course.

Pansy poked Stella. "Your punch is better."

Stella nodded in agreement. There was enough lemon juice in Hilda's recipe to eat the enamel right off your teeth, even if your teeth were store-bought and hurting like hers were. She couldn't wait to get home and take them out.

Hilda was still holding the floor during the social time. "I bought two of the most *precious* dogs last night. You wouldn't *believe* how beautiful they are! Those little darlin's have just stolen my whittle heart."

Stella mimicked sticking her finger down her throat. Pansy smothered a laugh in her hanky.

"What breed?" Minnie Draper asked. "I'd like to get a little dog, maybe a Scotty or an Irish terrier."

"Oh, mine are large dogs. I prefer a dog that can go for walks with you, not something I have to carry back. One is a French poodle, and the other is a mastiff."

Yep, Stella thought. *Those could be big dogs, very big*. But then someone Hilda's size needed a dog to match.

"What are their names?" Frances asked. Stella knew the retired schoolteacher was always interested in names. Frances remembered the name of every child she ever taught, and all of their parents, aunts, uncles, and distant cousins. Made her kind of boring sometimes, Stella thought, and then felt guilty. Frances was a dear.

Hilda primed her lips and rolled her eyes. "Well, I wanted to choose dignified names, but Thurvis isn't as enthusiastic about pets as I am, so when he kicked up such a fuss I gave in and let him name them."

"What did he choose?" Stella smelled blood. From the look on her face, Hilda didn't want to talk about this, so talk she must. "I'll bet the mayor came up with some dandies."

Thurvis Throckmorton spent a lot of time in his office since he took over as mayor, and unkind people hinted it was the only place he could go to get away from Hilda. Thurvis was good enough at the job, though like Hargus Conley, he didn't do much. He held the title of mayor of Morning Shade, and he listened to people complain, though he seldom acted on anything. A do-nothing lawman and a do-nothing mayor. Stella snorted. Pity she didn't have the job; she'd straighten out people, and she was just the lady who could do it.

Hilda had hesitated long enough that Stella thought she wasn't going to answer, but she finally raised her eyebrows and said, "My husband was a big fan of ventriloquist Edgar Bergen's dummy, so he named them . . . appropriately."

"He named them Charlie and McCarthy?" Stella asked.

Hilda twitched. "He named the poodle Mortimer, and the mastiff Snerd."

"Fine names," Stella said. Inside she was busting a gut. Mortimer and Snerd! She'd have given a dollar to see the look on Hilda's face when her "babies" were named. Trust Thurvis to do something goofy like that, but considering the way Hilda bossed him around, maybe he did it on purpose to get back at her.

Judging from the pained expression on Hilda's face, he'd hit a home run.

* * *

Stella hit the Citgo early next morning, craving her cup of latte. Pity how a soul can get addicted to the stuff—*snap*—that quickly. Other regulars were already there, chattering among themselves.

"Guess what happened last night?" Pansy said as soon as Stella sat down.

"What? Hargus overdose on Chocolate Cow?"

Pansy made a face. "Be serious, Stella. This is important. We have a *Peeping Tom.*"

Stella sat up straighter. "Get outta here. Where did he peep?" Adrenalin rushed.

"Helen Brewer's house. Scared her into a fit."

"What kind of fit?" Stella asked. This was important. Who in Morning Shade would go around looking in windows? Nothing like this had happened before—not here in Morning Shade anyway.

"I don't *know* what kind of fit." Pansy sounded exasperated. "But Hargus said she was so scared she could barely talk. He thought she wasn't going to let him in the house. Took a while to calm her down so she could tell him what happened."

Frances shuddered. "I can't bear the thought of someone peeping in my window. It's a violation of privacy."

"Among other things," Stella agreed absently. As soon as she could get away without rousing suspicion, she would go by Helen's and get the lowdown. Hargus couldn't catch a Peeping Tom if his life depended on it. He'd need her help.

Thirty minutes later and out of breath Stella knocked on Helen's door. She was surprised to see the curtain over the nearby window being cautiously inched aside. One eye peered out at her then disappeared. After a few moments, she heard locks click.

One, two, three.

Helen had the house barricaded like a fortress. She must really be scared. "That you, Stella?"

"It's me. Let me in."

The door slowly swung open and Helen appeared. A very haggard-looking Helen. "Guess you've heard about what happened to me."

"Pansy told me about it." Stella advanced into the living room, noticing the buckets of water beneath the windowsills as well as the three locks on the door. Helen followed close on her heels. Something was up all right. Helen was scared right out of her gourd.

Helen perched on the edge of her chair while Stella sat down on the couch. "I tell you, I've had things scare me before, but nothing like this. I thought my heart had stopped."

"That *would* be scary," Stella agreed. Fatal too. When a body's heart stopped . . . well. She'd rather think about the new mystery.

Helen sniffed. "Hargus didn't seem too upset, but he'd better get his mind off those race cars and start doing his job. I wouldn't want anyone to go through what I went through."

So, enough already. Get to the point. "What did you go through?"

"Well," Helen said, drawing her breath out, "I was sitting right here watching *Andy Griffith* reruns. I just love Sheriff Taylor; don't you?"

"Can't say I've ever thought about it." Good grief. Andy Griffith? If you were going to waste your time drooling over a movie star, why not go for the gold? Give her Arnold Schwarzenegger any day. The muscle on that man gave her a fainting spell. Her husband, James, had been a well-built man, but Arnold had the edge on him.

Stella pulled her thoughts back to the Peeping Tom. "What happened then?"

"What happened when?" Helen looked confused.

"You were watching Sheriff Taylor," Stella coached.

"Oh. Oh, yes. Well, I just sort of glanced toward the window, and guess what I saw."

"I wouldn't know." And if Stella wanted to find out before the good Lord called her home, Helen was going to have to speed up. After all, she was eighty-seven. She didn't have enough time left for these long-winded conversations.

"Well . . . there was this *man* peering through my window."

"Was that all he was doing? Staring?" Unless she missed her bet, a man hadn't stared at Helen in years.

Helen frowned. "Isn't that enough? He was all bent over with his face up against the glass and staring right at me. I just thought I was going to crawl right out of my skin."

Stella glanced at the drawn shade covering the window. "You had your shades up last night?" Helen never had her shades up at night. Stella had walked past here many a night, and all the shades and curtains had always been pulled like something was going on inside that Helen didn't want the neighbors to know about.

"Of course not." Helen sniffed. "I never leave my shades up at night. And I'll not be leaving them up in the daylight anymore either. You never know who's going to just step right up and stare at you."

"If you had your shades pulled, how did you know it was a man staring at you?" Helen was as nearsighted as a bat. How could she see anyone looking in the window? This mystery wasn't going anywhere. Stella was wasting her time.

But Helen was persistent. "I saw his silhouette, of course. He was tall. You could tell that from the way he had to bend over, and he had a lot of hair standing up in front like a lion's mane. Maybe it was a beard—I'm not sure—but it was long and unkempt. Hung clean down to his shoulders. Real mean he looked. He was up to no good, I can tell you."

So okay, maybe she did see someone. Probably a vagrant

from the railroad tracks that ran in back of the house. From the sound of her voice she was really spooked.

"So what did you do?"

"I threw my knitting right straight up in the air. Slipped four stitches! And screamed! I screamed so loud I even scared me. Guess it scared him too because he took off like a shot, and I called Hargus."

"And Hargus said you had imagined the whole thing."

"Not at first. He came and looked around, but you know the bad weather has let up, and it hasn't snowed for a couple of days, so there were no footprints."

Stella sat wrapped in thought. It sounded like Helen had really seen something. She'd go by tomorrow and talk to Hargus, but chances are he wouldn't tell her anything. She'd have to do some sleuthing on her own.

Imagine, a real Peeping Tom in Morning Shade.

After the case of the crooked letters, which Stella had solved with a small amount of help from Hargus, she'd thought nothing else would happen in this one-horse town. Now she had another mystery on her hands.

God was good.

But in case God changed His mind, she thought she was going to stop by the new kennel and see what they had on hand. She needed a hobby. If this Peeping Tom didn't pan out, she had a long winter facing her, and she needed something other than community service to pass the time.

I was going through the house, pinching dead flowers off my house plants when I heard Stella come in. No problem telling who it was because she had this odd habit of slamming the door and then opening it again and closing it softly. I'd never been able to figure that one out—why she had to shut it twice. Just shut it normally the first time and be done with it, but Stella never did anything the easy way. I heard her clumping down the hall, moving faster than usual.

She breezed into the living room. "Heard the latest?"

I recognized the tone. Something had happened to excite her. "About what?" These plants were a mess. Needed to be thrown out and replaced with artificial ivy, but I hated those plastic-looking things. Pansy Conley had a room full of the artificial plants.

"We have a Peeping Tom in Morning Shade."

"You're kidding." I stood there, still debating what to do with the dying foliage. I'd never realized how difficult it was to do normal two-handed tasks with one hand.

"Tom who?"

"Not Tom Who—a *Peeping Tom.* He peeked in Helen Brewer's window last night and scared the licorice right out of her."

"That's terrible." And to think I forgot to pull the shades half the time. No longer. I'd see they were yanked closed so tight a mosquito couldn't penetrate.

Stella set something down on the floor and related her recent visit with Helen. "You think Hargus can solve this?"

"I don't know. He's done all right so far."

"Yeah, with a lot of help from me."

"Now, you better be careful. A Peeping Tom is undoubtedly a pervert, and you'd better let Hargus handle this one."

I turned around—staggering backward, my jaw dropping to the floor when I saw the huge cage in the middle of my Persian rug. A snake—a very large thick *snake*—coiled in the bottom of the confine.

"Merciful heavens—*what* is that?" The ugly reptile lifted its head and its tongue flicked.

"A snake. You don't have to worry. I'm not going to do anything dangerous, but I know Hargus will need help if Helen really did have a window peeper."

"A snake!"

Stella glanced at the cage. "A bull snake. Bought it from the new kennel. I was reading the other night about how you can train snakes. Thought I might train a snake to get our slippers—maybe the morning paper—"

"Are you nuts?" I gave the cage a wide berth, my eyes fixed on the reptile. "You can't train a snake to fetch slippers and bring the morning paper."

Stella's jaw jutted out. "The book said I could."

"Just where do you plan to keep this snake?"

"In my room—you won't have to worry. I'll take care of him. You won't have to do a thing."

"You bet your sweet life I won't do anything. If that thing gets loose in the house—"

"It won't." Stella stepped over and jiggled the lock. "You have to be a genius to get the cage open."

Uh-huh. I'd heard the difference between genius and stupidity is this: a genius has limitations. I shook my head. This was really testing my patience. "You have a tendency to raise my blood pressure; you know that?"

Stella grinned. "Makes life exciting, doesn't it? You figure Helen really saw something? You know how nearsighted she is."

I shoved Captain aside with my good foot. Back raised, he was crowding my leg cast, eyeing the snake. He glared up at me and walked over and slapped Frenchie. The poodle yelped and shot under the recliner. Claire cowered behind the wastebasket, and the green macaw croaked, "GIVE IT A REST, MATE."

I was so used to our zoo (that now included a nine-foot bull snake) I barely noticed. "You talked to her. What do you think?"

"I think she believes she saw something. She's scared sure enough, but you know it doesn't take much to scare Helen."

Not like some women I could think of. Stella Diamond could lick her weight in wildcats with one hand tied behind her back. My mother-in-law was one tough cookie. I hoped I could be just like her when I reached her age—if I lived that long.

Stella mused thoughtfully. "I'll give Hargus until tomorrow. If he hasn't come up with anything yet, I'll give him a hand." She picked up her snake. "I think me and Boris will take a nap."

"Boris."

"Yeah. Boris Karloff. If Hilda can name her dogs after Edgar Bergen, I can name my snake after Frankenstein."

Well, I thought when she turned and lugged the cage up the stairway, *the name's fitting.*

* * *

That night I woke to the sound of a siren and flashing lights. I stumbled out of bed and fumbled for my robe. By the time I managed to get downstairs, CeeCee and Stella were already there. We stepped out on the porch to see Hargus's police car stopped in front of Helen's.

"The Peeping Tom," Stella said, grabbing her chest. "He's back!"

"You stay here," I ordered. "I'm going to see what is going on. Where's the snake?"

"In my room, locked tighter than a lockjawed clam."

If only the *snake* were a clam.

It took me a while to navigate the distance, but I managed. I didn't see Hargus, but Maury Peacock, my neighbor, was standing on the sidewalk dressed in Bermuda shorts and a SpaghettiOs-colored sweatshirt that read "I started out with nothing and I still have most of it."

"What's going on?"

Maury peered at me. "That you, Miz Diamond?"

No, it's my twin sister from Podunk. "It's me, Maury. Where's Hargus?"

"He's chasing a bear."

I stared at him. We had to get this man off his medicine. We don't have bears in Morning Shade. Oh, maybe a black bear out in the boonies, but none ever came into town. That's not saying they couldn't. I glanced around uneasily.

"What bear?"

"I can't rightly say. I never made its acquaintance."

I sighed in frustration. Victor Johnson, my neighbor on the opposite side, walked up and I turned to him in relief. "What's going on, Victor?"

"All I know is that Helen called Hargus and said there was a bear in her backyard."

Oh, right. First we have a Peeping Tom and now a bear. I wondered if Helen had been in Maury's medicine. I looked toward my own front porch, hoping CeeCee had been able to talk Stella into going back inside, but no such luck. She'd stay out until her curiosity was satisfied and she'd probably catch cold.

Hargus rounded the corner and I hailed him. "What's going on? Did you find the bear?"

He took a hitch in his pants. "There wasn't no bear. This is the second time Helen has called me out on a wild-goose chase, and I've done told her not to do it again."

"But she must have seen something."

"She did. She saw Hilda Throckmorton wearing a fur coat and walking them two dogs of hers."

"Oh." I breathed a sigh of relief. Bear. Peeping Tom. What was this town coming to? "How did Hilda take being mistaken for a bear?"

"Not well." Hargus wiped his forehead with a white hanky. "I never knew anyone could talk as fast as that woman. And loud . . . I couldn't drive a word in edgewise if I'da took a hammer and tried. I don't want to *ever* tangle with Hilda again. If Helen sees any more bears, she can hunt them herself."

He stumped off toward his car, and I figured he was planning to drown his sorrows in a can of Chocolate Cow. I carefully worked my way back across the street to fill Stella in on the excitement and get her inside before she caught pneumonia. But this Peeping Tom thing had us all unnerved.

* * *

The following night we watched the ten-o'clock news and then trailed up to bed. CeeCee locked the poodles in the kitchen and covered the birdcages, her normal evening routine. I had tried shutting Captain in my office, but after he shredded two reams of paper and scattered it all over the floor, I decided I didn't want to push him any further.

We had just settled down when the phone rang. I closed my eyes, wondering if it would quit if I just ignored it. I heard CeeCee run downstairs and in a few minutes she was knocking on my door.

"That was Helen! There's an alligator or maybe a crocodile crawling along her fence line!"

I opened my eyes wide. "You can't be serious. This is Morning Shade, in the dead of winter. We don't have alligators. Particularly this time of year. Do we?" Suddenly I wasn't so sure. I swung my feet over the bed and reached with my one good hand for the robe I had discarded earlier.

"I'll go see about it," I said. "I don't suppose she'll calm down until I do. Hargus warned her not to call him again after Hilda read him the riot act."

"I'll go with you. Give me a minute to get dressed."

By the time I had pulled on my clothes and swiped a brush through my hair, Stella was awake, fully dressed and feisty. I turned to confront her. "You are *not* going. Don't even think about it."

She drew herself up to her full five feet. "Don't take that tone with me. I'm not a child, and I'll go if I want."

I stared at her without blinking. That always got her. But not tonight . . . "Use some sense, Stella. It's cold out there. And dark. You could fall and break something. Be reasonable."

"I don't feel like being reasonable. I'll be waiting downstairs for you." Her lips firmed and she did an abrupt about-face. If I'd had a flyswatter I'd have whacked her across the rear. I was still ticked about that snake—trying to train a snake. What book had she gotten that from? I'd have to keep a closer watch on her trips to the library.

When I got downstairs, CeeCee was rummaging through the junk drawer looking for flashlights. We found three that worked and started across the street to Helen's. I wasn't looking forward to this. I didn't want to tangle with whatever was out there in Helen's backyard. It was Helen's; she could keep it. I'd give a lot to hear Hargus's police car right about now, siren blowing and lights flashing.

Stella was mincing along, taking short steps. Maybe my warning about falling and breaking something had borne fruit. Break a bone at her age, and it could be a long time healing. But tell the invincible woman that. I had my cane, and my gait was sort of a half skip and a jump along. Give me a few more days with this cast on my foot and I could outrun any alligator. I thought about Sherm and hoped he never learned how I disobeyed his orders to keep off my foot, but with the cane I could manage around the house, and I'd stay in my recliner tomorrow.

Helen opened the door when we hit the porch like a bomb squad. Her hair was in rollers, and her eyes resembled a deer's caught in a headlight. She pranced. She squirmed. "It's at the fence line—crawling along with that big mouth snapping at everything in sight."

Now that was comforting to hear. I was supposed to go back there, me with a bum ankle and bandaged left hand, wrestle a full-grown gator, or a croc, and do what? Drag it up on the porch?

I don't think so.

Helen refused to accompany us, so the three of us set out wielding flashlights, *our* eyes wild and our hair standing on end. CeeCee picked up a stick, and Stella had a rock in her hand. I had my flashlight and my cane—both in my right hand. I guess I was praying as hard as I've ever prayed. A paraphrase of my favorite memory verse ran through my mind: *"Greater is He who is in us than he who is in the world."* Did that cover alligators?

Stella clutched my arm, dragging her feet. If that gator took a run at us, she would be a deadweight pulling me down. We sidled around the side of the house, gripping our lights. CeeCee moved slightly ahead, and I was proud of her. My girl. Ready to sacrifice her life for mother and grandmother. A cold wind sighed through the bare branches of the old elm tree. A winter-white moon shone uncaringly overhead.

Suddenly a gray shape loomed out of the darkness.

CeeCee quickly pinned it with her flashlight and moved on. Nothing stirred. Like a beacon, all three lights swerved back in unison. A log. A big gray log with a protruding branch lay on the property line. Helen's alligator.

My knees sagged with relief. I was going to hang that woman for sure. Stella sighed deeply, and I gripped her arm. "Don't you *dare* faint. If you do, I'll wring your neck."

"That's what I've always liked about you, Maude—your compassion." Life surged back into my mother-in-law's voice, and I realized that she wasn't as fearless as I thought.

"I'm going in that house and *throttle* Helen," she gasped. "My heart's beating like a yard dog's."

"Mine too," I confessed. "As gator hunters, we're a wash-out."

CeeCee joined us; she'd been off investigating the log. "So who gets to tell Helen about her alligator?"

"We'll all do it," I said. I was afraid to turn Stella loose in this mood. I might have to bail her out of Hargus's jail if she really got started. And I'd be stuck with the snake.

Helen was waiting for us on the porch. "Well, which was it, a crocodile or an alligator?"

"Neither," I said, restraining Stella with my good elbow. "It was a log."

"A log? Well, go figure." Helen at least had the decency to look shamefaced.

"A bear last night," Stella groused. "An alligator tonight. You've got a regular Noah's ark going here."

"Get some sleep, Helen," I said, cutting Stella off. "We'll be going home now."

We traipsed back across the street. I for one was thankful it was *just* a log, but I wondered what that poor frightened woman would find to worry about tomorrow night.

Stella, of course, had the last word. She turned and yelled over her shoulder. "I don't care if a parade of monkeys riding elephants and tooting kazoos marches down Main Street, don't call me! I'm not interested." She climbed the porch steps, entered the house, and a few seconds later slammed her bedroom door.

I looked at CeeCee and shrugged. "Bet she woke Boris."

"**Okay.** Where is the worthless thing?" Stella pawed through a dresser drawer Monday afternoon. Patience wasn't her best asset. "Bunch of silly laws—why does anyone have to prove they can drive? Another way for the state to get your money." When her fingers seized on the rectangular card, she shouted. "Yes!" In her hand lay the key to freedom. Independence. Self-reliance.

Adjusting her glasses, she peered at the license. She hadn't driven in years—no need to. She either walked or Maude took her anywhere she needed to go, but she'd kept up her license. She wasn't a fool. She'd didn't want to take that test again. You never knew when life would throw a curveball, and Maude breaking her ankle plus hand surgery to boot, was a spitball slider.

Name: Stella Diamond
Weight: 104
Height: 5′0″
Hair color: Gray
Eyes: Yes

She snickered. The card didn't really say yes, but she'd always wanted to answer that way.

Birthdate: 5-2-1916

The year looked old even to her.

Blowing imaginary dust off the license, she smiled. "Who says you can't get yourself where you need to go, ole gal?"

Moments later she'd descended the rear steps, free of ice now, and made her way to the yard. A blustery wind stung her cheeks, but a clear sky looked promising. Stella dragged the heavy cover off the old Cadillac and then stepped back and surveyed the 1974 Fleetwood four-door sedan. They just didn't build automobiles like this anymore: V-8 overhead valves, automatic climate control, rear-window defogger, and padded footrests.

The car was a classic; Stella knew what she had. Purchased new in October '74, the old car still reeked of appeal. Paid thirteen thousand, one hundred twenty dollars for the vehicle—still had the sales receipt in the glove box. The little compact jobs that were being built these days were bound to get a body killed. This beauty had staying power written all over it. Sixty-three thousand on the odometer. New rubber in '86; new battery in '90. Stella had the cream puff detailed every year though she hadn't driven in—what?—six, seven years? Maybe longer.

But driving was like riding a bicycle; the skill might be a bit rusty but you never lost it.

She unlocked the door and slid behind the wheel—easing forward to peer over the long, long hood. Boy, this baby was long. She'd forgotten how long.

She reached for the key and turned the engine over. The motor sputtered to life. Giving the pedal a couple of pumps, Stella watched in the rearview mirror as blue smoke rolled from the exhaust. Nothing to worry about—just a little oil on the manifold.

She revved the engine, reliving earlier days when she'd drive to the market every Saturday morning, then swing by Oscar's garage, where she'd sit and read an old copy of *Good Housekeeping* while Oscar's boys washed, waxed, and vacuumed the Cadillac. The car never warranted the attention, but Stella liked the cherry scent the boys sprayed on the interior. Lasted well into the next week.

Today the car smelled musty—and felt cold. She was surprised the engine had started, but like she said, car manufacturers didn't build automobiles like this anymore.

Now. What to do—what to do. She studied the dashboard, her eyes searching for the heater control. Oh, she knew nobody called it the "heater" anymore. Now it was "climate control." Politically correct, you know.

She pushed a button and a fan blasted cold air. She waited a good ten minutes for the interior to warm up. Then easing the car into gear, she carefully she hit the gas.

The motor revved.

She hit the pedal again.

Varrooommmm.

She wasn't going anywhere. Stomping the pedal to the metal, she clasped the wheel, intent on moving.

VARRRRRRRROOOMMM.

What's wrong with this thing?

VARRRRRRRRRRRRRMMM. VARRRRRRRRRRMMM.

She was stuck. All this nasty weather and the wheels had mired in a rut. She'd rock it out. Stomping the pedal, she held on to the wheel waiting for the expected jarring jolt when the wheels broke loose.

VARRRRRRRRRROOM.

Blue smoke boiled.

Maude would have her hide for tearing up the yard.

VARRRRRRRRRRRRROOOOOOOOOOOOOOM.

Dad gum. This thing was stuck tighter than a tick.

VARRRRRRRRRRRRROOOOOOOOOOOMM!

She looked up when she heard a brisk rapping sound. Maury Peacock, swathed in a heavy coat, muffler, and hat appeared at the car's window.

What in the Sam Hill . . . she didn't have time to fool with *him* right now. Cranking the window down a fraction, she said, "Want something, Maury?"

Maury stood back, his breath leaving a vapor trail in the cold air. "Your car stuck?"

Well, of all the— "Does it look like it's stuck! Yes, it's stuck—now stand back. I'm about to break loose."

Maury took two steps backward.

VAAAAAAAAAAAAAAAARRRRRRRROOOOOOMMMMM!

Stella smacked the steering wheel. If this didn't beat all!

"Hey, Stella."

Stella ignored Maury and hit the gas pedal. The engine revved.

Maury's hands flew over his ears.

Stella flung open the driver's door and got out. Kneeling, she studied the back wheels, surprised to see them sitting on solid ground.

"Hey, Stella."

"What is it, Maury?" Couldn't he see she was busy?

"I don't think you're stuck."

Just like a man. She stood up, hands on her hips. "So what do you think's the problem, Mr. Fix-It?"

"I think you need to put the car into gear."

Stella felt her jaw drop. She leaned in the driver's side and checked the transmission setting. N. Neutral.

Bother.

"I knew that—just warming the engine a little," she said.

Maury wandered off, and Stella sheepishly climbed back behind the wheel. When she slid the gear into D the Cadillac sprang forward.

So she was a little rusty. Maury didn't have to make a case out of it.

Stella pulled alongside the house and eased the car onto the driveway. Good thing Maude was in her room napping. All that fuss about imaginary crocodiles and alligators at Helen's last night had worn her out. She'd taken a pain pill after lunch and said she planned to sleep the entire afternoon, which was good, because Maude would be as nervous as an old sitting hen watching Stella practice driving. It was making *her* a little edgy. But if she was going to haul Simon and Duella to Shiloh three times a week, she had to recover her driving skills.

Once she had the Cadillac rolling, Stella headed for the street. The first trial run went smooth as glass. Once she mastered the feel of the wheel she'd be off and running.

Traffic was nonexistent on Main Street so she practiced repeatedly pulling in and out of the drive. She noticed Maury had gone back in his warm house, watching her from the comfort of his large bay window. Making fun of her was more like it. She could see him eyeing every move she made. Thought he was so smart—too bad he'd caught her in her first mistake.

She didn't like anyone watching her—made her nervous. Why didn't he go take some of those pills that made him loony as a bedbug?

Pulling up close to the house, she braked, preparing to

maneuver the car back into its original spot. She carefully slid the gear into R. Foot barely touching the gas pedal, she backed up slowly. Piece of cake—

She frowned when she heard the soft *whack!* The sound startled her and she meant to hit the brake, but instead she hit the gas. The car shot backward.

Stella stomped the brake.

The car screeched to an abrupt halt. She glanced at Maury's window and saw him covering his mouth with his hand. So he thought it was funny, huh.

She eased her foot gently back on the gas pedal. She was a mite close to the house now. Slowly, slowly she crept backward. Bother. The siding seemed to be getting closer—but it wasn't moving. She was. Bother.

She stopped, pulled forward, and then tapped the gas pedal. The Cadillac rolled back.

Now the car was sitting directly below the kitchen window.

Not to worry.

She pulled forward, then eased the car backward again. Red taillights shimmered on beige siding. She was close—too close to the house. The car was sitting edgewise in the drive.

Maury's belly was shaking with ill-concealed mirth.

Okay, Stella. You can do this. She yanked the car into gear and puttered forward, then backward. The bumper was now flush against the side of the house.

An hour later, she vacated the car, exhausted. Cold. Hungry. Disgusted.

There weren't two inches clearance between the car and the house, but she gave up. She guessed there was something to be said for driving skills, and in her case, they'd rusted off the hinge. She'd have CeeCee move the car when she came home from work, and with any luck, Maude wouldn't look out the window and notice the Cadillac wasn't sitting in its usual place in the yard.

All in all, she hadn't squandered the afternoon. She'd practiced backing skills and other than accuracy, she done better than anticipated. Oh, she had taken out a row of hedges and the bricks circling Maude's tulip bed. And undoubtedly made Maury Peacock's day.

But she hadn't done badly.

With any luck at all, she'd be ready to make the trip to Shiloh by Wednesday morning.

* * *

"Are you in or out?"

Simon Bench—would-be passenger to Stella's newest quest, shook his head skeptically Tuesday morning. "I don't know, Stella. Five—six years is a long time—"

"You don't forget how to drive! Besides, I've practiced. I'm perfectly capable of driving the three of us to Shiloh."

Duella Parsons rolled her eyes and nervously blotted her lips on a napkin. She was wearing some ungodly shade of red lipstick this morning. "I agree with Simon. I think you should practice more before we all get in that Cadillac and risk our lives."

"Risk your life?" Stella snorted. "You always were too cautious. You got to live in the present."

"Precisely," Simon said. "And riding with you could be detrimental to our health."

Stella got up to refill her cup at Citgo's coffee bar. Other than the usual morning crowd filling thermoses and buying gas, snack cakes, and lottery tickets, the convenience store was quiet.

Stella topped off her cup and returned to the booth. "Are you in or out?" It wasn't a question; it was an ultimatum.

Simon took a bite of donut, swallowed, and then asked. "Are you sure Hargus can't drive us?"

"Ask him yourself—he'll tell you the same thing he told me. The days we do community service, he plans to stay overnight in Shiloh and drive back the next morning. Some stock-car buddy is rebuilding an engine and he needs Hargus's help."

Duella pleated a paper napkin, sending a skeptical look in Simon's direction. "Well, the whole idea makes me nervous, but I suppose we have little choice but to let Stella drive us."

Stella pretended to ignore the shades of negativity. "We don't have any choice. Judge says we have to go so it's settled. We leave at six-fifteen in the morning—weather permitting."

Duella brightened. "It could snow and we couldn't go."

Stella shot the hope down like a scud missile. "Weatherman's calling for clear skies and above-freezing temperatures."

"Oh, feathers."

Stella slid out of the booth, grinning. "Stop being such a pessimist. Doing community service will be fun—and it'll keep us occupied the rest of the winter."

"I'd think taking care of the house while Maude's down would be enough excitement." This came from a still-dubious Simon.

"I'm through with my work by nine o'clock. Maude's no trouble at all, and the Peeping Tom seems to have been nothing but Helen's imagination. I've got Boris—but he's as stubborn as a Missouri mule. Won't fetch a thing yet." Stella gathered empty paper cups and napkins and dumped them into the shiny trash receptacle. "I'll be waiting in front of the retirement home, 6 A.M.

sharp. Then Simon and I will pick you up ten minutes later, Duella. Everyone be on time. We have to be at the hospital by eight."

Simon sighed. "Shiloh is only a thirty-minute drive. What are we going to do with the other hour and twenty minutes?"

Stella gave him a long-suffering look. "We have to allow for trouble, Simon."

"Trouble? Car trouble? I thought you said the Cadillac was in good shape."

"It is in good shape, but you never know when you might blow a hose or a tire gives out. If we get there too early we can get a cup of coffee in the cafeteria."

Duella nodded sagely. "I think Stella's right. We need to leave early—in case of trouble. I hate to be rushed."

Stella left the convenience store in a good mood. She had marketing to do, and she wanted to stop off at Helen's and see how she was getting along. Poor soul.

Crocodiles in her backyard. That would be frightening if it had been true. But if she had imagined a bear and an alligator, maybe she had imagined the Peeping Tom too. Then again, maybe Morning Shade had a third, very interesting mystery on their hands.

A Peeping Tom.

Stella stiffened. The very idea of some pervert peeking through her window shade raised her hackles.

One thing was certain: If there was a Peeping Tom, she'd collar him. That, Morning Shade could count on.

* * *

Wednesday morning, the Cadillac braked in front of Shady Acres residential care facility. A brief glance at the clock on the dashboard and Stella smiled: 5:59 A.M. You couldn't get more prompt than that. She might be old, but her organizational skills were still tight as a drum.

The front door opened, and Simon walked out. Dressed in khaki Dockers and a green wool sweater beneath a heavy down jacket, he briskly covered the distance between the car and porch.

"Morning, Simon," Stella greeted when he got in on the passenger side. He looked downright spiffy this morning.

"Morning, Stella." He had to open and slam the door twice before the latch caught. Seconds later, the Cadillac roared off, trailing blue smoke in the early dawn.

When Duella exited The Antique Store she and her sister owned, cold morning sunrise caught the flame in her permed locks. Twin sister, Luella would still be sleeping at this hour. Neither Duella nor Luella were morning people.

Crawling into the backseat, Duella settled uneasily on the beige leather. "Morning all."

"Morning," Stella and Simon parroted in unison.

Stella glanced in the rearview mirror. "Better buckle up."

"Don't worry. I plan to." Duella reached for the seat belt. A second later Stella heard the snap.

Duella grabbed the back of her neck when Stella hit the gas and the Cadillac peeled out, leaving a black streak on the pavement.

Stella gripped the wheel as she tooled along the highway, reveling in the knowledge that it was all coming back—the motion, the feel of the wheel beneath her hands. She'd missed driving. Even when Maude was healed, she'd not bury the Cadillac under a cover in the yard and let others drive her where she needed to go. She had her independence back.

She jerked the wheel as a semi boiled past, rattling the car chassis.

Simon clutched the dashboard, on point now.

Stella eyed him. "Sit back and relax." The man was a bundle of nerves—too much caffeine.

"That was close, Stella."

"What?"

"The truck that just blew past us. You're crowding the centerline."

"No backseat driving," she warned as the Cadillac hummed along.

Duella leaned up to gawk over the driver's seat.

Stella shifted, moving her back with her forearm. "Don't do that. You're making me a nervous wreck."

"Speed limit is sixty-five—you're doing sixty-eight."

"So? No cherry top is going to stop me for going three measly miles over the speed limit." The car didn't have cruise control, but even if it did she wouldn't use it. She liked operating the gas pedal herself.

"There's a car coming up on your left!"

"I see it—it's a dual-lane highway, Simon."

"Left," Duella reminded when the big red SUV drew closer.

"I see it."

Stella glanced in the rearview mirror. The sucker was riding her tail now—inching forward, trying to get around. The big black bumper towered above the Cadillac.

"Get off my tail!" Stella shouted.

Simon clutched the dash. "Just slow down and let him go around."

"Not on your life!" Stella mashed down harder on the gas. "These cocky young kids think they own the road—look at him. Talking on a cell phone, drinking coffee, chewing his fingernails, and messing with his hair in the rearview mirror." She cranked down the window and stuck her head out. "Hang up and *drive!*"

The Cadillac veered to the right shoulder, and Stella whipped the wheel back to the left.

"Oh dear." Duella clung to the back of the seat, lower lip quivering.

An air horn sounded. Stella bristled. "Will you look at that—he's got him a big ole horn." She stuck her head out the window. "You got a horn, buddy! Well, blow it out your ear!"

Simon's knuckles turned white. "Come on, Stella. Let him go by."

"I've heard about road rage. He's going to have to learn there are other folks on the highway."

The speedometer climbed and vacillated between seventy-four and too-fast.

"I think you should let him by." Duella reached in her purse for a hanky. "The speed limit's sixty-five and you're going seventy-four . . . seventy-five. Seventy-six now!"

"Yada, yada, yada. No backseat driving. I'll back off when he does."

The SUV surged closer to the Caddy's bumper, the driver laying on his horn. Stella bit her lip with determination and set her focus on the centerline. When the moron wouldn't let up, she leaned her head out the window and shouted, "I know the jokes, buddy! All you can see is a pair of hands on the wheel—well, Stella Diamond's driving, sir! These hands may be old, but they're skilled!"

The Cadillac swerved to the right then the left.

"He can't hear you!" Simon shouted. "Roll up that window and let him pass!"

Duella patted her hair. The open window had snarled the flame red locks into a fur ball.

Stella turned to glare at Simon. "Why should I let him pass? The jerk needs to be taught a lesson."

"Not by us!" Simon closed his eyes when Stella momentarily lost control of the wheel.

The car hit the shoulder, tires grabbing traction in spinning loose gravel. Gunning the motor, Stella wrestled the vehicle back to the pavement. She flashed Simon a satisfied grin. "I've still got it."

"Pull over, Stella. I'm driving."

"No way. This is my car."

Duella went limp. She lay back, covering her eyes with a forearm. "She's going to kill us all."

The SUV crowded her back bumper.

Stella braked. Tires screeched.

The SUV driver hit his brakes.

Duella moaned.

"Stella!" Simon shouted when she gunned the engine, and they shot on down the road.

Coming up fast now, the SUV tailgated the Cadillac, the driver clearly furious.

Stella calmly hit her brakes. Red brake lights flashed.

SUV tires screeched.

Seconds—and a series of obscene gestures—later, the SUV driver turned off at a convenience gas and grocery store.

A serene smile played along Stella's lips. She shrugged and made clucking noises under her breath. "Chicken."

Simon slumped in his seat as the Cadillac tooled on down the highway.

* * *

Shiloh General Hospital was a small but fully equipped medical center. As predicted, the trio arrived early. Stella, Simon, and Duella headed for the coffee shop. A little before seven, they got on the elevator and rode to the first floor, where a smiling woman wearing a white lab coat and carrying a clipboard met them in the reception area.

"Ah—right on time."

Eleanor Pierson rattled off what they could expect with community service. Each one would be assigned a particular area. Simon would man the surgery-information desk along with hospital auxiliary volunteers. Duella would work in the flower room, and Stella would assist in art therapy.

"What's that?" Stella asked. Their footsteps echoed down hushed corridors.

"Art therapy is rather unique medicine. When a patient is diagnosed with depression, stress, anxiety, or grief, coloring helps the person to regain permission to be creative."

"Never heard of such a thing."

"Sometimes the simple act of coloring empowers a person and often can be a source of intense pleasure."

Stella snorted. Coloring. If that didn't beat all. It seemed like a gross waste of time.

Eleanor deposited Simon at the surgery desk and then walked the two women to the flower room.

"Duella, you'll sort the arrangements when they arrive and put proper room numbers on them. Later, you and one other volunteer will deliver the flowers to the patients." Eleanor smiled. "You'll enjoy this particular job. Flowers and mail are always a fun place to work."

Duella nodded. "I'm sure the job will be more relaxing than the ride over here." She shot Stella a censuring look.

Five minutes later, Eleanor led Stella to a large, airy room with various folding tables scattered around. The coloring room. Already several patients sat at a big table, coloring. Boxes of crayons littered the oak surface.

The auxiliary volunteer, dressed in pink, introduced Stella to the group. "Everyone—this is Stella. She will assist me for the next few weeks with your coloring therapy."

Dispassionate eyes turned to view the newcomer. One elderly man met Stella's gaze, picked up a black crayon, and snapped the stick into two pieces. A young Hispanic boy, who looked to be in his early teens turned dark, cynical eyes on her.

All righty, Stella thought. *Two more men with a serious attitude.*

She was going to enjoy this punishment.

The house was hospital quiet. I didn't know how to handle the silence. I could get around all right in my cast. Walking was just slow and awkward, and I was tired of being an invalid. Being waited on got old fast.

Stella was gone to her community service, and CeeCee, of all things, had taken a part-time job at the new kennel. Of course she loved animals, and working for a kennel was the ideal job for her. I told Stella there was no way I'd look after Boris—even if the house caught fire. She said fine; she'd expected as much. Truthfully, I think training a snake wasn't all she'd thought it would be.

"I'm working in a kennel, Mom! And Rick said I could board the animals there—except Captain. I thought we'd better keep him with us."

Right, I thought. But *boarding the other animals* were the magic, persuasive words. "Did you mention Grandma's bull snake?"

"No—Rick sold that snake to her. Said he didn't want the thing back. I think he's scared of it."

Who wasn't? "Honey, I think that's great, but what about my

typing?" The promise—the emergency-room vows: *I won't let you get behind in your work, I promise.*

"Oh that! It'll be a breeze, Mom. I'll do it when I get home each night. I'm only working a couple of hours after work."

Well, CeeCee had gone to work, and she had put the dogs and the birds in the kennel. Boris lived a solitary life in Stella's room, and my dictation was still lying untouched on the office desk. Captain acted as lost as I felt. Mostly he slept or prowled and howled. He was about to drive me crazy.

I had started back at my morning devotionals, something I had neglected after Herb died and my household was turned upside down. Now my life had changed again and I didn't like it. My ankle would heal; so would my wrist. But I, who had thought I wanted a quiet house, was bored to tears. Since Stella was so busy, she wasn't popping in and out driving me to distraction. I hated to admit it, but I missed her.

I managed to carry a cup of tea to a cozy rocker by a sunny window and leaned back with my Bible on my lap. I had been reading in Psalms this week, and I had forgotten how much I loved Scripture. I read Psalm 5 out loud, and Captain crouched at my feet as if he were actually listening.

"'O Lord, hear me as I pray; pay attention to my groaning. Listen to my cry for help, my King and my God, for I will never pray to anyone but you.

"'Listen to my voice in the morning, Lord. Each morning I bring my requests to you and wait expectantly.'"

He hadn't heard my voice in the morning for some time, but I was determined to do better. A plaque Stella had hung on her bedroom wall came to mind; it said "Slow me down, Lord."

Well, I had been slowed down, and it was up to me to make the best of it. The work on Jack Hamel's book was coming along well because CeeCee had offered some good insights. Things I hadn't thought of. She was a fast typist too, when she squeezed in a few minutes to work, but that had sort of fallen by the wayside right now because she was so wrapped up in Rick Materi at the B and G Kennel. It was Rick this and Rick that. I was getting worried about this Rick. Cee thought he was *wonderful.* I hoped she was right, but her judgment on men hadn't been all that great so far.

I got up and hobbled into my office, thinking about pecking out a few revisions with one hand. It hadn't come to that yet, but time was passing. Deadlines don't go away because the author can't type. Stella had offered to learn, but I had managed to head her off. I could imagine what a disaster that would be.

Captain perched on top of my file cabinet as if expecting me to get to work. I wish. Instead I pulled out my hand recorder and started dictating into it. Jack Hamel had an excellent story to tell, but I didn't believe I had ever had more trouble working on a book. First I couldn't read his notes—still couldn't—and now I couldn't use the computer. CeeCee promised to catch up on the typing tonight. I was just frustrated to be left out of the action, so to speak.

The day passed somehow and I heard Stella's car jerk into the drive. She drove with one foot on the brake and the other on the gas, and only the good Lord knew which one she would push next. So far she hadn't rear-ended anyone, and no one had hit her, but I figured it was just a matter of time. I kept her automobile insurance paid up and my prayer lines open.

The car door slammed, and a few minutes later I heard her coming in the front door. Slammed it, opened it and shut it gently. Stella's signature.

"Hey, Maude."

"In here."

She wandered into the living room, looking weary but alert. I would never have thought of putting Stella in charge of a coloring class for people with depression, but it seemed to be working. Stella had a new focus. Maybe she would forget about the Peeping Tom, which seemed to have died down anyway. Helen was still upset when anyone mentioned the incident, but then she always did have a hair-trigger fear factor. She'd eventually settle down.

"I stopped by the deli and got a rotisserie chicken for dinner. Thought that would be easier than cooking."

"Good idea." I didn't even want to think of her driving through the crowded parking lot at the Cart Mart. "Tomorrow is your day off, isn't it?"

"Sure is. I'm looking forward to it, but you know what, Maude?"

"What?"

"I'm starting to enjoy this coloring class. Those poor people need cheering up, and I'm doing my best to meet the challenge."

"I'm sure you can make a difference." I could just see her, arms akimbo, looking over her glasses and ordering them to be happy. They'd cheer up or else.

"There's this one boy—he's Hispanic." She shook her head. "He got his head in a mess of trouble."

"That's too bad. Is he depressed?"

"Nope. Just surly, but I'm surly right back, so it's working out."

She sat down in her favorite chair. "Never thought I'd ever say it, but I miss CeeCee's menagerie. House seems downright dull without those dogs and birds. Captain does his best, but he doesn't have any incentive to misbehave without the poodles to make miserable."

"It's so quiet around here I feel like screaming just to make noise. I even turn on the television sometimes during the day." Something I never did without feeling guilty because I wasn't working. Now I could watch TV all day, but I couldn't work and I missed writing. Never thought I'd say that either.

"Boris could keep you company. He gets lonely."

"Did he say something to you?"

"Of course not. But I'm gone a lot lately. You want me to bring his cage down tomorrow morning?"

"No thanks."

Stella got to her feet and headed toward the kitchen. "Well, God has a way of kicking us out of our rut once in a while. I suppose it's good for us."

"Probably so." What was that I had read the other day? "The only difference between a rut and a grave is that the grave is deeper."

I still wished I could type.

Stella crept down the stairs before the first cold rays of daylight dappled the kitchen floor. Breakfast was on her this morning. Bran muffins, chamomile tea, orange juice, and mixed frozen fruit. Good food and good for you. Maude was upset because she couldn't work, and she was going to eat herself into an early grave.

Strange woman, Maude. Complained all the time when she was working, and now she was disturbed because she couldn't work. No understanding some people. She wandered outside to get the morning paper. Wouldn't be long before Boris could help—but then again she was beginning to think whoever wrote that article on snake training didn't know beans about bull snakes.

Felt like snow. Sure hoped it didn't. Could she drive to Shiloh with snow on the ground? Probably she could, but would Simon and Duella ride with her? Probably not. Couple of wimps. But the young man with the dark eyes—Manuel—now he was a challenge. Bitterness ran deep in that young man's blood. She'd like to know what was bothering him—and she'd find out, given time. He liked to stir her up, but he didn't know who he was dealing with.

She returned to the house and sat down at the kitchen table and turned to the obituary page. Seven today. A body would think Morning Shade was an unhealthy place to live unless he looked at the age of these folks. Most of them had gone past their allotted span. Like her. Her time was coming. She could feel it in her bones.

Clyde Delmer: ninety-six. Didn't say what was wrong with him. Probably ate himself to death. She'd noticed him at church dinners. His plate always needed sideboards. She tried to eat smart, herself.

Hank Collins. She knew him. She used to work at the power plant, and he'd always stop and visit when he came to pay his bill. Nice man. His wife had died three years ago. Eighty-eight. One year older than her. Lord willing, she'd hold on for another year. Sometimes, she didn't know why she should; then again, Hargus needed her. Probably couldn't hold his job without Stella Diamond.

"What's burning?"

Stella jumped when Maude hobbled into the kitchen.

"What?"

Maude fanned the air. "Where's the smoke coming from?"

Stella blinked at her and sniffed. The bran muffins. Oh, shoot. She'd been so busy reading the obits she'd forgotten them! She got to her feet and hurried to the stove. "Open the door and let the smoke clear out in here. We don't want the smoke alarm going off."

Blamed thing sounded like the last trump. She hadn't forgotten the time before when she had burned something, and Maude had called the fire department. *Let's not go there again.*

Maude thumped to the door and swung it open, fanning smoke with a dish towel. "What were you doing?"

"Fixing breakfast." Stella dumped the tin of charred muffins in the trash. "How do you feel about toast?"

CeeCee rushed into the room. "Something's burning!"

Maude herded the last of the smoke out the door. "Breakfast."

"Oh. What was it?"

"Muffins." Stella said. "I guess I shouldn't try to help. I make a mess out of the simplest thing. You won't have to put up with me much longer. I'm on my last legs now." She peered at Maude and CeeCee over her glasses.

"Oh, Grandma, you'll outlive all of us. Don't worry about it. I'll fix toast."

Stella smiled; she could always count on CeeCee. Maude was unpredictable.

"I'll scramble eggs." Maude opened the refrigerator door. "Don't look so upset, Stella. Accidents happen."

Stella primed her lips. This wasn't like her daughter-in-law. Usually Maude was strung as tight as a high-wire act. Something was going on and she'd like to know what.

"Tell you what, Maude. You're getting awfully laid back. You think that medicine's too strong for you? One Maury Peacock in the neighborhood is enough." Poor old Maury was nuttier than a caged squirrel last month when the doctor had him on Vicodin and Valium after toe surgery.

Maude turned around to look at her. "Are you out of your mind?"

Stella could feel her cheeks getting warm. Try to do something nice, pass on some good advice, and look where it got you. She drew herself up straighter. "I'll have my breakfast at Citgo."

* * *

Wednesday morning, when Manuel Rodriguez stalked out of color therapy, Stella snagged his shirttail. "Come with me, funny boy."

The boy yelled, "Help! The old codger's hurting me!"

"Nobody's listening, twerp." Stella collared the young man and hauled him off in the direction of the cafeteria. The troubled youth didn't go quietly; doctors' and nurses' eyes followed the shouting match down the hospital corridor.

"Let go of me, old woman!"

"Pipe down, pip-squeak. You might be bigger than me, but I'm stronger." Actually she was as strong as a bull. Must be those vitamins she took or else . . .

Why, the boy was all mouth! He was loud and brittle, but he wasn't putting any force behind his words. Stella dragged him into the cafeteria and sat him down at a table near the ice-cream machine. She bent, and in a two-minute stare-off, she asked, "Chocolate or vanilla?"

Manuel refused to look at her.

Gripping his chin between both hands, Stella turned him to face her. "Chocolate or vanilla? Simple question."

"I don't like ice cream."

"Okay, we'll play it your way. Cone or dish?"

The boy still refused to cooperate. Okay. She'd dealt with mulish natures more than once. She had all day.

"Sprinkles or gummy bears?"

He jerked his arm free, his features sullen. "What do you want, old woman?"

Stella slid into the opposite chair. "For starters, knock off the old-woman garbage. I'm old; it shows. So what's your point?"

He looked away, his posture stiff and unyielding.

"Second—" Stella grinned at a passing nurse with a question on her face. "Patient throwing a tantrum."

The nurse smiled and walked on.

"Second," Stella continued, "I'd like to be your friend."

"Ha. Why would I want an old has-been like you for a friend?"

Stella shrugged, overlooking the insult. "I figure friends aren't that easy to come by—for you or for me. Can't ever have enough friends—not good ones, anyway. To tell the truth, I'm eighty-seven, and I can count on one hand the number of good, tell-'em-anything kind of friends I have."

"So no one likes you. What d'you want me to do about it?"

"So—" she reached over and turned his face back to meet hers—"how come you don't like me? I've never done anything to you—never laid eyes on you until a week ago."

His dark eyes flashed, and then he dropped his face into his hands. "Go away. I don't have any friends, and I sure don't want you for one."

"Well, that's too bad because I want you." Stella reached over and grasped the boy's hand. For a millisecond she encountered resistance. The hand was tough—like the young flesh had known hard labor in its years.

"What are you doing in here? I know scum when I see it, and you're not scum, son. A young man like you ought to be enjoying life."

His hand dropped away, and he sneered. "Tell Judge Rowten your sad story."

Stella calmly got up and drew two dishes of chocolate soft serve, to which she added chocolate sprinkles. Setting a dish in front of the young Hispanic, she softened her tone. She could be too abrupt—scared folks sometimes.

"Sorry, but I would like to be your friend if you'd let me. I got a nine-foot bull snake. Want me to bring it to class?"

The boy picked up the spoon and studied it. His dark eyes mirrored bitterness and a toughness that Stella suspected didn't go all the way to the bone; she would bet on it.

"Want to talk about it?"

The boy shook his head.

"You sure?"

Rejection. Curt denial.

"Well then, eat up. No use letting good ice cream go to waste."

Hesitantly, the young man dipped the spoon into the frozen custard and methodically began spooning ice cream into his mouth. No warmth. No softening. Stella suspected there was a whole lot of hurt in this child. Hurt so deep mere words weren't going to unearth the pain.

But he was eating the ice cream, she noted. And that was progress.

* * *

Thursday morning, Stella strode down the sidewalk toward the Citgo under a full head of steam. She couldn't get young Manuel out of her mind. No good deed ever goes unnoticed. She'd read that somewhere, and she'd done a good deed by trying to make friends with the boy. Even offered to bring Boris to class, but he wasn't interested. Most folks weren't when she mentioned her new acquisition. Sure sounded good at the time . . .

Seemed like her mind was crammed with useless bits of information—some of it more appropriate than others.

By the time she had eaten an egg-and-cheese English muffin,

the regulars were starting to dribble in. The waitress with the pink hair took her plate and brought her a refill on latte. Nice girl, once you got past the hair. Looked like she'd stuck a wet finger in a light socket.

"You need anything else, Stella?"

"No, Delphinium. This will do. Thanks."

What kind of mother would name her daughter Delphinium? Did she go through a seed catalog looking for something special? Too bad she didn't hang in there until she reached the *R*s. Nothing wrong with Rose.

Stella sipped the steaming latte. If someone had named her Delphinium, she might have dyed her hair pink too. The thought put her in a better mood.

Frances came in, wearing a flowered print dress under an L.L.Bean barn coat and a bright pink scarf tied over her beehive hairdo. Stella had known Frances for lo these many years, and she'd never seen her with a different hairstyle. Black as coal—Frances called it "dark ash." Stella snickered.

"Morning, Stella. It's good to see you back in your old haunts. I'll be glad when this community-service thing is over. It's not the same when you're not here."

The remark, of course, made her feel lower than dirt for laughing at her good friend that way. "It's good to be back. What's going on?"

"Not much. Haven't heard anything about Peeping Toms lately. Guess he got an eyeful the first time."

"Not peeping through Helen's window, he didn't. You'd need X-ray eyes to see through those drawn shades. She seen any more bears or alligators?"

Frances laughed. "Not that I've heard of. I did hear that Hilda swore off walking her dogs at night. Poor Thurvis is stuck with that particular chore, and he's not fond of those two dogs."

"Well—" Stella turned to stare at a pickup sitting at the pump—"seems like trouble takes its own sweet time coming around."

"Why, Stella Diamond! Are you suggesting you'd welcome a new mystery—a Peeping Tom!"

"Shoot, yes. Better than sitting around watching concrete dry."

"But you have your community work. And Boris."

Stella shrugged. Lackluster life at best. Except for Manuel. She had a heart for that young man.

Simon joined them, setting his coffee down before he stripped out of his jacket. "Ah, a day off. I'd forgotten what a luxury freedom can be. When you're retired with nothing to do, you forget those little treasures like a day to yourself."

The talk turned to general topics and Stella tuned it out, thinking about the Peeping Tom and wondering why he'd never come back. That was real disappointing. Over two weeks had passed, and nothing. Zip. Nada. She roused to hear Pansy complaining that nothing exciting ever happened anymore.

"You want excitement?" Simon asked. "Try riding to Shiloh with Stella behind the wheel. I've stomped the floorboards out of the passenger side, and Duella has broken out in hives."

Stella stiffened. Nothing wrong with her driving. Simon and Duella needed a nerve transplant. Scared of a little thing like running a couple of red lights. Just plain chicken.

Frances leapt to her defense. "If you don't like Stella's driving, why don't you drive?"

"She won't let me. It's her car."

"I never saw anyone who liked to complain more than you

and Duella." Stella sniffed. "I'd think you might show a little gratitude."

"I'll show gratitude to the Almighty if we survive. I'll say one thing for your driving, Stella; it's done wonders for my prayer life."

"Not to change the subject," Pansy said, "but who *do* you think Helen saw that frightened her so much? Hargus said she was shaking like a blackberry briar in a high wind. She didn't talk in complete sentences for days."

Frances shuddered. "I've not seen anyone around town that looked like who she described—hair like a lion's mane—and furthermore I don't want to. I've taken to pulling my window shades at night, even though I'm on the third floor."

"The man had a beard," Stella said. She doubted anyone would go to the bother to haul around a three-story ladder for the gratification of peeping at Frances, but then what did she know? Who'd have thought he'd peep at Helen? If Mr. Tom Peeper ever peeped in her window, she'd peep back. That would fix him. Fight fire with fire was her motto, and strike the first match when at all possible.

Simon got to his feet. "Well, I need to get busy. Got a lot of things to do today before I have to report for community service tomorrow."

Stella glared at him. The way he talked about her driving, he just might be walking. Do him good. Give him time to find his manners.

He grinned at her. "Don't be mad, Stella. I was only teasing. You do a fair job behind the wheel."

She sniffed.

"I do appreciate the ride, though it is a trifle interesting at times. See you in the morning?"

She thought about it and then nodded. "I suppose." She couldn't make Simon walk to Shiloh. He and Duella didn't mean any harm.

"You leaving, Stella?" Pansy asked when she and Frances got to their feet.

"No. I think I'll stay here for a while. Keeps me out of the house."

They left and she had another latte.

Hargis came in, got a cup of coffee, and carried it to her table. "You busy?"

"Do I look like I'm overworked?"

"You know what, Stella Diamond; you got a mouth on you."

"Yeah, the Mouth from the South—that's me." Last time she looked, Arkansas was still part of the South anyway.

"Well, see if you can control it. I got something on my mind." Hargus peered at her from under bushy eyebrows. "You hear any more about this Peeping Tom at Helen's?"

"Not a thing. You?"

Hargus's lip quivered. "Nothing. Helen was scared blue when I got there, but it seems like if a man peeked in that window he'd peek in somewhere else. I ain't seen anyone around that even comes close to meeting Helen's description. You'd think he'd stand out a country mile in Morning Shade."

"No one turned evidence?" She was proud of herself, learning cop lingo. She squinted at Hargus to see if he'd noticed, but he wouldn't notice anything that didn't look like a race car. Got a real one-track mind, and it jumped the track more often than not. "You think he's from out of town? Like over at Ash Flat? They got some weird lookers over there."

Hargus nodded. "I'd thought about that. Reckon he'll be back?"

Stella pursed her lips, trying to look wise. She liked this sitting and sharing information, the way the real fuzz did. Pity Hargus didn't indulge in this sort of thing more often. If he'd ask, she could be a real help to the boy.

She shook her head. "Who knows? Could be just passing through?"

"And then again . . ." His voice trailed off.

Stella shook her head. Pansy's boy. She had to let bygones be bygones and help him out. "Maybe Hilda Throckmorton knows what happened that night. You ask her if she's seen anything unusual? You know we can't trust Helen's eyesight."

"No, and I ain't going to talk to Hilda. You know what she called me?"

Stella's eyes rounded. "What?"

"A do-nothing, interfering busybody. I ain't been called names like that since I left home."

Pansy called her own son a do-nothing, interfering busybody? Shame on her. Got to hand it to Hilda, though; she had a way of pinpointing the problem.

The morning freight rumbled through town and Stella turned her head to listen. "Hargus, we're a pair of idiots."

He bristled. "Now don't you start. I'm getting tired of all this name-calling, particularly since I'm the one getting called."

"No, listen; what do you hear?"

"Can't hear nothing but that train whistle blowing at the crossing."

Stella had thought about railroad vagrants once—then the idea completely slipped her mind. "That's right. And where do those railroad tracks run?"

"Through the lower corner of Morning Shade. So what?"

Stella sighed. Hargus needed a vocabulary makeover.

Teach him some new words. "So this. *Who* rides the freight trains?"

Hargus squinted. "The engineer, I guess; who else?"

Stella sighed. Seemed like she always had to do his thinking. "Drifters, Hargus. Hitching a ride without paying, getting off in a town, bumming a meal. During the Depression there were lots of drifters in Morning Shade."

Hargus grinned triumphantly. "I wasn't born then."

Stella glowered. "Well, listen up. What if one of those drifters came through town the other night, and he was hungry, and he looked in Helen's window?"

"Why would he want to do that? Helen ain't nothing to look at anymore, and she sure ain't much with her hair up in curlers."

"Maybe—but she screamed like a fire engine and scared him off."

Hargus seemed to absorb the idea—or at least it looked like something penetrated. "You know, you just might have something there."

Well, came the dawn. It took the boy a while but he finally arrived.

Hargus shoved to his feet. "I guess that solves the problem. I'll get back to the office now. If you need anything else explained, Stella, just give me a call."

For once Stella was speechless. Sat right there and listened to her, and then pretended he'd come up with the answer. When it came to brass, Hargus could outfit an entire marching band.

A few minutes later she had another thought. What if she was wrong? What if there had been a real Peeping Tom? Helen might be overly excitable, but she must have seen something out of the norm that night. She needed to talk to Helen again. She glanced at her watch. Plenty of time before lunch. She'd drop by, do a little snooping, see what this thing was all about. If there was a Peeping Tom . . . man, she hated to get her hopes up.

Helen was in full lockdown mode. At least two locks on all of the doors—some of them new—window shades pulled down tight in broad daylight. Stella shook her head. Poor woman. She looked like a basket case, lips trembling, hands shaking. Whatever anyone else thought, Helen was sure she'd had a close encounter with something.

Stella sat down in the rocker, and Helen perched on the edge of the couch.

"Nice of you to come by, Stella. No one else seems to care. I tried to talk to Hargus, but he just says, 'So what?' I don't think that's nice."

Yeah, Stella had run into that problem herself a few times. "Helen, I want you to think hard; are you sure you saw a man that night? You don't think that maybe you mistook say a tree branch or something like that to be a prowler?"

Helen nodded vigorously. "Positive. Saw him silhouetted against that window shade, big as life. Maybe bigger."

Stella thought about how to put this discreetly. "You know the freight goes through town."

Helen's brows shot up. "Well, everyone knows that. Couldn't miss it, the noise it makes. Goes right in back of my house—hear it every night."

"Hargus and I have just about decided your Peeping Tom could have been a vagrant who'd got off in town, and when you screamed it scared him so much he moved on down the road."

"Hmmm. You think so?" Helen shook her head dubiously.

"Well, yes . . ." Didn't she?

"I don't know. Seems to me you and Hargus don't have any hard proof of that, so to speak, and I believe I saw someone. It would be hard to convince me otherwise. I'll keep my doors locked until I know for sure. You can't be too cautious anymore. It's not the world we grew up in."

She had that right. The world had changed a lot in the last eighty-seven years. Stella got up from the rocker. "I'll be running along. Got to fix lunch. Since Maude's accident and surgery, my load's increased something terrible." Although it would be a cold day in July before she fixed breakfast again. Let CeeCee and Maude fix their own. "If anything else out of the ordinary happens, let me know. Want me to bring my snake over some night and let you see him?"

"Oh . . . I don't think so. But thank you anyway."

On the way home, Stella decided Helen liked being the only house the Peeping Tom had hit. She liked the attention—made her feel important in a funny kind of way.

Maybe she didn't want the mystery to be solved.

* * *

CeeCee looped the keys to the postal truck over the ring that housed them and reached for her coat. Grandma was in Shiloh today so Mom would be alone. She needed to start dinner. Something easy tonight: soup and sandwiches. She absently thought about the abandoned stack of revisions lying on Mom's desk and determined to do better.

Rick had been waiting at his mailbox today with a cup of coffee and a small box of miniature chocolates. She'd seen the miniature boxes at Wal-Mart. They didn't cost much, but it was the thought that counted. She'd never dreamed when she started driving the route that it would lead to anybody like Rick Materi. After her disastrous marriage to Jake, she'd thought she'd never trust again, but Rick was different.

She climbed their back-porch steps and pushed open the door. "Mom? I'm home."

"In here."

Maude was sitting in front of the TV doing nothing. Just sitting there. CeeCee swallowed the lump in her throat. She didn't remember ever seeing her mother when she wasn't busy, working around the house or sitting at her computer. It hurt to see her so . . . helpless.

She forced a smile. "You look comfortable, but your fire's about to go out." She walked over to the fireplace and put a large piece of wood on the dog irons. "There, that will catch in a minute."

"I'd have done it myself, but I can't lift the wood with one hand."

Of course she couldn't. Guilt washed over CeeCee. She could take a break from her mail route long enough to come home and see if Mom needed anything. Iva, her boss, would understand.

"I saw Rick again today."

"Oh?" Maude raised her brows

CeeCee smiled. "He is the most thoughtful man. You'd really like him. I'll have to run you by the kennel some night and let you meet him."

"I'd like that."

CeeCee mentally winced at the cautious tone in Mom's voice. "He really is a nice guy."

"I'm sure he is." Maude reached for the *TV Guide.* "If he's good to you, I'll like him."

"He's good to me," CeeCee said. And she meant it. "Very good."

They heard the Cadillac roar into the drive. Maude put the magazine aside and sighed. "Every day I expect the highway patrol to come by and tell me Stella's wiped out half the drivers on the state highway."

CeeCee laughed. "She's done all right so far, although I think Simon has a few more white hairs than he did. I know she doesn't have any business driving, but she has the license and the car, and she's so bullheaded she won't listen to common sense. Besides, how else would she get to her community service?"

"True," Maude said. "But I still don't like the idea of her out on that highway by herself."

"She has Simon and Duella."

CeeCee giggled at Maude's resulting look.

We were watching *Wheel of Fortune* when the phone rang. I noticed CeeCee took off like a shot to answer. It had been a long time since my daughter had shown such passion for life. Rick Materi had done that for her, but I didn't know beans about the new man in town. Hadn't met him, actually. Just heard about his "ravishing dimple."

In the time it took Vanna to turn a vowel, a winded CeeCee appeared in the doorway. "That was Rick. He wants me to come; he has a sick animal. Do you mind if I leave for a while?"

"Why would I mind?" Stella asked. "I'm going to sit right here where it's warm and relax. You don't know how hard it is to keep all those people coloring inside the lines. Between the patients and arguing with Manuel, I'm worn to a frazzle."

"I'm not tired. Care if I ride along?" I said. This was my chance to finally meet wonderful Rick with the ravishing dimple. "It would do me good to get out of the house for a while."

After a bit of obvious mental debate, CeeCee shrugged. "Sure, come on. I'll get your coat." She hurried from the room.

Stella peered over her glasses. "Might be a good idea for you to check out this Rick person. Never met a perfect man, but it sounds like this one must come close."

"Now, Stella."

"Anything too good to be true usually is."

CeeCee came back with my coat slung over her arm. "Here you go. We'll be back after a while, Grandma."

"Better have your key handy. I'm too old to be waiting up for anyone."

The kennel was a short mile and a half from home. CeeCee helped me out of the car, and a large man with the worse comb-over I have ever seen hurried out of the small building to help.

"Mom, this is Arnold Biggert. He's the kennel vet." CeeCee held the passenger door open wider, and Arnold took my arm and gently helped me into a wheelchair.

When I sent Cee a questioning look, she explained. "We keep the chair around for injured animals too heavy to carry."

Once inside the kennel I looked around; the operation was small but nice. I glanced at Arnold Biggert and wondered why Rick needed CeeCee tonight? Rather thoughtless, I felt, but maybe I was being overly critical. I knew the young kennel owner came from a wealthy Texas family. Probably used to being waited on.

A man with a football build bustled into the room. "Ah, there you are darlin'; thanks for coming out tonight."

I eyed this blond Greek god, admittedly searching for the dimple. It was there, and I had to admit, it was ravishing. When he smiled the whole room lit up.

So this was Rick.

"Rick, this is my mom."

He strutted toward me, smile a little too confident, manner a little too brash, hazel eyes way too experienced for my taste.

It was as if Jake Tamaris had been reincarnated. I held out my right hand and he clasped it tightly. "Maude. I'm so glad to finally meet you. CeeCee is a godsend."

CeeCee beamed and I wanted to smack her. Just got rid of one jerk and here's another. I'd mind my manners, though. "Hello, Rick; so nice to finally meet you. CeeCee speaks highly of you and the kennel."

He looked around, self-gratification on his face. "Give me time, and the B and G Kennel will be a household name in this part of Arkansas."

Well, it beat football, but not by much.

Arnold loomed over me like a mighty oak. I blinked and he grinned. I felt my lips twitch in a nervous smile. My stars, the man was big—and that hair. Looked like a bowl of fettuccine caught in a windstorm.

"Mrs. Diamond. Mighty proud you dropped by. CeeCee's told me a lot about you."

I shot Cee a frigid glance. "I hope it was all good."

"Can't wait to read one of your books. I'm a stranger in town, been here a few weeks, but you know how it is, hard to get acquainted."

I knew. Small towns tended to be cliquey. And that hair didn't help any.

"I was wondering, Mrs. Diamond, if you might enjoy going out to dinner some evening?"

My head snapped around so fast I almost got whiplash. "Pardon?"

He smiled, and his eyes crinkled at the corners. "You and me. I'd sure like to take a pretty lady like you out to dinner."

"Ah . . . well, I don't go anywhere right now." I glanced at my foot cast. "Poor health, you know."

He nodded sympathetically. "I heard about your accident, but you don't need to worry. I'll get a wheelchair and tootle you around in style."

Tootle me? Well, that was one way of getting attention, but if I wanted to be "tootled" around I wouldn't pick Arnold to do the tootling. "I don't know, Arnold. Going out isn't much fun when you have to go in a wheelchair."

He leaned toward me, expression grave. "I'll tell you what, Maude—may I call you Maude?"

I nodded. His manners were impeccable.

"You don't want to withdraw from life because you had a little trouble. Now, I'm not going to take no for an answer."

I stared at him. "You're not?"

"No, ma'am, I'm not. You put your glad rags on tomorrow night, and we'll go over to the Chinese Wok in Ash Flat. That will perk you right up."

Swallowing, I glanced at Cee and saw her grinning from ear to ear. *Mercy. Why didn't I stay home?*

* * *

I tossed and turned that night—kept thinking about Arnold and tootling and appalling comb-overs. Give me a chrome dome any day.

The next morning my editor on Jack's book called. He wasn't pushy, but I could tell they needed the finished book to put into production. I finally swallowed my pride and asked for an extension—another month, six weeks at the most. The editor was more than happy to accommodate. I hung up the phone thinking I needed to have a serious talk with CeeCee. She had to stay home a couple of nights and work on the manuscript. Rick could do without her; I couldn't.

I heard Stella coming in and pasted a smile on my face. Keep a stiff upper lip, and all that.

"Hey, Maude, guess what?"

"No clue. What?"

"I was just over at the Cart Mart and Thurvis Throckmorton was in the next aisle talking to Hargus. Now there's a pair."

I had to agree. "Were they talking about the Peeping Tom?"

"Nope. Thurvis was madder than hops. Seems like him and Hilda have nightly tiffs about those two new dogs of hers. You seen those beasts? The mayor was telling Hargus he'd accused Hilda of paying more attention to the pooches than to him, and Hilda said the dogs were more interesting."

I belly-laughed. Thurvis shouldn't have been airing family problems in public, but I could just hear Hilda saying that.

"That's what she said: 'the dogs don't prop themselves in front of the TV every night and watch ESPN.' She makes him take the dogs for a nightly walk. Hargus told him to buck up and refuse, but Thurvis said it got him out of the house for a while, and sometimes the dogs were better company than Hilda."

"Well, with Thurvis and Hargus out and about at night, I guess Morning Shade's the safest it's been in a long time."

Stella sniffed. "You know what, Maude? I got me a feeling."

I sighed. Stella and her intuitions—which were amazingly astute. "What is it this time?"

"Kidding aside, I don't think we've heard the last of this Peeping Tom. Got a feeling right here—in my left elbow."

I hoped it was just her arthritis acting up again. Her driving was costing me sleep. I didn't need to worry about Stella mixing it up with a Peeping Tom too.

A body can only handle so much and I'd about reached my limit.

I stepped back from the mirror, frustrated. I wasn't seventeen anymore. The bloom in my cheeks was now a wilted tinge—aided only slightly by Cover Girl blush. It wasn't that I was trying to look seventeen—far from it. Tonight's "engagement" with Arnold was just another milestone, one I wasn't happy to cross.

Dating.

I hadn't dated in forty years. What would I say? How would I act—silly, like a young girl on her first movie date? Goodness knows I wasn't excited about tonight's venture, but Arnold had been so insistent, and a plate of sweet-and-sour chicken might do me good. Not my hips, but me, personally.

I checked my makeup one final time and decided I'd done about all I could do for a woman with a crutch and a wrist bandage. It wasn't like this was a notable engagement. I categorized tonight like this: two lonely people and a plate of egg rolls. The parallel made me feel better. One glance at my watch and I hobbled into the living room to await Arnold's arrival.

Stella wasn't any too happy about my venture into the singles' world. She hadn't said as much, but I knew her looks, and the one she gave me when I came into the room clearly said it was too soon for me to be acting like the merry widow. I headed her denigration off at the pass.

"Tonight is not a date. I simply agreed to have dinner with Arnold. The man's new in town and doesn't know anybody."

"Humph. Has he tried church? That's what churches are for."

I stared at the cage sitting beside her chair. "You know I don't like Boris to be in the living room."

"He's our guard snake."

Guard snake. Stella's less-than-subtle way of letting me know she highly disapproved of my dinner plans.

Stella turned back to Vanna White and *Wheel of Fortune*. Audience applause saved a strained silence.

I eased into my wheelchair and reached for a hard copy of my work-in-progress, figuring I might get a little editing done before Arnold got here. I must say, the edits on Jack Hamel's book were easy—relatively small things that I could change without toppling the book structure. The second half of the advance royalties check arrived today, and I was breathing easier.

When would I learn that God never failed? In the throes of financial insecurity I often resorted to hair pulling, worrying about circumstances beyond my control. Later, when the money was safely in the checking account, I'd look back and marvel how good God had been. Never failed me—never. If only I could learn to hang on to that reassurance—to trust God with every aspect of my life without the slightest apprehension. I was working on the problem, but I still had a way to go.

The doorbell chimed the "Battle Hymn of the Republic." When the melody ended—I was nearly on my feet with my hat across my heart—I looked at Stella. "Did you change the tune?"

She nodded. "Tired of 'Dixie.'"

I laid the manuscript aside, hoping that she'd answer the door. When she hit the volume button and Vanna's voice got louder, I knew my mother-in-law was in full pout.

"Stay where you are," I called sweetly. "I'll get it." It isn't like I'm *handicapped* or anything.

"Too soon," Stella muttered under her breath.

"It's not a *date*. It's an act of kindness." If Mel Gibson was at the door, it would be a date. Arnold Biggert, with the comb-over, was a simple act of kindness.

When I opened the door Arnold smiled, and I must say that he had the nicest, most sincere smile I'd seen in a long while. The greeting was like a breath of spring air on this cold January night.

"Arnold," I said.

"Maude." He extended a small bouquet of purple irises. The delicate floral scented the icy air. I spotted a portable wheelchair sitting to the side.

"Where did you find irises this time of year!"

"Actually—" he stepped into the warm foyer—"I grow them myself." He flashed another amiable grin. "It's a hobby."

"Well, it's a wonderful hobby. Thank you so much." I turned to ask if Stella would mind putting the bouquet in water, but I saw that she had conveniently disappeared. The cage was gone too. Vanna turned another vowel on the blaring set. "I'll only be a moment, Arnold."

"Can I help?"

"My coat—it's the blue one. Hanging on the hall tree."

* * *

Warm air greeted me when Arnold helped me out of the wheelchair into his pickup. The truck was a late model and had a rich burgundy leather interior. After seating me and buckling my seat belt, the vet shut the door and walked around to the driver's side. I sat in the toasty truck's interior and wondered if we'd make strained conversation on the drive to Ash Flat.

To my surprise—and relief—our conversation came as effortlessly as breathing. The miles ticked by with hardly a break in conversation. We talked about nothing, actually. Small talk. My injury and Arnold's recent move to Morning Shade.

How did he like small-town living? Liked it fine. He'd lived in Oregon most of his life and welcomed the slower pace.

Never married.

I was about to ask why a man his age had never married, but he beat me to the punch.

"Always been too busy," he said. He admitted he was married to his business.

I could well understand; sometimes writing consumed my life to the extent that I felt like I was married to the occupation. Like marriage, my career and I had our ups and downs, but I suspect that my love ran deeply—more deeply than I understood. Writing was an integral part of me, and I suppose I couldn't stop if I wanted. At times I felt the process left me drained and empty, but what would I do without the mental release?

I started to relax. I needed this night out. Maybe Arnold would turn out to be a trusted new friend.

"CeeCee tells me you're a mystery writer. I'll have to read one of your books."

I chuckled. "I've published twenty-two mysteries."

"Twenty-two! You must be a best seller!"

Maude clammed up. No, she wasn't a best seller. She'd like to be a best seller, but so far she'd failed to make any of the big best-seller lists. And now with the Hamel ghostwriting project and her injury, she didn't know when she'd have another Diamond mystery published.

"Do you write under your name?"

"M. K. Diamond. That's my pen name."

"M. K. Diamond." He shook his head. "That's nice. Never met a writer. You're my first."

Arnold flipped on the turn signal and entered the right-lane exit ramp to Ash Flat. I was determined not to look at him, because if I did my eyes would go straight for the comb-over, and I didn't want that. A man had a right to wear his hair any way he saw fit, but goodness' sake, couldn't he look in the mirror and see that he'd created a fashion monster?

"Yes," he said, picking up the earlier thread of discussion. "Haven't had much time for women the past few years. My first attempt at true love turned out to be a disaster. I was young and didn't have enough sense to know that I couldn't push my attention on a woman who didn't want it. I'd wait beside her car every night for her to get off work, and sometimes I'd follow her home to make certain she got there without any trouble. She lived in a rough section of town.

"I finally learned my lesson," he said. "Also spent two years in a penitentiary for a white-collar crime. Learned my lesson there too." He glanced over and smiled.

I grinned lamely, not daring to look at him. *I'm on a date with an ex-con. Please, God, don't let Stella hear about his past.*

"Have you met Dr. Phillips yet?" I asked, keeping my tone chatty.

"The other vet in town? Yes, met him a few days ago. Rick and I were having a sandwich at the café when we bumped into him."

"Nice man."

"Seemed real friendly."

Five minutes later the pickup wheeled into the parking lot of The Chinese Wok. Business was slow on a weeknight so we had our choice of parking spots.

My thoughts were still reeling when we entered the hut and located a booth near the back. I thought maybe I should further explore the penitentiary remark, but I felt loath to bring it up again.

Arnold's eyes were on the large buffet filled with steaming entrees. "I'm having that," he announced when the waitress brought pots of hot tea and sat them on our table.

Grinning, the older lady bowed. "Two?"

Arnold looked to me expectantly, and I agreed. "Two buffets."

Over dinner we chatted. I didn't bring up the past and Arnold refrained from saying anything more about the stalking incident. My eyes could not stay away from the comb-over. Heavily gelled, swept to the right side in lengthy wisps of graying strands.

"What about this Peeping Tom?" Arnold dipped a piece of crab rangoon in sweet sauce.

"I don't know what to think—pretty scary, actually."

"Does Hargus have any thoughts on who might be doing this?"

I shook my head, dousing an egg roll in duck sauce. "Stella—my mother-in-law—she likes to try her hand at sleuthing. She and Hargus are working on the Peeping Tom incident, but there's only been one and they haven't come up with any useful leads. Actually, Helen's so nearsighted the incident might very well be only a figment of her imagination."

"Well, if there is a perpetrator, they can be facing time," Arnold observed. .

Of course he would be sensitive to such matters. I didn't say anything figuring "time" meant jail time, and I didn't much want to bring that up again. I wondered if CeeCee knew about Arnold's past. Had she encouraged her mother to date an ex-con? That didn't sound like my daughter. . . . That didn't sound like anybody I knew.

Before I realized it, it was nine o'clock and the restaurant was closing. The waitress set chairs upside down on tables. A young boy dragged a large broom out of the closet. While Arnold paid the bill, I made a quick stop at the ladies' room. All in all, it had been an enjoyable evening, a pleasant diversion on a cold winter night.

"We'll have to do this again," Arnold said on the drive back to Morning Shade.

I wasn't sure I'd go that far—I'd have to think about this jail thing. Arnold certainly had been all gentleman, and I knew youth sometimes did things that they lived to regret, but I didn't want to upset Stella. Two dates would officially signify the end of mourning, and I wasn't ready to let go of Herb. Not yet. Maybe not ever. Besides, nothing irritated me more than to see a widowed woman go nuts after a spouse's death. I knew perfectly normal women who jumped right back into dating before their husband's belongings were cleared away. I wasn't going to go that route. I was going to give Herb a decent mourning period—however long that might be. So I brushed off Arnold's suggestion, saying I wasn't getting out much these days. He seemed to understand, but I figured he would be calling again soon.

I unlocked the front door and heard the phone ringing. Tossing my keys on the foyer table, I hobbled to the living room. "Stella?" I called out. Was that snake downstairs?

Captain opened his eyes at the sound of my voice. The cat yawned and stretched. My eyes switched to the sofa and found it empty.

"CeeCee!" I shouted when the persistent shrill ring jarred me. Wheeling to the end table, I jerked up the cordless.

"Maude?" It was Stella.

"Where's Boris?" I asked her.

"In my room. Why?"

"I just got home. Where is everybody?"

"CeeCee's at the kennel. I'm at Shady Acres."

I glanced at my watch. "What are you doing over there at this time of night?" I knew that Simon, Frances, and Pansy would be getting ready for bed at this hour. Bridge rarely lasted past eight o'clock, and this wasn't the normal bridge or Farkle night.

Unmistakable resentment colored Stella's voice. "I've been calling for the last hour. Did you just get in?"

I downplayed the lateness of my return. "I've been home a little while. What's going on?"

"Did you enjoy dinner?"

Mentally sighing, I tried to think of a way to soothe her ruffled feathers. Of course she was loyal to Herb; so was I, and I can't say that I hadn't felt culpable all evening—like I was dishonoring my late husband by even sitting in the same booth with another man.

"I'm glad to be home, Stella." And that was the truth. My world was here—in this house, with my daughter and mother-in-law. I wasn't seeking a new life; I liked the one I had. Stella had hurt enough when she lost her son, and I wasn't going to hurt her more.

"Well, you missed all the excitement."

"I did? What's happened?"

"The Peeping Tom—he was here."

"There? At the retirement home?"

"Yes, scared Peaches half out of her wits. We're trying to calm her down."

"Is Hargus there?"

"Of course—we're working the case. There were two of them tonight, Maude. *Two* Peeping Toms. We got a blockbuster case on our hands this time."

"Two. Did they leave any clues?"

"Haven't found anything yet. Me and Hargus briefly searched the grounds, but Hargus's batteries went out on his flashlight. He's getting new ones now. We're going out again as soon as I get Peaches settled."

I heard the old excitement in Stella's voice—the cutting-edge adrenaline she got when things started to happen. "So, you didn't have all that much fun tonight. Too bad—but Arnold didn't look to be your kind. Didn't think you'd have any fun. Well, I'll be home as soon as I can—but don't wait up. Might crack the case wide-open; then I'll be in later. I'll check in on you to see how you're feeling—make you a cup of warm tea if it's not too late."

I smiled. Had I said that I *didn't* have fun tonight? Funny how a person hears what they want to hear. "A cup of tea would hit the spot. Be careful, Stella."

"Ten-four."

"You're certain, Peaches? You can't give us anything other than the man had a face only a mother could love, and his partner looked weird?" Stella reached for the Kleenex and put the box in the distraught woman's hand. "One man was old; the other extremely ugly? Is that all you can tell us about the Peeping Toms?"

Peaches nodded and then buried her face in a tissue. "What else can I say? It was so unnerving—I was fixing popcorn in the microwave, and I happened to look up and there they were, *two of them* peering in the window." She shuddered. "I'll never be the same. Wait. Come to think of it, I believe one of the men was long in the jowls. . . ."

Stella exchanged dubious looks with Hargus. "You said the window shade was pulled."

Peaches nodded, owl-eyed. "I wouldn't dare leave my shades open at night. Not with all this nonsense going on."

"If the window shade was down, how can you be certain of the two men's features?" How could she be certain they were men? Maybe someone—a woman—or two women from the retirement home went outside, got confused, and peeked in windows trying to find their way back?

Peaches lifted her face momentarily. "You don't believe me?"

"We believe you," Stella said. "But with the shade pulled all you'd be able to see would be silhouettes, at best." She wanted a mystery as bad as Hargus, but they might be making a mountain of a molehill.

Stella didn't know what to make of Helen and Peaches. The two women swore the Peeping Tom—or Toms, as it were—were male, and one was ugly. First thing out of Peaches's mouth tonight was "the perpetrator was *so* ugly you'd have to tie a pork chop around the man's neck to get a dog to come around."

Not much to go on. Was it possible both women were so nearsighted they couldn't accurately see anything about the perpetrator other than there was one—or two now—and they imagined they could distinguish features? Stella shook her head. "If that's the case, and they are men, then it narrows our field of suspects."

"Yeah," Hargus agreed, shifting to the opposite foot. "Narrows our suspects for sure. I've been thinking; maybe someone's playing tricks—youthful pranks. Yet if what Peaches and Helen are saying is true, then we have to rule out teenagers and go more with the drifter theory." He took a hitch in his pants. "Suppose a couple of homeless could be riding the rails—peeking in folks' windows."

Peaches dabbed at moisture pooling in the corners of her eyes. "I do declare I've never been so frightened. Makes a body scared in her own home."

Stella reached over and patted her hand. "You're safe, Peaches. Take a sleeping pill, and you'll feel better in the morning. Meanwhile, me and Hargus are going to take another look around." Their earlier foray had produced nothing, but maybe they'd overlooked something. There'd been so much confusion going on—Peaches sobbing and everybody trying to calm her down.

Hargus dropped a couple of new C batteries in his flashlight and switched it on, blinking when the light blinded him.

Peaches caught her breath.

"Turn that thing off," Stella said shortly. "She's spooked enough."

Buttoning her coat, she motioned for Hargus to follow her. The two negotiated dimly lit hallways, speaking in hushed tones. It was late, and an uneasy silence had settled over Shady Acres residential care facility.

A cold front had dropped temperatures into the low teens when Stella and Hargus exited the building. Hargus flipped on the flashlight and ran the beam around the outside of the porch perimeter. Stella didn't see or hear anything but the faint tinkle of wind chimes hanging at the west end of the building.

"Let's have a final look around before we go home."

Hargus nodded. "We could have missed something."

The two fell into synchronized step and rounded the building. Hargus skimmed light over the deserted grounds. "I'm glad you told Peaches we were going to look around."

Stella nodded. "I didn't want her to be upset if she saw or heard anything at her window in the next few minutes."

They paused to investigate a row of ice-coated shrubbery. Other than a blue Wal-Mart sack tangled in the branches, nothing unusual came in sight. They walked on until they were standing beneath Peaches's window.

Stella lowered her voice. "Be careful—we don't want to set her off again." She cocked an ear at the sound of a distant train whistle. Glancing at her watch, she noted the time. Hargus moved the beam closer to her.

"Eleven-thirty freight," she said.

Hargus nodded. The train raced closer, the engineer laying on the horn. Soon a long line of cars whipped past, rumbling into the distance.

"Don't logically see how a man—or men—could hop off a train traveling that fast, scare the wits out of a body, and then hop back on," Stella mused. She listened to the disappearing *clickity-clack*.

"Couldn't." Hargus huddled deeper into his sheepskin-lined jacket. "They might jump the train, but they couldn't reboard without cracking a skull."

Stella agreed. "So if the culprits are drifters, they'd still be in the area."

Silence fell between them. Stella wondered if the two men were looking at them right now—plotting evil. They could be crouching anywhere along the steps and curving, dimly lit walkways.

Hargus switched off the light. "It's late. I have to go."

"Hold on." Stella eased toward a row of dwarf Alberta spruce bending low to the ground. The shrubs still winked brightly colored Christmas lights. Weather in Morning Shade had been so bad that groundskeepers were behind in maintenance.

"Come on, Stella. It's cold." Hargus's voice came to her in the inky blackness. Overhead, clouds blocked the stars and moon.

"Hold the light over here—in this direction."

Grumbling, Hargus switched on the beam and flashed it in her direction. Minuscule snowflakes danced in the powerful ray. "It's starting to snow," he groused. "Let's go."

"Move the light here—ten inches to the left of my left foot."

Hargus flooded the area with light, illuminating a rock and another Wal-Mart sack.

Edging down the row of shrubbery, Stella kept her eyes on the ground. Surely the culprits had left some clue: a bent twig, a footprint. A scrap of paper or a cigarette butt.

Ah-ha!

Adrenaline surged. Stella bent over and snagged a piece of white. Her fingers closed around the object, and she pulled it out of the hedgerow. For a second she and Hargus stared at the object. A shoe—a sneaker. But lo and behold what a sneaker!

"What's that?" Hargus moved in for a closer look.

"It's a shoe."

"I can see that! Who wears a shoe that size?"

Stella turned the shoe over in her hand, searching for a size. "Great balls of fire. It's a size fourteen."

"Fourteen!"

"One of the men must have lost it when they heard Peaches scream."

Hargus took the shoe out of her hand and turned it over and over, studying the footwear. "They caught Bigfoot, didn't they?" he asked.

"Bigfoot was a *hoax*. Appears the man who started the legend died a few months ago, and his son confessed his father's prank."

"What about the Lox Ness monster."

"That's Loch Ness," Stella corrected. "Don't know anything about him other than to say with certainty he isn't our suspect."

"Nobody around these parts wears a shoe this size." Hargus fished something out of his coat pocket and dropped the shoe into the black garbage sack. A closer search of the site produced no further evidence.

Snow fell in large flakes now, coating Stella's and Hargus's coats and hats.

"I say we're wasting time." Hargus blew on his fingers, stomping one booted foot then the other. "There's nothing more here—and even if there were, it'll be here in the morning."

Stella nodded. She was a mite stove-up herself. "We'll come back in the morning," she said.

Hargus grumbled something, but he followed her to the parking lot.

A size-fourteen shoe, Stella thought. A sizeable clue—in more ways than the obvious.

CeeCee had breakfast duty Monday morning: cereal, fruit, juice, and coffee. I knew she and Stella thought I was putting on weight, which I was, but constant sitting and eating did that to you, and those were my major activities these days.

Stella approached the table with her teeth in, for a wonder. She sat down and waited for CeeCee to bless the food. It made my heart sing to see CeeCee's gradual spiritual reawakening. I could remember the bitter, disillusioned young woman who had tried to turn her back on God not so long ago. It was good to hear my daughter giving thanks.

Stella picked up her spoon and held it. "Did I tell you about the shoe Hargus and I found at Shady Acres?"

I poured milk over my Cream of Wheat. If she'd talked about that shoe once, she'd mention it a hundred times. But the size was interesting . . .

"Find out who it belongs to, Grandma?" CeeCee asked.

Stella's eyes sparkled. Even if this was a much-to-do-about-nothing mystery, the excitement had revived my mother-in-law. Now she fairly bristled with animation.

"Not just any shoe, mind you, a size-fourteen sneaker."

CeeCee playfully gaped. "Who wears a shoe that size? Bigfoot?"

I laughed at the idea of the elusive Bigfoot showing up in Morning Shade. "I don't think he wears shoes. Where would he go to buy them?"

CeeCee giggled. "Now he has one shoe off and one shoe on. What's the nursery rhyme?"

"'Diddle, diddle, dumpling, my son John,'" I finished, and we both laughed.

Stella's lower lip drew in. "Will you get serious? Bigfoot was a hoax, and you both know it. This is a real clue. The only one we have, and it's not funny."

"No, of course it's not," I hastened to assure her. "I guess it just struck us wrong. I'm sorry, Stella. We'll behave."

CeeCee sobered. "You know, Peeping Toms really aren't all that funny. I don't know anyone in Morning Shade who wears such a large shoe."

"There must be someone," I mused. A thought hit me. "You don't think Gary Hendricks is pulling another one of his stunts?"

"No," CeeCee interjected practically before the words were out of my mouth. "Gary wouldn't do anything that foolish."

"He wouldn't?" She knew Gary's tendency for practical jokes, and leaving a size-fourteen sneaker lying around would be right up his alley.

"I know one thing," Stella said. "There is a Peeping Tom—and maybe two."

"I hate to hear that." I stirred cream in my coffee. "I was hoping Helen had been mistaken and Peaches—well, we all know Peaches."

Stella drained the last of her cup and set it down. "Not to worry. Hargus and I are on top of the case. We'll have the pervert in custody shortly."

CeeCee got up from the table and began clearing dishes. "I may be late tonight. Rick wants me to stop by and help clean the new puppy cages."

"Thought that Biggert man's working for him," Stella said. "How come he can't clean cages?"

CeeCee flushed. "He can, of course, but I agreed to help with the work for free boarding for Frenchie, Claire, and the birds."

"I'd about as soon have the dogs and birds back home than have you driving around alone at night with a Peeping Tom on the loose," Stella groused.

"I never thought of that," I exclaimed. What kind of mother was I to let my daughter take foolish chances? "Cee, maybe you should—"

"Mom—I'm *careful.*" She interrupted me, something CeeCee seldom did. She must be upset. "What do you think will happen to me driving home from the kennel? It's not more than five minutes away."

Twin spots of color brightened her cheeks. I recognized the signs. Her temper was on a fast rise. "Don't get huffy," I said. "We only worry about you because you're ours."

She wasn't mollified. "I'll stop by and see Rick. If he needs help, I'll stay, and I consider that my business."

"So do we," I said mildly. "No need to come unglued."

CeeCee appeared to soften. "I just don't want anyone to interfere with my relationship with Rick."

"What makes you think anyone would?" I asked. Although it was exactly what I planned to do; Rick Materi was wrong for my daughter, and I didn't want her hurt again. So shoot me.

"This is completely off the subject," Stella said. "Who do you think owns a size-fourteen sneaker?"

CeeCee rinsed the dishcloth and hung it to dry. "I haven't a clue. Sorry, I have to get to work." She left the kitchen and a few minutes later I heard the front door slam.

I raised my eyebrows. "She's royally ticked."

Stella nodded. "I've got to figure out some way to trace that sneaker."

Well, of course, first things first. Talk about a one-track mind. I supposed CeeCee would eventually cool down, but I didn't like the way Rick was beginning to monopolize her time.

I didn't say so, but if the Peeping Tom or Toms wore that shoe, he wasn't anything I wanted Stella to tangle with.

Deep snow lined CeeCee's postal route that morning. One glance at the Hendricks rural box and she knew she had two choices: leave the truck and slip-slide her way to the receptacle, or take the small shovel she carried in the back of the vehicle and scoop out a path. She opted for the shovel.

Sliding out of the mail truck, she picked her way to the back and opened the hatch. Moments later she wedged the tool into the biggest drift, keeping an eye on the house. Hendricks, town buffoon, didn't appear to be around this morning.

Actually, she hadn't seen Gary in weeks other than briefly at church. The guy had a few redeeming qualities, though she'd had to take a long hard look to unearth them. Gary was the town's scoutmaster, and the boys loved him. Some said he took the place of many a busy or indifferent dad at town functions.

Rumor was he had a new girlfriend. CeeCee found that highly suspect, but in a tiny way, she was glad for the irrepressible prankster. Apparently he'd met and fallen for Karen Asbury, a young, inherently shy young woman who worked in the children's book section in the library. Scuttlebutt said the two fit like a key and lock, though Karen was nothing like the outgoing Gary. She was reclusive, serious, stern. CeeCee shook her head; she couldn't imagine the two together, but what did they say? Opposites attract.

CeeCee grunted and heaved a shovel of snow aside. Overnight, a system had dumped eight new inches on Morning Shade, and flakes were still falling.

She turned when she heard a car crawling down the street. The blue Cavalier slowly forged through deep snowdrifts and stopped beside her. The driver rolled down the window. "Morning, Miss Postal Lady."

"Good morning." She hefted another shovelful of snow to the side.

Gary quickly slid from behind the wheel, and moments later he was wielding a shovel beside her. "Sorry—I should have had this cleared earlier, but I baked cinnamon rolls this morning, and I wanted Karen to have one before they got cold."

Warm cinnamon rolls. Had a guy ever baked cinnamon rolls for her? CeeCee shook the thought away. Jake certainly never did; Rick brought donuts to the kennel on Saturday mornings, but he always set the box on his desk and told everyone to help themselves.

Wasn't quite the same as having a guy drive in eight inches of fresh snow to deliver warm rolls.

"That's nice of you. I'm sure Karen appreciates your thoughtfulness."

A smitten grin spread across Gary's wind-chapped features. "Yeah—she does. She's nice, CeeCee. Have you met her?"

"Once." CeeCee pitched a shovelful of snow to the side. "I like to visit the children's section in the library. I love the books—and the cute little animal statues they have around. Have you seen the kangaroo?"

"Looks real, doesn't it?" Winded, Gary stood back and leaned on the shovel handle. His eyes grazed her. "How's things going with you and Rick?"

CeeCee flushed, suddenly feeling unnerved.

Admittedly, Rick attracted her—fascinated her—made her juices boil in a way they hadn't since Jake died. It was way too soon to think about love. At this point in her life she wasn't sure if she'd recognize love if it walked up and spit on her, but the handsome kennel owner was a welcomed diversion from salt-and-vinegar potato chips and watching *Law & Order* every night.

Mom bothered her though. She kept hinting that Rick was just another Jake Tamaris incarnate, but CeeCee knew different. She'd lived with—and loved—the real Jake, and Rick, though he bore some similarities to her deceased spouse, wasn't Jake.

Yes, like Jake, Rick loved sports, idolized football, liked to laugh, and had a fondness for pricy things: cars, clothing. But *unlike* Jake, Rick had an honest streak running through his veins. She may not like everything he did or said, but she was fairly certain that the Rick she saw was the real Rick. He wasn't given to illusions, and he'd openly told her more than once that when it came to women and money he couldn't be trusted.

How's that for honesty? At least she knew that if she fell for him she was creating her own misery.

Gary's voice drew her back. "Hey." He reached out and tapped her gently on the forearm. "You don't have to keep shoveling. You can hand me my mail."

CeeCee felt a sheepish grin crawl up her face. When she thought about Rick the whole world disappeared. "Sure thing. Hold on a sec." She stored the shovel in the back of the LLV and walked around to the side.

Gary followed. "Care if I pick your brain?"

"About what?" CeeCee reached in a bin and extracted a banded bundle.

"Women." He shook his head. "I'm not good at mind reading."

CeeCee laughed. "Most men aren't. What do you need?"

"I want to do something special for Karen. You know, I want her to know that she's special."

CeeCee wondered why more men weren't blessed with Gary's sensitivity. He could be a buffoon, have ill-timed streaks of pure insanity, but lately she'd noticed a caring streak penetrating his prankster heart.

"Well—" CeeCee handed him the mail—"you could caramel an onion and give it to her."

He had the decency to blush. "*Au contraire.* Very foolish attempt to gain a woman's eye."

CeeCee grinned. "I wouldn't advise repeating the act."

Gary absently thumbed through his envelopes and flyers. "What could I get Karen that says, 'I like you. Really like you.'"

CeeCee shoved her hands in her coat pocket and debated the challenge. Not many men had asked her advice on matters of the heart—come to think of it, only Gary. She felt a strong urge to help him because surely Karen couldn't approve of his practical jokes. She was too austere . . . too conservative.

"Perfume?" She offered.

"Too ordinary. I don't think she wears perfume."

"Maybe a day at a spa—you know, massage, pedicure, facial, haircut, makeover."

Negative. "She's not like that. She likes simple things."

"Okay. Simple."

"But nice."

"Simple but nice."

"But memorable—something she won't forget."

"Golly, Gary. I'm not Santa Claus."

He flashed another grin. "Sorry—I just—"

"Want to tell her how much you like her."

He nodded, his brown eyes solemn now. "That's not easy for me to convey to a woman."

"Give me a few days and I'll try to come up with something simple, nice but definitely worthwhile and exciting."

His face brightened. "You're on!"

She motioned to the cavernous drifts burying his mailbox. "If you want to do something to make me happy, have this cleared away by tomorrow morning."

He snapped a brisk salute. At times the guy could be downright . . . appealing . . . in an odd sort of way.

"Will do, sir!"

CeeCee opened the truck door. "Fall out, Sergeant."

"Colonel, sir! As you say, sir!"

When she drove off she glanced in her rearview mirror and grinned when she saw Hendricks shoveling snow like a man possessed.

Well, like she said, at times Hendricks could be downright human. Her thoughts flashed back to Christmas when he had carameled an onion, wrapped it in brightly colored red cellophane, tied it with a green ribbon, and left it in the mailbox for her Christmas present.

She shuddered.

Could a zebra change his stripes? She hoped for Karen's sake it could.

Stella roared off in the Caddy, and Captain and I had the house to ourselves. Whoopee. To think I used to pray for solitude. I used to pray for a lot of things that I'm beginning to see were selfish, self-centered requests. When had I become a whiner—a person who wallowed in self-pity? Self-pity was never an attribute that I admired, and I'd never thought of myself in that light, but lately I was beginning to see that what God had so richly given me I considered a millstone. I was blessed to be able to share my faith through stories.

CeeCee had made chicken and noodles for me to reheat. Lately, I alternated between my crutches and a cane, since it seemed to help my ankle to switch off once in a while, but I still got frustrated trying to work with one hand. Never expected to think this, let alone say it, but I'd be so glad to be able to type again. This forced inactivity was making me recognize and count my blessings. I was finding I had more than I had ever realized.

Was that odd or was that God?

I heated water in the microwave, dropped in a tea bag, added honey and carried the finished product to the living room and my recliner. CeeCee had bought me something like a child's sippy cup, only this one was insulated to keep hot things hot and cold things cold. After I had burned my tongue a few times, I got the hang of drinking from it. I could hook one finger through the handle and still grip my cane. If I ever spilled the contents, I'd probably have first-degree burns on my good leg. Serve me right for being so stubborn, but I wasn't about to give up my morning tea.

Two cups of coffee for breakfast, nine o'clock tea, and a repeat on the coffee for lunch; I was caffeine wired.

Once I settled in my chair, tea on the table, telephone within reach, Bible on my lap, I was ready for my morning devotions. Psalms again—63:7-8: "I think how much You have helped me; I sing for joy in the shadow of Your protecting wings. I follow close behind You; Your strong right hand holds me securely."

I spent a few moments dwelling on the beauty of the passage. I write words, but mine never have this grace and majesty. I relaxed as I meditated on the contents of the message. The shadow of His wings. What a wonderful place to rest. My right hand might not work, but His right hand upholds me. I sat there for a minute, feeling truly blessed.

My thoughts eventually wandered back to the Peeping Tom. Why would anyone want to go around peeping in windows? Morning Shade never used to have problems like this. I didn't know what this town was coming to.

The phone rang and I reached for the receiver.

Arnold Biggert. "Morning, Maude. How are you today?"

"Very good, Arnold. Yourself?"

"Couldn't be better. Thanks."

So come to the point. Or is this something I don't want to hear?

"I had a nice time in Ash Flat the other night."

"Chinese food is my weakness." I felt like I should add something about appreciating him taking me.

"I was wondering if we could go out again tonight?"

Well, scratch that. The man didn't need any encouragement. Stella was finally settling down. "Oh, Arnold, I'm sorry, but I have rewrites to do. This manuscript is on a deadline, and CeeCee and I have to work every night this week." I ignored the strong disappointment suddenly gripping my stomach. Going to dinner sounded great. Did I dare risk Stella's disapproval again?

He cleared his throat with a rumble like a drum solo. "You couldn't take off a couple of hours? We could eat here in town."

I couldn't imagine where, unless we went to the Citgo, and wouldn't Stella love that. I realized Arnold was waiting for my answer.

"No . . . I'm in the middle of this book, and I really do need to stay home and work. I'm sorry. Some other time?" Now why had I said that? He'd be sure to ask again and I'd be sure to make another excuse.

"Some other time."

He hung up and I felt like an insect. He was so gracious. I'd had a wonderful time talking over dinner, and after a while I'd even stopped noticing the comb-over. If it had been Sherm now. . . would I be less considerate of Stella's feelings? I jerked my thoughts back into line. *Grow up, Maude. You're a widow with responsibilities. What man would want to take you on?*

My immediate concern had better be the manuscript. I couldn't type unless I mastered the art of putting a pencil between my teeth and tapping on the keys. My "easy ghostwriting money" suddenly wasn't so easy. If CeeCee didn't get busy and insert the revised material, I would be up that well-known creek without a paddle.

My daughter's good intentions were gradually eroding. She spent more and more time at the kennel. Stella and I had to be careful what we said about Rick. Just the barest hint of disapproval put her in a huff.

So go the life and times of Maude Diamond.

Stella was so excited about the sneaker she had trouble keeping her mind on the art-therapy class. Complete waste of time, anyway. Grown people sitting around coloring. Mack Johnson broke more crayons than a preschooler.

Give those folks something to do and they'd forget all about being depressed. Look at her, eighty-seven years old, on a downhill slide, and you didn't see her sitting around coloring. She had a mystery to solve.

She had an idea so brilliant it stunned even her. Turn the class loose on the shoe! See what they'd come up with. Manuel was smart—smarter than most kids his age. Smart alec—but brain smart too. There must be all sorts of brainpower lurking behind those bored expressions.

She'd tried to get the class interested in the case once before, but she didn't have the shoe then. Well, she didn't exactly have it now. Hargus had insisted on keeping it, because he was what passed for the law in Morning Shade. She sniffed. Poor boy. He couldn't find his back pants pocket with both hands. He'd be sunk without her help.

She clapped for attention. "Hey, listen up."

Most of the group ceased work. Manuel didn't though. Trust him to be the worm in the apple. Downright pigheaded. She hurried on before they went back to their coloring. Most of them had the attention span of a two-year-old in a candy store.

"You remember I told you about Morning Shade's Peeping Tom?"

Several heads nodded.

"Well, we have a solid clue." Stella noticed Manuel had stopped coloring; his dark eyes focused on her now. She warmed to her subject. "Guess what it is. A size-fourteen sneaker."

"Whooee!" Nella Arthbuckle exclaimed. "Fourteen. Now that's a good size foot."

Zeke Wilkins cut loose with a braying laugh like a donkey in a rainstorm. Stella had forgotten how he could get on her nerves. "My old granddaddy would have said he had a 'firm understanding.'"

Stella peered at him over her glasses. Zeke was about as funny as a trip to the dentist, and his old granddaddy must have been a couple of pickles short of a barrel.

"As I was saying—" she started over—"that's a rather unusual shoe size. Kind of hard to come up with anyone in town with a foot that big."

Susan Hoskins patted her ash-blonde hair cut in a stylish wedge. "I admire a man with a sense of humor," she said. "I wear a five-B width myself."

Stella snorted. Sure she did. And the moon was made of Limburger cheese. Those sandals she wore looked like rubber rafts.

Rita McElheny joined the conversation. "Put an ad in the paper: 'Shoe found, return to owner, no questions asked.'"

Stella debated the suggestion. No questions? How could she find out anything if she didn't ask questions? "We're talking about a criminal here. Of course we're going to ask questions. Nice try, though," she added when Rita looked downcast.

Lawrence Horseman chuckled. "Reminds me of that old song we used to sing about a gal named Clementine. Believe she wore a nine." Lawrence started singing in a passable baritone. "'Herring boxes without topses sandals were for Clementine.'"

Stella grinned. That was an old one. She used to sing Herb to sleep with that song when he was an infant. Now he was gone, and she was living with his widow, who had started dating again.

She wouldn't have thought it of Maude.

"How about this?" Rita offered. "Is there some sort of gathering where you could get people to take off their shoes? Then you could check the footwear for size."

Stella nodded her head slowly. "The only place I can think of would be church. But how could I get them to take off their shoes?"

"Well, when I had my carpet cleaned, I wouldn't let anyone walk on it until it dried," Rita said. "Usually took three days to fully dry."

"Bingo," Stella pointed at her with a black crayon. "That would work. Let's see, if I had the sanctuary cleaned on Saturday the carpet would still be wet on Sunday."

"Oh yes, indeed," Rita said. "It takes a long time to dry in winter."

"I'll have to pay to have it cleaned," Stella mused. "Shouldn't cost that much." She didn't think Hargus would help. That boy was so tight he pinched a nickel until the buffalo bucked.

With everyone sitting inside in their sock feet, she'd have

plenty of time to check shoe sizes. With a plan like this, she couldn't miss. She'd have that Peeping Tom cornered before Hargus could pop open another Chocolate Cow.

The class had gone back to coloring, and Stella was so relieved to have a plan of action that she sat down beside Mack and colored a nice landscape for Maude. She figured it would lend a touch of class to the kitchen when she taped it on the refrigerator.

* * *

Stella stopped by Hargus's office early the next day to tell him about the shoe plan. She hoped he would help her comb through the footwear on Sunday morning, and maybe offer to help pay half on the carpet-cleaning bill. She'd already called the Hidy-Tidy Carpet Cleaners and made arrangements for them to do the work.

Hargus offered her coffee, and she accepted a cup, stirring in a teaspoon of creamer. He leaned back in his chair, listening to her for a change. She thought how professional it felt sitting here talking about crime.

"So what do you think? Isn't that a good plan or what?" Stella asked.

"What?"

She stifled an exasperated snort. "Don't get smart. You have a better idea?"

He shrugged. "It's okay. Might work. But we got another problem."

She sat erect, nerves keyed to the max. "What now?"

"The Peeping Tom struck again last night."

"Hot dog! Where this time?"

"Farley Birks. High school principal. Just walked right up and looked straight in his window."

Stella shook her head. "Did Farley get a good look at him?"

"Nope. Like Helen and Peaches, he had his shades pulled down. You know Farley."

Stella sighed; she knew Farley all right. So fussy he reminded her of that Mister What's-His-Name who used to do the toilet-paper commercials. You wouldn't catch Farley squeezing the Charmin.

Hargus steepled his fingers. "He left a little souvenir there too."

"He did?" Stella was all ears. "What this time? The other shoe?"

"A woman's corset. One of those old-fashioned ones with whalebone stays. You know the kind."

Stella laughed so hard she almost lost her bottom plate. "He left a corset at Farley's?" They had a practical joker on their hands—sounded for the world like one of Gary Hendricks's pranks. "Wouldn't you have loved to see Farley's face when he found it? Has he recovered from the shock yet?"

Hargus grinned. "He got a little excited all right. What kind of criminal have we got here who wears a size-fourteen sneaker and a woman's corset?"

Stella eased to the front of the chair. "Cross-dresser with big feet."

"We only found one shoe," Hargus reminded her.

"A cross-dresser with a big foot and a peg leg," she amended. "We're in trouble. No one like that lives in Morning Shade."

"We got another problem," Hargus said. "I saw Pete Gyres in the mercantile and he was ordering a new pair of—get this—size-fourteen sneakers. Seems like someone has stolen one, just one, of his grandson Todd's shoes."

"Land, I had forgotten that boy," Stella said. "Got feet like Bozo the Clown. But who would steal just one shoe? So you think Todd's peeping in windows?" Wouldn't put it past a teenager.

"Couldn't be. Todd was here in early December; then he went to spend a few weeks with his maternal grandmother. Still there, Pete says. So that means we have no idea who put that shoe there, but it wasn't Pete's grandson.

"I say we got ourselves a peg-legged, shoe-stealing, corset-wearing Peeping Tom," Hargus said. "We got a job on our hands. Think we're up to it?"

"We are if anyone is." Stella grinned. She'd humor the boy, let him think he was helping. Whose idea was it to check everyone's shoe sizes on Sunday? Hers, of course. What had he come up with? Nothing—pure-dee nothing.

"Still think we should check the shoe situation. Make everyone take off their shoes Sunday morning."

"Why? The sneaker must belong to Pete's grandson."

"We can't afford to leave a stone unturned. Sounds like it's Pete's boy's shoe, but then the culprits might be playing tricks on us. Sounds like we got a prankster behind these peeping incidents."

"Gary Hendricks?"

"Could be. I'll do a little snooping around."

* * *

Stella was hotfooting it to the Citgo an hour later when she saw Hargus drive by with Maury Peacock in the cab of his GMC. Curious, she abandoned Citgo and instead beat a path to City Hall.

By the time she got there, Hargus was elbowing Maury into

the mayor's office. She bent low, trying to catch her breath. Was Maury the Peeping Tom? Was Hargus cutting her out—giving her false information when he knew all along Maury was the town peeper? He would if he could. He'd do anything to get a solved case in his favor.

In his dreams.

She marched inside to see Maury standing before the mayor, twisting his hat in his hands, indecision on his face.

Thurvis didn't seem all that happy either. "Maury, you know you're not supposed to be smoking in the city limits," the mayor was saying. "You were at the town meeting when the smoking ban was voted into place."

Maury nodded. "I was at the meeting, Mayor, but I don't know this City Limits place. Don't remember seeing anything like that in Morning Shade and it don't sound like a place I'd go anyway."

"No, Maury, I mean inside town."

"Inside Town? We got *two* new businesses here? Where in tarnation are they and what are they?" Maury bristled. "They sound like joints, and I've never gone to joints in my whole life. I'll have you know I've been a deacon in the Living Truth Church most of my adult life, and 'the lips that touch liquor shall never touch mine.'"

Thurvis screwed up his face. "I'm talking about you smoking. Now you owe a two-hundred-fifty-dollar fine."

"For what!" Maury demanded. "For not going to those places? Did we pass a law that I got to go to somewhere I don't want to go? I'm not paying it." He shook his head. "It's not the money; it's the principle of the thing. A man has to take a stand somewhere."

Thurvis took a deep breath and wiped his forehead. "How

do I get into these things? I never liked that no-smoking ordinance in the first place, and I'm starting to purely despise it. Never mind, Maury; I don't have the constitution for this. Case dismissed."

Maury shook his head. "I don't know what the constitution has to do with it. You can't tell me it says I have to go to places like that, because I don't believe it. That wonderful document was written by men who believed in God. They probably wouldn't have gone to that City Limits place either."

Stella followed Hargus out of the mayor's office. "What's going on, Hargus?"

He sighed. "I caught Maury smoking his pipe and hauled him in, and I ain't never going to do that again. It's more than I can stand. He's got Thurvis so confused he don't know what he's doing, and I ain't far behind."

Maury slapped his hat back on. "I don't know what this town's coming to. Peeping Toms, fancy places no decent folks would go to, and we got a *thief* too."

"A thief?" Stella asked. "Something been stolen?"

"My wife's girdle."

Stella peered over her glasses. Was he for real? His wife had been dead long enough for even someone as goofy as Maury was, to have missed her. "You're wife's gone, Maury."

He nodded. "Yep, she's singing with the angel band, but she didn't take her girdle with her. Somebody stole it. I'm getting ready for a spring garage sale, and I hung the missus's unmentionables on the line to air fluff—"

"Air freeze," Stella interrupted. "It's January."

"Whatever," Maury waved his hand dismissively. "Anyway, someone stole that girdle. Took it right off the line. Left the clothespins, though."

Stella threw Hargus a hard look. They knew where that girdle was. It had turned up on Farley's front porch.

"Maury, you know anything about a size-fourteen sneaker?" Stella asked.

"Why would I know anything about a shoe that size? My wife didn't wear a fourteen shoe. She wore a six. Think I don't know that?"

"Never mind." *Should have known better than to ask,* Stella thought. Ellie Peacock hadn't worn a size-fourteen anything. Stella would have noticed that for sure.

I sat on the front porch, mentally reviewing the Hamel revisions. The rewrites had been a struggle, mostly because CeeCee had been getting less and less dependable, but they were going to strengthen the work.

I sat back to watch the birds swooping low to snatch pieces of popcorn on the sidewalk. A young girl and her grandfather were the only others in the snow-covered walk this afternoon. The little girl reminded me of CeeCee when she was that age. CeeCee. I sighed, thinking about my little girl.

She would promise to be home early and then come dragging in almost every night well past midnight. And sure she would have an excuse; Rick needed her for one thing or another. It seemed like she was spending all her free time at the kennel, but I knew the situation had gone way past working for free boarding. She was infatuated with Rick Materi, and it troubled me. I hated to see her end up with another Jake Tamaris, but what could I do? She hadn't listened the first time and she wouldn't listen now. All I could do was pray. I was learning that God would answer, but in His own way and in His own time. I had to accept and trust.

Stella dozed in her chair when I came in around four o'clock, chilled to the bone. I didn't blame her; there wasn't much on television worth watching. I slipped out of my coat and gloves and hung them on the hall tree about the time a car door slammed; in a few minutes the front door opened and CeeCee came in. She was home early.

"Hi, Mom. Got those revisions ready for me to type?"

Stella rushed in where angels and I didn't dare tread. "You're home early. What happened?"

CeeCee shrugged. "Rick had a meeting with a customer tonight, so I helped Arnold for a while but he said I should come home and help Mom."

"Arnold said that?" I had to quickly catch my grin before Stella caught it. "That was nice of Arnold," I amended like it wasn't a big deal. But it was a big deal—to me.

Later, I watched CeeCee's fingers fly over the keys. She was fast; she'd have the remaining changes keyed in shortly. Unfortunately she kept one ear cocked for the phone, and I knew that if Rick called she'd be gone in a flash.

I went through some of the new material she had added and noted again her emerging talent. She seemed to enjoy the work too, or she would if she could quit listening for the phone.

Would CeeCee end up being a writer like me? Would I be happy about it? Writing wasn't an easy life, but when the muse called, those of us to whom God gave the writing gift, have to answer.

CeeCee worked like a Trojan and finished the entire stack of revisions I had set out for her. I was overjoyed. The most work she'd done in weeks. I could face tomorrow's schedule with confidence. A few more nights like this and I'd make that deadline. CeeCee went upstairs to bed, followed by Stella. I stumped into the kitchen for a glass of water.

The outside light shone through the window shade, illuminating the room so that I didn't bother turning on the overhead light. I filled a glass of water at the sink and stood there drinking it, thinking of how quiet the house was. Call me crazy, but I missed the dogs and the birds. It was like part of the family was missing—the irritating part, but still an important part.

I turned back to the window and dropped my glass. Glass shattered when it hit the sink, but I barely noticed. There, silhouetted against the window shade was the outline of a man. Long hair, lots of it, just the way Helen had described it.

And ugly.

I screamed.

CeeCee and Stella bolted down the stairs and both hit the kitchen in time to keep me from falling. They helped me to a chair, staring at me like I had lost my mind.

"You all right, Maude?" Stella quavered.

I jerked around to gape at the window. "The Peeping Tom! He was there—saw him plain as day, silhouetted against the window shade. He looked exactly like Helen and Peaches said."

Stella sank down in a chair, her face the color of dried leaves. "He came here? Knowing I was after him? The nerve of that man."

"You know who he is, Grandma?" CeeCee asked.

"Of course not," Stella said. "Whatever gave you that idea?"

"You did," I said. "You said he knows *you're* after him."

"Well, if he lives in Morning Shade, he must know I'm after him." She appeared to be regaining spunk. "Everyone knows I'm Hargus's right hand."

"Not everyone, surely," I protested. Surely there were a few lucky people who hadn't heard the news yet. I was getting my breath back, and my heartbeat had slowed to something approaching normal.

CeeCee had stepped out onto the porch to look around. Now she returned, shaking her head. "Nothing out there. Didn't see anyone."

"Tell you what," Stella said. "There was a motorcycle gang hanging out at the Citgo the other morning. Seems like they were on their way south when one of the hogs broke down. They were hanging around town with nothing to do while they waited for the garage to get in a part."

"You think one of them is the Peeping Tom?"

"I don't know. They seemed friendly enough, real polite, but some of those men were big. They had a lot of hair too. Long and shaggy and full beards."

"That would fit the image I saw. But this is the fourth incident—how long have the motorcyclists been hanging around?"

"Who knows—I just noticed them this week. Drink an awful lot of latte."

"I've seen them ride by the kennel a couple of times. Their hogs rattle the windows." CeeCee walked to the sink, careful not to step in the broken glass, and drew a glass of water.

My heart still sat in my throat. What if they had seen CeeCee coming from the kennel and followed her home? She caught my expression and shook her head. "Don't go there. I've got sense enough to know if anyone is following me. I'm careful."

"I hope so."

Stella got up from her chair. "I'm going back to bed." She stopped in the doorway. "Some of their women aren't pint-sized either. Most of them could use a good girdle. I'm going to talk to Hargus tomorrow, see what he thinks. They could be the ones causing the trouble."

The following morning, CeeCee stopped by Gary's, happy to see him waiting at the mailbox. Since they'd formed the habit of sharing dating experiences, she now looked forward to their daily chats. He leaned on the mailbox, listening while she talked.

"It's not that Rick means to be bossy," she explained. "But sometimes I feel like I'm just one of the help."

"You talk to him about that?"

She nodded. "He apologized, and I think he was surprised that I'd feel that way. Maybe after Jake I'm just being paranoid. I expect men to let me down."

Gary shook his head. "Not all men are like Jake. You'll find someone—if not Rick, then someone else."

"Like you found Karen?"

He grinned, reaching out to lightly tweak her nose. "Like Karen. She even laughs at my silly jokes."

CeeCee laughed. "I think my sense of humor's been stunted recently."

"We don't all laugh at the same things. How's Rick's sense of humor?"

"Not all that great." She sighed. "Especially if the joke's on him. He needs to loosen up and learn to laugh at himself."

"Not a bad trait," Gary agreed.

"Yeah, well, I've got to go. People are waiting for their mail."

"The roads are better today, but there are still some slick spots. Drive carefully."

"I will. Tell Karen I said hello—we'll all have to get a sandwich together one of these nights when Rick isn't busy."

"Great idea. Hey, CeeCee?"

"What?"

He leaned closer—so close she caught a faint hint of Calvin Klein cologne. "Be careful. Don't get in over your head until you're sure what kind of guy Rick really is."

"I will, Gary, thanks."

She drove away, thinking about what Gary had said: there would be someone for her. She just desperately hoped Rick would be that someone.

What was so awful about that?

Yet something told her it was awful, and she'd best beware. CeeCee had learned a long time ago to listen to her instincts; they were rarely wrong.

* * *

"That's right—slip your shoes off and leave them here in the foyer."

Stella stood guard over the Living Truth Sunday morning services. Worshipers flocked into the small church unaware of the peculiar demand that awaited them.

Farley Birks vocally objected to Stella's bizarre request. "Take off my shoes? What sort of nonsense is this?"

"No nonsense. Just had the sanctuary carpet cleaned and it isn't dry yet."

Farley leaned over and untied his Florsheims, but not without serious grumbling. "Never heard of such idiocy."

Farley's wife slipped out of her boots and looked none too happy herself. "Are we supposed to walk on a wet floor?"

"Just a trifle damp," Stella said. "Nothing to worry about, but you know how a damp carpet can pick up dirt. No sense in having it cleaned if we just get it dirty again."

Farley rolled his eyes, but he padded into the sanctuary in his stockinged feet.

For more than twenty minutes Stella oversaw footwear hitting the floor and fielded complaints. Now she was getting somewhere. If the Peeping Tom was in the congregation, he'd soon be exposed. Maybe if she solved the mystery, personally fingered the culprit, folks would be more forgiving for having to attend worship service in their socks. The request did seem a trifle irreverent. She grinned. The look alone on Frances's face when she had to slip out of her pumps and mince down the aisle without her shoes was worth it. Dampened her dignity a bit.

Guilt pricked Stella's conscience. *Lord, am I thinking more of finding the right-sized shoe than I am about worshiping You the way I should?* She remembered all the times she had gotten upset at Hargus, thinking he was stupid and couldn't find his way out of a paper bag. Was she getting so full of Stella Diamond she didn't have room for the Lord? A major mistake, indeed.

Pastor Pat Brookes was the most vocal about parting with his shoes. "Honestly, Stella. I can't preach barefoot—whoever heard of having a church carpet cleaned on a Saturday?"

"Got a better price from the cleaning service, Pastor." And that was the truth. She'd gotten 10 percent off for the slight inconvenience, and since she was paying for it, she had to save wherever she could. Hargus hadn't offered to chip in 50 percent. Not even one percent. That boy was tightfisted.

Color flooded the youthful pastor's cheeks when he slipped off first one loafer then the other. Stella spotted a big toe poking through a hole in the black cotton sock. That had to be embarrassing.

The congregation continued to arrive and were swiftly relieved of their footwear. Tender-footed Maury Peacock limped to his pew, grousing under his breath something about wishing he'd stayed home to read the Sunday paper.

With that kind of attitude he might as well have stayed home. What a disposition to bring to the Lord's house. She watched Pansy take off her oxfords. If she'd thought about it, she would have expected Hargus to tell his mother about the plan, but it looked like he hadn't. So maybe he'd done one thing right, anyway, but she'd still take him to task for not helping.

Some partnership they had going. Him not bothering to show up—letting her take the flak from unhappy church members alone. If she did locate a likely suspect, for two cents she wouldn't tell him. She lifted her eyes toward the ceiling. "Lord, I didn't mean that."

Of course she would tell him. She'd just let him sweat a little first.

Mayor Throckmorton and Hilda arrived. Hilda didn't take kindly to Stella's jarring request. She peered down her nose as if she smelled something rotten, and maybe she did. Take this many shoes off and you could figure the fragrance level might be soaring somewhat. Stella wondered if the mayor's wife had a run in her stocking. Hilda didn't, but neither did she appear to warm to the idea of sitting shoeless in the chilly sanctuary.

"Really, Stella! Why is this necessary?"

"Just cleaned the carpet. Not quite dry yet." Better not say any more than necessary. Not so easy to get mixed up that way. She had to tell the same story every time. Let them start comparing notes and coming up with different reasons for the discarded footwear and she'd be in more trouble than a cat on a griddle.

"No one said a thing to me about having the carpet cleaned!" Hilda complained.

"Didn't want to bother you," Stella said. "Everyone knows how hard you work."

"Well—"Hilda fanned herself with the morning bulletin—"true, but I think I should have been told about the carpet. We could have brought in fans and left them on overnight."

"My—" Stella smiled—"why didn't I think of that?"

When eighty stocking-footed members swelled to their feet for congregational singing, Stella quickly closed the double doors to the sanctuary, dropped to her knees, and began pawing through footwear, Rockport by Rockport. She paused once, staring at the mound of Life Stride, Merrells, Naturalizers, and Bostonians. Where *was* Hargus? He was supposed to be helping her. Balancing her weight with both hands, she got to her feet, groaning when she heard dry bone sockets pop. Mercy she hated getting old.

To her right, a sizeable pile of shoes had started taking shape. Men's loafers, women's pumps, sneakers. Smelly Adidas. She'd let the infants and small children keep their shoes on. There wasn't a baby or child in the congregation with a size-fourteen shoe. Stella didn't think there was a man or a woman with feet that big either; she'd have noticed something like that.

Creeping to the double doors, she cracked the heavy oak a

fraction and searched for Hargus. She spotted him seated third pew from the front. The worm. He never sat down front, but today he'd sneaked in the back way and outsmarted her. He knew if he sat up close she wouldn't call attention to his leaving. Real wily. Too bad he didn't show the same ingenuity when he worked a case.

Easing the door shut, she returned to the pile of shoes. Pastor Pat rarely ran over on Sunday mornings—especially winter Sunday mornings. Folks liked to get home to a pot roast and enjoy a cold, lazy Sunday afternoon. She took a nap herself. If this shoe search didn't work out well, she might not be too quick to come out of her room this afternoon. Maude wouldn't be happy when she heard about this. Good thing she decided to stay in and off her foot this morning.

The shoe mountain had everything imaginable with sizes ranging from three narrow to twelve and a half wide—that clodhopper belonged to Hilda. The mayor wore a ten and a half. That had to be rough on Hilda. Stella snickered then quickly sobered when she caught sight of her own tens. Cinderella she wasn't.

You need to let up on Hilda.

Stella shook the nagging thought from her conscience. She knew she was hard on the mayor's wife—sort of became a habit to think negatively of the old gal. Wasn't a very Christian thing to do. Both she and Hilda put in a lot of time at church, and sometimes Stella thought she'd personally lost sight of her purpose to serve the Lord and not to bicker. She had to admit that Hilda tended to bring out the bicker faction in a body. Good Lord probably knew that. Truth be told, He might go in for a bit of bickering Himself where Throckmorton was concerned.

She looked up when the front door opened and a gusty wind

carried Tanzel Ramsey, church secretary, through the doorway. Everyone loved Tanzel. Early sixties, pretty as a picture and light as thistledown after her low-carb diet. Tanzel had served Living Truth for over forty years. If a job needed to be done, Tanzel did it.

This morning she was layered in heavy wool, her cheeks a rosy tint thanks to an icy wind. "I'm late," she mouthed. "Car wouldn't start."

Stella nodded, holding a finger to her lips to indicate the service was underway. Pastor Pat's muffled voice sounded from behind the double oak doors. His words seemed to have a bit of an edge this morning. Probably because of that bare toe. If Hilda caught sight of the protruding member, she would have a field day. Probably think it was sacrilegious or something.

Tanzel unwound her scarf and hung it and her coat on a foyer peg. Stella picked up another shoe and checked for size. She looked up a moment later to see Tanzel peering over her shoulder at the sizeable mound of footwear. "What's going on?"

"I'm checking shoe sizes."

Tanzel frowned. "I can see that. Why are you checking shoe sizes—and what are so many shoes doing here in the foyer?" She glanced at the closed sanctuary doors. "Isn't anyone wearing shoes this morning?"

"They were." Stella discarded a woman's size seven. "I had them remove them before they went into the service." The next question would be why, so Stella didn't wait for Tanzel to ask. "I figure this is the easiest way to check for possible Peeping Tom suspects."

"Oh—the Peeping Toms. At first, I thought Helen and Peaches might be getting excited over nothing; you know their eyesight is horrible. But when Maude had a peeper too, I started to take the allegations seriously."

Stella nodded. "They're for real, and the culprits have to be stopped."

Dropping to her knees, Tanzel studied the heap of leather. "Need some help?"

"I could sure use some," Stella agreed.

"Where's Hargus?" The secretary picked up a black pump and looked for the size. "Shouldn't he be helping?"

"He should, but you know Hargus. He's sitting third row from the front this morning, avoiding me." And that was the worst mistake of his life. After she finished with him, he'd be glad to help next time. If Hilda got too riled up about the shoe search, Stella just might hint it was partly his idea—which it was. That would fix him.

"Crafty." Tanzel located the size and pitched the shoe aside. "What size are we looking for?"

"Fourteen—in a sneaker."

"Then we can eliminate all these pumps and loafers."

Stella shook her head. "Not necessarily. The culprit likely wouldn't be wearing sneakers to church. If there's a fourteen in anything, we can start from there."

Tanzel nodded. "Good thinking. Does pastor know what you're doing?"

"No, and I don't intend to tell him. He wasn't any too happy about having to preach the morning message in stockinged feet." Stella bit her lower lip, wondering if she should mention the hole in his sock. Nah. Elly Brookes had enough to keep her busy; she didn't need to be embarrassed for neglecting sewing chores.

"Well, I've been meaning to ask if you'd changed your mind about the ladies helping with household chores—bringing in a few food dishes every week?"

"Nope, CeeCee and I are getting along fine. Might have to ask for help with some of Maude's typing, but right now we're managing."

"The ladies are dying to help—"

"We know they are, and we appreciate the thought. But we're fine for now. Really." Stella tossed another shoe on the pile.

By the time the service ended, the pile of examined footwear had mounted to a large heap. Stella pitched the last shoe onto the pile when she heard the congregation sing the first verse of "Just As I Am."

Apparently the Peeping Toms weren't among the congregation, and she felt tremendous relief. These stocking-footed folks were family; she'd be devastated to learn that someone among them had evil intent.

She stared at the pile of shoes. Instead of being sorted in pairs the way they were taken off, they were all jumbled in one big mess. Going to be a spell before people found their own. If they had been annoyed before, they were apt to be moving up to belligerent now. Might be a good time for her to leave early. If anyone said anything, she could say she had to get home to check the roast.

Having her own transportation came in handy this morning.

* * *

"You looked at every single pair of shoes Sunday morning?" Mack studied a crayon, his wizened eyes thoughtful.

Monday's art-therapy class was full. Stella noted the young, surly-looking teenager staring at his coloring pad. Resentment steeled Manuel's dark eyes.

"Every single one of them," Stella said. "Tanzel—that's our

church secretary—she helped. We even backtracked a couple of times to recheck certain member's footwear, but the congregation is clean."

"So back to square one." This came from one of the younger women—Rita, who'd recently miscarried.

Stella nodded. "Back to square one."

Zeke picked up the thread of conversation. "Any Peeping Tom incidents this week?" Stella first thought Zeke was going to be a troublemaker, but other than breaking a lot of crayons, he hadn't given her a minute's trouble.

"Not a one," Stella confessed. The trains ran regularly; the vagrant theory wasn't holding water so far. The Peeping Toms appeared to be the same two men—at least victims described the same character traits: ugly, old, wrinkled, one wore an old-time aviator hat; the other was hatless. Whoever was doing the peeking was staying put. Where were they hiding out? Hargus had checked the underpasses for signs of recent activity and nothing looked suspicious. No cold ashes to indicate there'd been a recent fire. Helen was holed up in her house like a mole, shades pulled even in daylight hours. Morning Shade was under siege, and Stella had to do something to restore the town's confidence.

She felt the burden of responsibility on her shoulders. She'd dressed Hargus down good for sneaking out of a smelly job, and he'd just shrugged and said, "So what?" in that detached way of his. Pansy ought to have taken a slipper to that boy's backside when he was young enough to handle. You couldn't do much with a middle-aged smart alec. He was too set in his ways. Mess with her and his ways were liable to undergo a change.

The coloring group bent to their papers. Stella knew they were doing their best to help, but the poor souls had their own set of problems. Manuel continued to keep his distance. Looked to be eighteen, nineteen and full of himself.

Stella reached over and put a crayon in his hand. "Here's the idea, bub. You're in here because you have a problem. I don't know what the problem is because nobody tells me, and I'm here because I've got my own problems. But this is how it works. Everyone here is equal. You got nothing to prove to me. We're all here for a common goal, and that's to move at our own pace and build a little trust and communication, if possible."

The young man's lower lip curled. "Gonna stuff ice cream down me again?"

"Cooperation helps. A lot of difficulties can be resolved and relationships improved if you'll get with the program. 'Course, it's up to you whether you want to cooperate."

Mack glanced up. "You've tried a stakeout?"

"Not yet; might try it next," Stella said, returning to the Peeping Tom mystery. First she'd have to talk Hargus into the notion. She didn't know how he'd feel about around-the-clock surveillance.

"The perpetrators haven't taken anything—I mean they're not doing anything other than looking into windows?" Mack asked.

"That's enough," Stella reminded. "They've got every woman in Morning Shade scared of their own shadow."

The young Hispanic gave a derisive laugh. "You're a *detective,* old woman?"

"Well—" Stella leaned back and carefully peeled paper off her crayon—"I'm an old woman. And you're a young whippersnapper with an attitude who needs to be taken down a notch." She looked up and met the boy's black, hate-filled eyes. "You're looking at the woman who can do it."

Auxiliary volunteer Teresa Stout violently shook her head. Under her breath, she reminded Stella, "We don't speak to our patients in a threatening tone. We're here to help."

"I'll help. Give me two days with the boy, and I'll straighten him out."

The boy threw the crayon on the table, and the chair legs scraped. Manuel Rodriguez left the room.

"Make that three days," Stella amended. "That's a troubled boy."

18

Monday night around 8 P.M., the Throckmortons' back door opened and Thurvis stepped out. Shivering, he glanced up at a full moon and huddled deeper into his fleece-lined overcoat. Pulling his hat brim low, he whistled for the dogs. Mortimer and Snerd surged between his legs and shot outside, almost upsetting him.

"Easy, easy," the mayor said shortly. Leaning over, he snapped a leash on Snerd, but Mortimer was half a block away by now.

The kitchen light illuminated Hilda's solid frame, clothed in a white chenille robe. Multicolored hair curlers stood up like Velcro antennas. "Don't be gone long, Thurvis. *CSI*'s on in thirty minutes. I don't want the babies to get overly chilled."

"I'll be back shortly, dear one."

Thurvis set off briskly, trying to keep up with the mastiff's awkward lope. Snerd dragged the mayor by the leash in a vain attempt to catch Mortimer.

Thurvis rounded the corner, puffing. Now out of Hilda's sight, he quickened his pace. Crossing Main Street, he headed—as he did every night—to the park bench on the corner. The streetlight was out, thanks to Fred Lassiter of the city works department. The mayor and Fred had swapped favors; Fred disconnected the streetlight, and in turn, the mayor backed up Fred's story about having to work Thursday nights.

Fred bowled in a second weekly league Thursday nights. His wife wasn't happy with one bowling night. She would have gotten peevish at a second.

The bargain seemed a fair enough swap. Cigars and bowling balls for two small—actually gray-colored—lies. Borderline deception. The mayor wasn't particularly proud of lying, but he did love cigars. Bowling *was* work, when properly executed, and if Thurvis didn't get to enjoy his nightly cigar he'd likely be shooting out streetlights in frustration.

Mortimer loped back when the mayor and Snerd approached the darkened street corner. Leaning down, Thurvis unsnapped the mastiff's leash. "All right—be back in fifteen minutes, boys."

Tongues lolling, the dogs bolted for freedom.

Sinking down on the bench, Thurvis fumbled in his coat pocket and took out a Montecristo. Lifting the Cuban import to his nose, he inhaled, closing his eyes with sheer ecstasy when the rich scent of Dominican and Honduran hand-rolled tobacco penetrated his senses. If anyone had been looking—which they weren't, since the bench sat well back in the darkness—he knew they'd probably think that Mayor Throckmorton's expression strongly resembled Hilda's when she bit into a fried Twinkie at the fair last summer. He grinned. Ah yes, it had been said many times in many ways: women were all right as far as it went, but there was nothing like a good cigar. Truer words were never spoken.

Ah.

For a millisecond, guilt reared its ugly head. A city ordinance wasn't to be taken lightly—especially by the mayor. More than one Morning Shade resident was sitting home right now, chewing gum, eating LifeSavers, sucking on peppermints in an attempt to kick the habit. Smoking was a bad addiction—nobody would dispute that—but sometimes a man just didn't care. Especially Thurvis, who'd smoked cigars for over thirty years. No one with an ounce of compassion wouldn't see the problem.

If Hilda hadn't been so single-minded, he could have smoked in the comfort of his own home, with no one the wiser. And if Fred's wife had been more understanding, he wouldn't have to fool her about the second bowling night. Put that way, they didn't have a choice. They were forced to sneak around to do what they should have been able to do without any guilt at all. He felt better about the cigar.

Flame flared briefly when he lit up. He puffed once, twice, three times before he could get a draft going. The smell of aromatic tobacco drifted on the cold air. Leaning back on the bench, he puffed. And drew. Contented sighs whispered from the darkened bench. February air carried the scent of deep dark tobacco.

Stella rounded Main Street, wishing she'd started home earlier. Pansy had wanted to play a second round of Farkle and she had given in. Now it was past dark, and the wind was as cold as a well digger's ankles.

She could have driven to Shady Acres—well, no she couldn't have. Maude was kicking up a fuss about her driving—threatening to have the Cadillac's distributor cap removed. That would be rotten. To make things worse, the streetlight was out, and if it weren't for the moon she wouldn't be able to see her hand in front of her face.

Her footsteps slowed when she neared the corner. She paused, sniffing the air. Smoke. Tobacco smoke.

Someone was smoking a cigar.

Briskly stepping behind a barberry bush, she peered through the hedge, catching sight of a rosy glow beneath the darkened streetlight. The glow would dim and then get brighter. Dim, bright.

Something shot past her leg, and she whirled to catch sight of Mortimer and Snerd, the mayor's dogs, loping across the Fergusons' lawn. Hilda's babies—which could only mean that Hilda was smoking.

Or Thurvis.

Stella's hand shot up to cover her mouth. *Mayor* Throckmorton was breaking the no-smoking ordinance? Shame on him. A city official—breaking his own law.

Marching from behind the bush, Stella headed toward the rosy glow. The light grew bright, stayed on a moment, and then she saw it suddenly sail through the air and land on the opposite side of the street.

Well.

Walking straight at the bench, she called out, "Is that you, Thurvis?"

When nobody answered, she kept walking. "Might as well come out, Mayor. I smell the smoke."

Silence.

Seizing the bull by the horn, she waded into the darkness and collared the first thing her hand touched. Hauling the mayor into the moonlight, she wagged her finger in his face. "Shame on you, Thurvis Throckmorton!"

"Now, Stella—" The mayor's uneasy laugh made her even madder. "I wasn't hurting anybody—just happened to find an old cigar in my coat pocket and thought I might light up a few minutes while the dogs had their nightly exercise."

"*Shame* on you, Thurvis. You're not exempt from the law—no citizen in Morning Shade is exempt from the law!"

"Shhh," Thurvis glanced down the darkened street. "Okay, you caught me. We'll let this be our little secret, won't we? I won't smoke anymore, and you keep quiet about what you just saw."

"In a pig's eye." Trying to get her to lie? And her an officer of the law. Or almost. In everything but name.

"Now, come on, Stella. There's no use getting hard-nosed

about this. I've smoked for thirty years—you can't expect a man to quit overnight."

"Other men—and women are doing it."

"Well, I'm not other men," the mayor snapped.

"I'm making a citizen's arrest."

"Now hold on." Thurvis jerked his jacket tail into place. "You can't make a citizen's arrest. You're carrying this sleuth thing too far. Why don't we just forget this little matter and you get back to work on the Peeping Toms—"

"Thurvis Throckmorton. You're under arrest for breaking the no-smoking ordinance."

"You can't do that!"

"Just watch me."

* * *

The following morning Thurvis walked into City Hall, shed his coat and hat, and then calmly walked into his office. He greeted his secretary, Mary Beth Higgins, and sat down at his desk.

Stella sat opposite him in the overstuffed chair, waiting, just as he had expected. Well, he knew how to handle complaining citizens.

Picking up the complaint, he read in a solemn tone. "Thurvis Throckmorton, you have been served with a citizen's arrest for breaking the smoking ban. How do you plead?"

Thurvis looked up. "Guilty," he mocked. Eyes back to the paper.

"I sentence you to a two-hundred-fifty-dollar fine and issue a stern warning that if you're caught smoking within Morning Shade city limits a second time, the fine will double. Do you understand, Mr. Throckmorton?"

Thurvis looked up. "I do, Your Honor."

"Pay the court clerk," the mayor said and whacked a gavel on his desk.

Stella smiled, gathering her purse. "Very cute, but remember. I'll be watching you, Thurvis. And I won't mention this to Hilda unless I catch you breaking the ordinance again."

"You won't catch me smoking again." He smiled.

The mayor watched her close the door behind her before allowing a grin to seep across his cagey features.

* * *

CeeCee hummed under her breath and counted her blessings—and she had too many to count. Living with Mom and Grandma; enjoying her pets without worrying the animals were bothering Mom. CeeCee wasn't crazy about the parrots, but then she hadn't really chosen them. Found the birds abandoned in one of the houses on her mail route. She missed Burton, her pug, which died a few months ago. Just died. But she guessed life was like that; here one day and gone the next. Made a person think, didn't it? Burton would have liked the kennel, and he would have loved Rick and Arnold.

The dark cloud hanging over her head since Jake died was finally starting to lift. There'd been times when she'd thought it would never happen, but now she could think about tomorrow without falling to pieces.

She was glad she lived in Morning Shade. A great town with good people.

She let the postal truck idle in front of Minnie Draper's box while she thumbed through Minnie's bundle, making sure she had it all. Craft magazines, credit-card offers, daily paper, and the usual handful of catalogs. Minnie must send off for every one offered. What did she do with a Victoria's Secret catalog?

CeeCee chuckled. Judging from the way Minnie dressed and the way she kept house, she must not order much, but catalogs and brochures provided interesting reading. Grandma called them "wish books."

She honked at Walter Dupont's house and he hustled out, pulling on a denim jacket. "Howdy, CeeCee. Got me a present?"

"Sure do, Walt. Looks like a pair of Redfoot boots."

His face lit up with a smile. "Best boots a man can buy. Comfortable and weatherproof. Can't get Redfoots around here. You ought to get you a pair. Just what you need."

"I'll give it some thought, Walt. You take care." Sure. She chuckled and drove on, thinking that she needed a pair of clumsy boots. Just what the well-dressed woman would choose!

The Sullivans' Saint Bernard loped to intercept her. She hit the gas and sped past before he cleared the end of the drive. She'd learned how to handle pesky bumper-biting dogs. As many as there were on her route, she'd had to. Of course, it got a little trickier when she had to stop and put mail in the box.

Gary Hendricks was bent over shoveling snow away from his curb. Seemed like they'd had a lot of the white stuff this winter. It was beginning to get old. She grinned watching him. She'd trained him well. If he wanted her to listen while he talked about Karen, he had to keep the ground around his mailbox cleared. She slid to a stop and he leaned on his shovel.

She lowered her window. "Morning. Can I talk you into cleaning the road in front of the rest of the boxes on this lane?"

"Not a chance." He grinned, happy and relaxed. Karen had been good for him. "You have any problems on your route?"

"No, I was joking. Most of the streets are cleared, and I drive in the ruts to the boxes that haven't been shoveled. I deliver to the door for some of my older people. I'd hate for them to fall and break a limb."

Gary sobered. "You're special, CeeCee. No wonder I was attracted to you. Rick's a lucky man, and I hope he realizes it."

CeeCee smiled awkwardly, surprised. Compliments were rare in her world. "Thanks, Gary. I appreciate that. How are things with you and Karen?"

He beamed. "Great. Just great. I'm so blessed to have found her. I don't mind admitting I was disappointed when you turned me down, but it's all worked out for the best, hasn't it?"

"I guess it has." For Gary anyway. She had Rick, sure, but Mom and Grandma hadn't accepted him and probably never would. She didn't like to think that she might have to choose between Rick and family members.

Gary correctly interpreted her gloomy expression. "Maude still doesn't like Rick?"

CeeCee shook her head. "It's silly. She insists on comparing him to Jake. He's not anything like Jake."

Gary's features turned grave. "I never met Jake, but from what you've told me, I'd hate for you to get hooked up with another one like him."

"I won't," CeeCee said shortly. "I do have common sense. Sorry, but I've got to run. Tell Karen I said hi."

"I'll do that," he promised. "She asks about you often."

"Well, that's good." Her lips twisted in a wry grin. Gary wasn't her type though he had wanted to be, and half of Morning Shade had tried to pair them off. She hadn't liked Gary or his practical jokes as a prospective suitor, but he made a great friend.

She finished the route and drove back to the post office. Snow had melted and pooled where people had tracked it into the lobby. CeeCee volunteered to mop the floor before someone slipped and fell.

Daphne Baker came in, moving cautiously on three-inch heels. In this snow? What kept her from breaking her neck? CeeCee pushed the mop, thinking that Daphne also had on enough makeup to open her own cosmetic shop.

Now she fluttered over to talk, lips curved in a superior smile. "CeeCee. How sweet of you to keep the floors clean for us. *So* thoughtful. I'm sure all of this snow makes your job *much* harder."

CeeCee stared at her blankly. Did Daphne think she was the janitor?

The woman smiled. "I've been over to the kennel to ask Rick's advice on my precious tabby cat. She's been off her feed lately."

"Well, I'm sure he can help you."

"Oh yes, he's always helpful." Daphne giggled and the sound reminded CeeCee of a nervous hungry cat.

With curly blonde hair and peach-glow complexion, Daphne looked like a cover girl for the Meadow Fresh Dairy Barn, until she opened her mouth. *Not Rick's type,* CeeCee thought. She had never been able to see why any man would be attracted to Daphne. That giggle alone would drive her crazy.

"Rick is such a sweetie. I'm going to invite him over to dinner some night to pay him back for all the free advice he's given me."

"How nice of you." CeeCee gritted her teeth and tightened her grip on the mop handle. Women swarmed around Jake . . . er . . . Rick, all the time. He laughed about it, but so far he hadn't been snared by any of his rather too obvious admirers.

Daphne teetered over to a row of postal boxes to pick up her mail. CeeCee thought, unkindly, that from the back view, she waddled like the south end of a northbound goose. CeeCee gave a last vicious swipe at the floor and walked to the back room to put the mop away.

Iva smiled sympathetically. "Don't let Daphne get to you. You know what she's like. Showing her an unattached man is like throwing a hungry dog a bone."

CeeCee laughed. "Rick is big enough to take care of himself. I'm leaving now. Got to go to the Cart Mart and pick up something for dinner. I sure hope it doesn't snow tonight."

"Me too." Iva leaned her elbows on the counter. "I like snow, but it's possible to have too much of a good thing."

CeeCee did a quick run through the grocery store and headed home, dreading to face Mom and Grandma. Rick was coming to pick her up for dinner and a movie. She'd get everything ready for the evening meal before she dressed to go out. Mom wouldn't be pleased.

At first Mom or Grandma hadn't said much, but lately Grandma had become more vocal about her absences. It was hard not to snap back, but she'd been brought up to show respect. However, maybe it was time to point out that she was grown and perfectly able to make her own decisions.

She pushed open the front door. "Yoo-hoo! Anybody home!"

Maude hobbled into the kitchen where CeeCee was putting groceries away and sat down at the table. "Rough day?"

"Not too bad. The roads are clear. If another big snow doesn't come, the rest of the week should be all right."

"That's good." Maude yawned. "I'm getting tired of sitting around. Be nice to get back to work. I'm actually looking forward to it."

CeeCee turned and said teasingly, "Is this my mom? The one

who would never write another word unless someone made her?"

Maude smiled. "The Lord has taken me down a notch or two, hasn't He?"

"He has." CeeCee dropped a kiss on the top of her head and set out the ingredients for dinner: spaghetti, canned sauce, frozen garlic bread, a nice green salad. That should be sufficient. She saw her mother eyeing the hamburger she had put on to brown.

"Are we eating early tonight?"

CeeCee stepped to the skillet and kept her eyes on the ground beef. "I have a date with Rick."

"I see." Maude picked up the saltshaker and wiped imaginary grains off the top, but CeeCee was aware of a chill in the air.

"I know I was supposed to work tonight, but I'll catch up tomorrow. I promise."

She couldn't meet her mother's steady gaze, guiltily aware she hadn't kept her promise to help in any way she could and not to let Mom fall behind. Her intentions had been the best, but she hadn't met Rick then. She'd get the manuscript done, if Mom would just have patience.

"Don't worry, we'll make that deadline."

"I hope so," Maude said, her voice dry.

Stella entered the kitchen. "Fixing supper early, aren't you? Upsets my stomach to eat too early."

"You can eat anytime you like," CeeCee said, trying not to sound out of sorts. "I'm just getting it ready. All you'll have to do is put the garlic bread in the oven."

"You going out?" Stella peered over her glasses. "Working at the kennel tonight?"

"I have a dinner date and movie with Rick."

"Date?" Stella asked. "Fancy that. And Maude has a new boyfriend, that Biggert man with the funny hair. Everyone's dating except me. Must be something in the water. Guess I'll have to find someone to take me out so I can make a fool of myself."

"Grandma . . ." CeeCee protested, but Maude got in first.

"I told you going to dinner with Arnold wasn't a *real* date."

Stella grunted. "You went out. You had dinner. You came back. That's a date."

"A very innocent evening," Maude pointed out. "I thought it would be good for me to get out of the house, and you know what? It was. I enjoyed myself. Is that a crime?"

Stella sighed. "People don't observe the old customs anymore."

"Look, Grandma, life goes on. Jake's dead, but I'm alive and I'm young." CeeCee slapped the spaghetti spoon down on the counter, spattering sauce. She'd had all she could take. They could finish their own dinner.

Forty minutes later she paraded downstairs, dressed in navy blue pants and a cream-colored sweater trimmed with yarn flowers in shades of rose, powder blue, and sage green. She looked good and she knew it. The few pounds she'd lost had been enough to make the pants fit loosely, and the sweater looked as elegant on her as it had in the store.

Rick, when he arrived, seemed suitably appreciative. "Wow, babe. Look at you."

CeeCee pirouetted in front of him. "It's new. Do you like it?"

"Love it. I'm going to be one proud guy tonight." He held her coat while she slid into it. His hands lingered on her shoulders, and she thought that he might have kissed her if Grandma hadn't chosen that moment to wander into the foyer.

"Not left yet? Thought I heard the door close. You seen my

teeth? I'm looking for my bottom plate. Guess I laid it down somewhere." She minced around, peering into corners, while Rick looked undecided as to whether to help or stay out of the way.

Captain sauntered in and eyed the newcomer with a malevolent gaze, while snarling deep in his throat.

Rick took a couple steps backward. "That's quite a cat. Had him very long?"

"It's a long story," CeeCee said. One she had no intention of repeating. Grandma was pulling this act on purpose. Probably had a piece of fish or something in her pocket to make sure the cat followed her.

She drew Rick toward the door. "See you later, Grandma."

Before Stella could answer, CeeCee closed it. She was going to have to do something to make Mom and Grandma understand they couldn't meddle in her life. If she had to move out and get an apartment, she intended to have the freedom to make her own choices. Good or bad.

Rick slipped his arm around her middle. "Chinese, Mexican, or steak?"

"Steak." Actually she would have preferred Mexican, but she'd overheard Rick telling Arnold that steak was his favorite meal.

"All right. That's my kind of eating and my kind of woman."

At the restaurant, the hostess smiled at Rick and she asked, "Table for two?"

Hey. There's two of us. See? I'm right here.

The attractive brunette led them to a secluded table. "All right?"

Rick grinned. "Perfect." He slipped her a twenty. "Can you get me a beer, honey? House tap's fine."

She demurely accepted the generous tip. "House tap it is. If you need anything else, just let me know. I'm Patty."

"Patty." He winked. "I'll remember that." She left and Rick

reached across the table to take CeeCee's hand. "It's good to have you all to myself."

Before she could concede that it was good to be alone with him, the waitress showed up balancing a beer and a large menu. "My name is Cindy, and I'll be your server for the evening." She hovered over Rick while he perused the entrees.

"Excuse me?" CeeCee said. "Menu. Please?"

"Oh, sure. Sorry." Cindy handed her a menu.

Rick closed his and quirked a questioning brow. "Steak and salad bar?"

"Fine." She didn't need all that food, but when had that ever stopped her? She was a light eater. When it got light she started eating.

The porterhouse steaks were lean, and the salad bar bountiful. CeeCee knew she was eating too much, but it was only for one night. She'd cut back tomorrow. Rick seemed to know his way around the place, and she was curious.

"Do you come here often?"

He speared his last bite of meat and thoughtfully chewed. "Not often. But the food's good and it's hard to find a decent steak around here." He glanced at his watch and CeeCee admired the tanned wrist against the gold band. "We're going to have to step on it so we can make the movie on time."

The dessert cart arrived—a glorious presentation of flourless chocolate cake, crème brûlée, strawberry cheesecake, and something that looked so rich CeeCee cringed.

"One crème brûlée." Rick smiled at the waitress. "And bring two spoons." He turned to CeeCee and winked. "A lady never eats a whole dessert."

Like she didn't know that—but actually she *didn't* know that. She always ate a full dessert and licked the spoon afterward.

Cindy brought the check, and Rick dropped a second twenty on the table. CeeCee glanced at the gratuity and thought maybe she was in the wrong business; she needed to give up the kennel and get a waitress job. Rick wasn't tight with money, and that was a point in his favor, CeeCee thought. Responsible, reliable, and generous. Why couldn't Mom see the good qualities?

Rick flashed a smile at the woman selling tickets at the theater, and she got so flustered she couldn't make change. And she was old enough to be his mother. CeeCee sniffed. Did every woman he met drool over him? Apparently so. But while he seemed to enjoy their attention, he didn't say or do anything to encourage them.

When they located their seats, he slid an arm around her shoulders and she nestled against him. It had been a long time since she'd felt like this. That last year with Jake had been hurtful, trying to deal with his lifestyle, which had gone on without her. Rick wasn't part of the celebrity game, thank goodness. And that was a *big* point in his favor.

The movie, a senseless romantic comedy, was a delightful mixture of the insane and in love. She was sorry when it was over and Rick removed his arm from around her shoulders. He pulled her to her feet, holding her against him for a minute before they joined the throng exiting the theater.

The ride back to Morning Shade passed too quickly. Snowflakes, big and fluffy as goose feathers, drifted slowly down in the glow of the headlights. Rick suddenly braked, catching her from sliding into the dash with his elbow. The Throckmorton dogs sauntered across the street, in no hurry to let the car pass.

"Guess Thurvis decided to walk them late tonight," CeeCee commented.

Rick tooted the horn and Snerd turned his head to look over

his hindquarters. "I think the mayor's crazier about those dogs than Hilda."

When they reached the Diamond house, they stood outside, watching the swirling flakes dancing around them. White powdered Rick's blond hair. He laughed softly. "You have snow on your eyelashes."

She smiled, and he drew her close, his lips meeting hers. She tasted snowflakes, which melted with the warmth of his kiss.

He slowly lifted his head to gaze down at her. "My snow maiden." His voice was husky. "Drive carefully tomorrow. I don't want anything to happen to you."

She stood inside the door, peering out the side curtain until red taillights disappeared into the distance. Then she turned the lock and slowly climbed the stairs to her room. Mom was wrong. Rick was nothing like Jake.

Breakfast was the only meal we shared lately. The only time the three of us sat down and actually conversed without shouting at each other from another room.

For me, my writing situation was getting desperate. CeeCee spent all her free time at the kennel, and I was falling further behind every day on the revisions. My daughter's solemn promise to help had proved to be as empty as my head must have been to agree to the carpal tunnel surgery. Why couldn't I have used a little common sense and waited until after I had finished Hamel's book before putting myself in a position where I had to depend on someone else to get my work done?

Stella hadn't come down yet this morning, so for a rare moment I had my daughter to myself. "Looks like the streets are clear again. The street crew does a good job. I worry when you have to drive on icy roads."

"I haven't had any trouble so far." CeeCee set a bowl and the box of cereal in front of me. Coffee or milk?"

"Both." I tried to think of a discreet way to bring Rick into the conversation, but she beat me to it.

"I had a great time with Rick last night."

"That's good."

She sat down, toying with the cream pitcher. "If you'd give me a concrete idea of why you are so against him . . . ?"

I dumped Oatie Boats in my bowl. "I would think that was obvious. He walks like Jake, he talks like Jake, and he's got an eye for the women like Jake."

CeeCee flushed. "That is so unfair. You haven't given him a chance."

"Sure I have. He can't help what he is, I guess, but I don't want you to make another mistake."

I had seen Rick earlier this week at Citgo buying gas, and the woman with him was someone I'd never seen before, but from the way she behaved, she must have been a very good friend. I did have enough sense not to mention the incident to CeeCee. She'd find some excuse—like the woman was a good client, but good clients don't sit on top of their accounts.

My once reasonable, insecure daughter slapped the glass of milk down so hard it slopped over onto the table. "Where's that so-called Christian nonjudgmental attitude you're supposed to have? Aren't we supposed to leave the judging to God?"

"It's not judging when it's a fact. The fact is that Rick Materi loves the women—exactly like Jake Tamaris loved the women. Does this conversation strike a cord? Didn't we have this same exchange—at this same table—five years ago?"

CeeCee sat across from me, her features set in stone. "Listen, Mom. I'm grateful for everything you've done for me. You've always been there to pick me up when I fall, but I'm a big girl now. I have the right to make my own decisions."

"Even if they're wrong?"

"Even then. I'm asking you to please stay out of my personal life."

At the moment I'd like to shake some sense into that pretty head; I only intended to help, but obviously she didn't see it that way. She waited, her eyes holding mine, and I wanted to cry. She had gone through so much with Jake, and now she was making the same mistake with Rick.

I swallowed my hurt. "All right. If that's what you want. I'll never mention the man again."

"That's what I want. If you can't say something nice, then don't say anything at all." There wasn't the least hint of compromise in her voice. I knew she was dead wrong, but my only option was to stand by ready to pick her up when her house of cards collapsed.

She sulked out of the room, and I used my napkin to wipe tears and blow my nose. Captain yowled, and I sighed. "You said it, cat."

Stella schlepped into the room, eyes half open. "CeeCee just left, glowering like a thundercloud. You two have words?"

"I tried to get her to see Rick Materi the way we see him."

"That's a thankless task." Stella filled Captain's bowl, which was a first. Usually she ignored him unless they were tormenting each other. Today they were buddies. Go figure.

She took a bowl from the cabinet and fixed her own breakfast. "You know, I'll be glad when you get back to normal. I like CeeCee, but you're a better cook."

"Well, it's nice to be missed. Anything new on the Peeping Toms?"

She smelled the open carton of milk and then poured some on her cereal. "The one who peeked in our kitchen. How tall was he?"

"How would I know? He was outside the window."

"How far up the window shade did he come?"

"I don't know . . . about so high." I measured maybe five feet with my hand. "Why?" The shoeless church sermon last Sunday had stirred up a hornet's nest. I hope she wasn't hatching up another idea like that one.

"Oh, just wondering." She licked her spoon and laid it back in the bowl. "Me and Hargus are having a strategy meeting this morning. I think there's something fishy going on here. Size-fourteen sneakers—a woman's corset. We're either dealing with a nut or we're looking for the wrong person."

"What wrong person? You don't have any solid leads, do you?"

"No solid ones. But I have a feeling." She touched her left elbow. "Right here in my knowledge bone. Something ain't kosher."

Later I stood at the window and watched her hurrying up the street to the Citgo. Knowledge bone. I pulled up the sleeve of my robe and stared at my elbow. Nothing. Not even an arthritis twinge this morning.

Stella found Hargus in his office midmorning. He was sitting with his feet on top of the desk, drinking coffee. Just what she expected. Not even a notepad and pen in front of him. It was a good thing she'd given this meeting considerable thought.

She sat down and pulled out her notebook. "All right now, here's how the cow ate the cabbage."

Hargus brought his feet down with a thump. "Hold on just a minute. I'm in charge of this meeting."

"Oh yeah?" She fixed him with her eagle-eye look. "Just who put you in charge?"

"Don't need anyone to put me in charge. I'm the law here and don't you forget it."

Who could forget that? But she had to go slow with Hargus. Push him and he got antsy. Let the boy think he was in charge, and the investigation would move along. "All right then, what did you have in mind?"

He scratched his head. "Well, nothing in particular. You got any ideas?"

Stella sat up straighter, fishing a ballpoint pen out of her purse. "I do have a plan."

Hargus pinned her with a smarty look. "I hope it's better than your shoe plan. All that did was make Hilda Throckmorton mad. She cornered me at the Citgo and chewed on me for a good five minutes. That granddaughter of Mildred Fasco's found out Hilda wore a size twelve and a half and told it all over town. Hilda was ticked."

Stella grinned. "Got hot, did she?"

Hargus shook his head. "Oh, *hot!* She was on fire, except I was the one scorched. She seemed to think the shoe idea was mine. You got any thoughts on how she might have reached that conclusion?"

"Now why would she think that?" Stella thinned her lips in an innocent line. "I explained that Saturday was the only day we could get the carpet cleaned. Who would have thought it would still be wet on Sunday?"

That isn't really a lie, is it, Lord? She didn't say she hadn't planned it that way, just asked who would think it. Like asking his opinion.

Hargus eyed her, jaw set like concrete. "If I didn't know better I'd think you set Hilda on me."

"Don't be silly. Why would I do that? Hilda is probably upset because the shoe gig wasn't her idea. Her bark's worse than her bite."

"Her bark's bad enough. I've never seen anyone who can talk louder and faster. It's no wonder Thurvis spends most of his time in his office. Gives his ears a rest."

Enough of this. She had things to do. "You want to hear my plan or not?"

"I'm not sure. Seems like everytime you have a plan I get in trouble. You're a jinx, Stella Diamond."

She tapped the pen on the table. Don't let him get started on that. Hargus was hard to turn off once he got the bit in his teeth and commenced running. "Have we decided the Peeping Toms come in on the freight?"

"We ain't decided nothing yet. We don't know where they come from."

"Well, say they *might* come in on the freight. We need to catch them in the act, not go looking for them after they've already left."

"How do you plan to do that? We got no way of knowing when they're coming. It's not like they send a postcard announcing their arrival."

Stella pressed her lips together. Deliver her from a smart-mouthed man. Sarcasm so thick you could cut it with a knife.

"We do a stakeout."

He gaped at her like he'd never heard the word before. "A stakeout?"

"Yeah, you know—a stakeout. It's a police word. You ever heard of it?"

His lip curled. "I've heard of it. What you planning to stake out?"

"The railroad tracks. If these drifters are jumping off the freight, we'd be there to catch them. Or not catch them, exactly. We'd have to wait until they did something, but we could follow them, and when they stopped off at a local window—we nab them."

"How we going to know exactly *where* they'll get off the train?"

"That's what we're going to stake out. I'll be at the north end of town, and you take the south. The railroad runs straight through the corner of Morning Shade. With us on the job, the culprits will be hard-pressed to pull off another caper."

Hargus shifted in his chair. "I don't know, Stella. These guys could be dicey. Maybe we ought to bring someone else in on this—"

"Baloney. We can handle this. You insinuating that I can't hold my own?"

"I'm not sure I can hold my own against 'em. They might not be anything to mess with. You go on home, and I'll do the stake-out."

Stella drew herself up, spitting mad. "Whose idea was this, anyway? Mine. I don't plan to stay home, so forget that. Now what time do you want to start this surveillance project?"

"I don't want to start it at all," Hargus groused. "But if I have to—guess about eight o'clock."

Stella shook her head thoughtfully. "Maude's been going to bed around nine. I'll have to wait until she's down for the night before I can sneak out. She'd have a royal snit fit if she knew about this."

She spotted a gleam in Hargus's eye. "You tell her, and I'll tell Pansy the truth about why you couldn't take her to dinner last week. Out with your racing cronies, weren't you? Leaving your poor old mother sitting home alone."

"Now cut that out. Blackmail is against the law."

"But you're not in a position to do anything about it, are you?" Stella got to her feet. "I'll be on the north end of town a little after nine. I'll count on you to be on duty on the south end earlier than that."

She left, hoping he wouldn't turn chicken. Of all the wishy-washy, sorry excuses for a lawman. Pansy hadn't done the world a favor when she gave birth to Hargus.

Now she had to worry about getting out of the house without arousing Maude's suspicions, which wasn't as easy at it sounded.

* * *

At nine-fifteen sharp, Stella crept downstairs and eased out the front door. She had dressed for the stakeout in black pants, a heavy sweater (swiped from CeeCee's room), and Maude's black windbreaker. A black scarf covered her white hair and black gloves covered her hands. At the north end of town she stopped near Willy Sims's barn. Long abandoned and let go to pot, it would be a safe—and fairly warm—place to conduct a stakeout.

She gave a passing thought to the fact that it would also be a good place to provide shelter to a couple of hoboes moonlighting as Peeping Toms. If she ran into trouble, she had her whistle. She touched the long wiener-shaped device dangling on a black eyeglass cord. One toot from this baby and she'd arouse the town. Stella Diamond still had enough lung power left to blow a nickel-plated, earsplitting, crowd-drawing whistle. You'd better believe it.

She settled out of the wind and started watching. Not that there was anything to watch. James used to say they rolled up the sidewalks in Morning Shade at ten o'clock. Not much nightlife going on here.

Not much life anytime, come to think of it.

Clouds drifted across the face of the moon. She used her penlight to consult her watch: 9:30. Only fifteen minutes since she had left the warmth of her room? Seemed like it should have been at least an hour. She wondered how Hargus was faring. She uncapped her thermos and took a swallow of hot chocolate. Steam fogged her glasses.

Ten o'clock came and passed with no activity. Eleven. Curiosity got the better of her. She should have come up with some way of communication between the two of them. Leaving her shelter, she made her way to the south end of town. No sign of movement. A town with no lights and no people was downright spooky. If she were home, she'd be in bed burrowed under the cover.

Sleuthing was tiresome work.

She reached the old oak where Hargus had decided to take up his position. A rumbling sound came from somewhere off to her right. She froze, listening. What was that? Never heard a noise like it before.

She turned her penlight in the direction of the noise. Hargus lay flat of his back on the cold, hard ground. As she watched, he took a deep breath and let it out with a sound like an angry warthog. His lips fluttered, and then he inhaled again.

How about that? She'd finally found something Hargus excelled in. The lad was a real snore champion. If they handed out prizes, he'd win the silver cup every time.

She switched off the light and made her way back to her outpost. Sorry excuse for a lawman. Sleeping. A whole flock of Peeping Toms could gallop past him and he'd never know it. They just didn't make lawmen the way they used to. Catch John Wayne sleeping? Big John never slept. Well, he had to sometime, she guessed, but he never snored during a stakeout.

Settling back in her shelter, she yawned. It was going to be a long night.

* * *

Stella jerked awake, blinking. Maude must have turned off the heat. She was half frozen. She stared into the surrounding blackness. What happened to the streetlights?

After a moment she remembered; she was on a stakeout. Must have dozed off.

A quick check of her watch in the glow of her light showed the hands at one o'clock. She got to her feet, stiff as a poker. If she knew what was good for her, she'd get back home and up to her room before Maude woke up. She wondered if Hargus was still sleeping on the job, or if he had gone home. Deciding that he had—probably an hour ago, she gathered her thermos and flashlight. No use making a body sick. This stakeout had gone well—not productive, but any detective knew that most stakeouts didn't come up with a single lead.

* * *

Early this morning, she met Hargus at the Citgo, and they discussed the stakeout over cups of steaming latte.

She fixed her partner with a cold stare. "Did you stay out all night?"

He looked as guilty as a politician caught with his hand in the public till. "Yeah, sure. You?"

"Of course." *Or most,* she didn't add. It was after one in the morning when she got home. "See anything?"

Of course he didn't. He wouldn't have seen the high school marching band if they had paraded by, as sound as he had been sleeping.

"Nothing. You?"

"Not a thing. But the stakeout went well."

"How do you figure?"

"There weren't any Peeping Tom incidents last night."

"Maybe not, but I'm not sitting out in the cold every night. I think one of my big toes got frostbite. We got to come up with a better plan."

What did he mean *we?* Every plan they'd had she'd thought up. So what if they didn't work? They were making progress.

Limited. But progress.

Stella took heart. Last night proved one thing: Peeping Toms didn't like cold weather any better than she did.

But she agreed about a new plan. She was a mite stove-up herself this morning.

* * *

Friday night at the kennel, CeeCee reached for the last donut in the box, but a male hand intercepted her. "Uh-uh, mine." Rick grinned and bit into the iced maple.

CeeCee swallowed the urge to say something. Taking the last donut was the sort of thing Jake would have done. She hated it when Rick showed her late husband's rude tendencies, which wasn't often, but enough to annoy her.

She got up and filed a collie's folder. "That's your third donut tonight," she reminded.

"Who's counting?" He licked his fingers and winked. "I don't have the weight problem."

The weight problem? Was that his less-than-subtle way of saying that she did? Her cheeks blazed.

She shoved the file door shut and returned to the desk. Snow drifted by the front window. Business had been nonexistent today. Morning Shade folks had kept their pets home and near a warm fire. Mrs. Curtis, a brave soul, had ventured out to bring her puny Pekingese in for an allergy shot, but that had been the only business.

CeeCee rearranged a stack of magazines, picked up an empty coffee cup, and tidied the small waiting area. "If you don't mind, I'm going to take off early."

Arnold Biggert had left two hours ago.

Rick shoved the last of the donut into his mouth. "There's

a box of surgical gloves and toilet paper you need to put up before you leave."

Surgical gloves and toilet paper would keep. A nagging headache at the base of her skull made her think more of home, a couple of aspirins, and a bowl of Grandma's chicken noodle soup.

"Hey—" Rick leaned over when she passed his desk and latched on to the corner of her sweater—"are we in a bad mood today?"

She shook her head. "I'll work Monday afternoon for a couple of hours. I can put the gloves and tissue up then."

Pulling her closer, he nuzzled her neck. Her knees turned to soup and her anger cooled. It wasn't Rick's fault that she loved maple-iced donuts—and she had eaten two already. Actually she should be thanking him for saving her the additional two hundred and twenty, sugarcoated, warm, mapley . . . calories.

Rick's breath felt warm against her neck. "You know you're my little sugar bear, don't you?"

"I know." She snuggled closer to his warmth. Sometimes he even felt like Jake—comforting, safe.

He kissed her lightly, then with more pressure. He tasted like maple icing.

"You're my one and only sugar bear," he repeated. "I'm crazy about you, CeeCee."

Of that she wasn't so sure. His one and only? Then who was making all the female calls wanting to speak to "Ricky" personally. CeeCee seriously doubted the women were all "customers" as Rick declared. The kennel was also a brokerage, and Rick's business was growing, but not at the rate of his phone calls.

"Can you walk me to my car?"

"Now?"

She nodded. "My old battery's been acting up lately and I'm afraid the car won't start."

"Babe—it's freezing out there."

"You have a coat, don't you?"

"Sure, but why go out if I don't have to. Tell you what. If your car doesn't start come back and get me and then I'll go out."

The least he could do was walk her to her car. She bit back the thought when the phone shrilled, interrupting the conversation. Rick motioned for her to answer it. Why, she couldn't fathom, since he was right next to the instrument.

The call was from a St. Louis pet-store chain. She handed him the receiver and reached for her coat. He was deep in conversation when she left, closing the back door firmly behind her.

Trudging through ankle-deep snow, she forged her way to the car and groaned when she saw that her windshield was buried beneath ice and several inches of new powder. Ice coated the door handle, and by the time she slid behind the wheel and started the engine her teeth were chattering.

While the heater warmed the car, she started the search for the long-handled scraper to clean the windshield. She fumbled under the driver's seat and then slid her hands across the cold fabric. Sparks flew. She cursed under her breath as she rummaged under the passenger seat. Grandma had borrowed the ice scraper earlier this week—had she forgotten to return it?

A thorough search turned up no brush. Great. Rick's refusal to help flashed through her mind. The car had started; he wouldn't be overjoyed about cleaning snow off her windshield.

She opened the door and got out. Now what? Wind whipped white stuff in heavy sheets. The storm was turning into a full-blown gale.

Ripping off her gloves with her teeth, she tried to hand

scrape the frozen windshield. The results were a broken nail and nine frozen fingertips. She paused, biting back tears. Her head throbbed. Nothing—not even a gale—could make her go back into that kennel and ask for Rick's help. If he cared anything about her he'd be out here helping. Instead, she'd bet he was still on the phone, feet propped on the desk, talking to a female customer. She'd have to drive home with an ice-coated windshield, stick her head out the window and inch her way to Main Street. Thankfully traffic was virtually nonexistent right now.

Suddenly Gary Hendricks's blue Cavalier turned the corner. The small, front-wheel-drive compact appeared to have no difficulty getting through the mounting drifts.

When the scoutmaster spotted her standing beside her car, he braked and rolled down his window. "Trouble?"

She had to shout over the blowing wind. "I don't have an ice scraper! Can I borrow yours?"

"Hold on!" He sprang out of the car, bareheaded and with ice scraper in hand, and maneuvered through the swelling drifts. CeeCee noticed he wasn't wearing boots, only casual loafers.

He approached her car, grinning. "What a day to be without a scraper," he teased.

"Grandma borrowed mine and neglected to return it."

"No problem." He took a manly swipe across the windshield, and ice and snow flew.

"I can do that," CeeCee objected. "I didn't mean for you to clean it." When Jake was alive she'd have to be up early on mornings like this to clean both his and her windshield. She'd even start the heater in Jake's car so when he climbed in, the interior would be warm as toast. They'd had garages, but Jake had crammed so much sporting gear in the cubicles there was no room for automobiles.

Gary brushed her protests aside and within minutes the windshield was free of ice and snow.

"Thanks so much," she said. "Can I pay you—"

"Pay me?" He frowned. "It's my pleasure to help. What about your tires?" He stood back, his eyes scanning the tread. "You need snow chains—or studs. This winter's turning out to be a beast."

"I know. Mom and I talked about new snow tires, but money's kind of tight right now."

"Tell you what." Gary pulled his coat collar closer. Snowflakes lay on his auburn lashes. "I have four fairly new snow tires sitting in my garage. I bought them for my old car, and when I bought the Cavalier it had snow tires. The old car didn't bring anything on trade-in so I kept the tires. They'll fit sixteen-inch wheels; they'd fit your car great."

CeeCee smiled. "Sorry—money's just so tight—"

"You'd be doing me a favor getting the tires out of the way. I stumble over the nuisances everytime I go to get in my car."

"You mean you want to *give* me the tires?" Nobody had ever given her anything as expensive as a set of snow tires. "You could run an ad in the *Weekly Trader* and probably get top price for them—especially this time of year."

"I could," he agreed. Then shrugged. "But it's too much trouble; I don't want to stay home and answer the phone."

"Boy—I don't know—"

"You need the tires, don't you?"

"Sure, I'd like to have them—"

"Then it's settled. How about I take the tires to Wilson's garage and you can have Bert put them on for you?"

"That would be super, Gary—if you're sure you don't need them."

"Nah, I'm glad to get rid of them." He turned and waded back to his car.

CeeCee suddenly felt an overpowering rush of gratitude. No one had ever given her anything—at least nothing she needed so badly at a time she needed it the most. And the benefactor was none other than Gary Hendricks. The guy who thought it so hilarious to put dry ice in a plastic Coke bottle and rattle the neighbor's last nerve.

And now snow tires had changed everything. CeeCee suddenly wanted to be nice to the guy—to show her appreciation. With a mental sigh she realized that CeeCee Tamaris could be bought for a set of steel-belted tires. "Hey, Gary?"

Gary turned back to face her.

"How's Karen this week?"

The scoutmaster's face lit like a Christmas tree, his eyes shown as brightly as the evening stars. "Fantastic!"

"Did she like the flowers?" Gary had wanted to do something special for his girlfriend and decided that he'd send fresh flowers every day. What woman wouldn't adore that?

He nodded, his warm breath rising in a creamy vapor. "She loved the flowers. She calls every time she gets a fresh bouquet."

"Which is every day?" CeeCee crossed her arms, grinning. Gary wasn't so naïve. He was a sensitive, caring man. Karen was a lucky gal.

"I'll have those tires to the garage by afternoon tomorrow," he said, and CeeCee swore he blushed.

"Thanks, Gary."

"Thanks more than you know," she whispered, recalling Rick's hesitancy to help.

22

Around four Saturday afternoon, my phone rang. I looked up from my writing pad, wondering if Stella would get it. CeeCee was still at Wilson's garage having snow tires mounted—tires that Gary Hendricks had given her.

I can't recall ever seeing my daughter so excited over anything as mundane as a set of tires, but her old treads were worn thin and she'd wanted to buy new ones for a while. I made a mental note to personally thank Gary for the thoughtful act. CeeCee said he was tired of working around the tires, but I knew this time of year he could have sold them in a minute.

The phone rang a third time, and I hurriedly thumped to the extension and fumbled for the Talk button.

"Are you making a snowman?"

"Pardon?" I recognized the vet's voice, but the question didn't register. Was *I* making a snowman? With a bandaged wrist and a broken ankle? I don't think so.

Arnold chuckled. "Just wondered what you were up to this snowy afternoon."

"My fighting weight," I complained. And if I didn't get moving pretty soon the observation would be more fact than fiction. All this inactivity was taking a toll on my waistline.

"I'm thinking hot pizza sounds good. Can I interest you in joining me?"

"Pizza?" We'd have to drive to Ash Flat for pizza, and I knew I didn't want to risk life and limb on a meal. "Isn't it snowing at your house?"

"Coming down like cornflakes. I was looking at the bird feeder a few minutes ago and noticed that it's nearly buried in the white stuff."

"Then we couldn't possibly drive to Ash Flat for pizza," I reasoned. I was fairly certain that I wouldn't want to go regardless of road conditions. I'd been home so much lately I was beginning to like staying in.

"Who said anything about Ash Flat? I'm talking the deli counter at Citgo. Ever eat their pizza?"

"On occasion," I admitted. Once I'd stopped for milk, and a fresh pizza was coming out of the oven. Before I left I'd eaten a couple of pieces and ordered three additional slices to take home for CeeCee's and Stella's dinner.

"Thanks for thinking of me, Arnold, but I guess I'd better stay in this evening. CeeCee's getting tires put on her car, and I'm not sure where Stella is—"

"I bumped into CeeCee not fifteen minutes ago. She and Stella are both at Citgo, eating pizza. I told them I'd call you, and we'd make a party of it."

I felt my defenses weakening. I had no practical excuse other than work, and Arnold knew I wasn't working full speed these days.

"Oh . . . I don't know. I'd have to get dressed—comb my hair . . ."

"Throw on a sweat suit and a ball cap," he said. "We're not going to the Ritz, just Citgo."

By the time he pulled up in front of the house I'd managed to do better than sweats and a ball cap. I'd found a nylon jogging suit hanging at the back of my closet and white tennis shoes on my dusty shoe rack. With a little styling gel, I'd wrestled my hair into some semblance of order, added a little blush and mascara, and decided I didn't look so bad. Weeks of inactivity had helped ease the pinched lines around my upper lip and the corners of my eyes. I was starting to look relaxed. Like the old Maude.

When Arnold rang the doorbell I picked up my cane and hobbled to answer. The cane was solid and served more as a walker, but I was getting around fairly well this afternoon.

I opened the door and my eyes immediately shot to the comb-over. Why didn't Arnold wear a hat? a cap? a turban? Was he proud of that . . . thing? Did he think it looked natural? It looked about as natural as a cow with a blackboard.

"I see you skipped the sweats and ball cap." His gaze skimmed me admiringly.

I smiled. "I thought I could do better than that."

He helped me into my coat and then checked to make sure Captain had water and food in his dish before he switched on a lamp. "It'll be dark by the time we get back," he said.

The brief drive to Citgo was uneventful; no one was out. New-fallen snow lay in uninterrupted patterns across my neighbors' lawns. Cold winter twilight made me realize that this drive was exactly what I needed to improve my sprits. The air was icy and crisp—a nice change from the stuffy house.

The teasing aroma of baking pizza filled the air as we entered the Citgo. The convenience store had a holiday feel about it tonight, like the expectant sense on Christmas Eve. Eight or nine people sat around the tables and booths, drinking coffee or mugs of steamy hot chocolate.

"Maude!"

"Good to see you!"

I greeted friendly voices and hobbled toward the booth where CeeCee and Stella scooted across the bench to make room for me and Arnold.

"Sorry, Mom; we started without you," CeeCee apologized.

"I thought I was slow," Stella joked. "You make me look like a teenager."

"You are a teenager," I joked back. "And a feisty one at that."

Arnold reached for my cane as I squeezed in beside CeeCee. Tonight my daughter's eyes had an extra special glow—she looked happy, earnestly happy tonight, and that made me want to stand up and shout praises to the Lord. I hadn't seen CeeCee this upbeat in a long time, and I had to wonder if Rick had something to do with her mood. *Dear sweet Lord, I hope not*. Rick wasn't good for her; I knew that sounded judgmental and motherish, but my instincts told me that if she got involved with Rick she'd be no better off than when Jake was alive.

But to my surprise, Rick's name didn't come up. Instead, CeeCee laughed and told about how Gary had found her ice scraperless. She sent a disapproving glance at Stella. "The poor guy waded in ankle-deep snow to come to my assistance. Had the windshield cleaned in nothing flat and then turned around and gave me four perfectly good steel-studded snow tires!"

Stella remarked that it was nice of Gary—the tires. Arnold said snow tires weren't cheap, and I agreed. I'd priced a set for the Buick last year and nearly fainted. Instead I had Herb's chains installed on the back tires, but they made a terrible racket.

Conversation turned to the Peeping Toms, and Stella filled Arnold in on the new leads, which were pitifully slim.

Before I knew it I'd polished off two pieces of sausage-and-cheese pizza and was about to reach for a third when someone mentioned ice cream.

"I shouldn't," I pleaded, but Arnold got up and came back a few minutes later with a heaping chocolate cone he'd gotten from the soft-serve machine. I loosened the top snap on my jogging pants, and devoured the cone without another thought. I hadn't been eating sweets lately, and I'd forgotten how much I loved them.

I couldn't believe I could be having so much fun and be so relaxed that time simply ceased to exist. It was ten-fifteen when I glanced up at the clock hanging over the checkout counter. I should have noticed the place was clearing out. CeeCee and Stella had left two hours earlier.

Arnold and I had lapsed into conversation about my years with Herb and his years in veterinary school at University of Cambridge. We drank so many cups of coffee that I'd lost count, but my bladder would remind me once I got into bed later. It had been years since I'd sat and talked with a man. I hadn't realized I was so starved for male friendship.

I'd even stopped noticing the comb-over.

Lamplight spilled out from the front window later when we turned into my drive. Arnold killed the engine and sat silent for a moment. The stillness was more compatible than uncomfortable.

Please Lord, don't let him be thinking about kissing me good night. The thought was so foreign and so funny I almost laughed out loud. Just the thought of a real kiss—a smack on the lips after all these months—why, right now my lips felt like two oversized beach balls, and I knew I would be a miserable kisser.

"Tonight's been fun. Thank you, Maude."

"It has been," I said. "Thank you for asking me. I'd have just stayed home, opened a can of soup, and watched reruns."

"Well, we couldn't have that." He turned, smiling. "I hesitated to ask you because I don't want to be pushy, but it gets awful lonely at my house on the weekends."

I knew the feeling only too well. Stella and CeeCee were in and out. For the most part I always had someone around, but not always someone to listen to me. Arnold was a good listener.

"Single isn't all it's cracked up to be," I admitted.

"No, single can be a lonely life. I watch happy families coming in and out of the kennel and I wonder . . . " His voice trailed off and he didn't finish the thought.

"You wonder if you haven't missed the best years of your life."

He lifted his eyes. "Sometimes I do. Yes."

"If it's any consolation, I think most of us wonder that, but in different ways. I wonder if I didn't marry too early and missed part of my youth."

"Did you have a good marriage?"

I nodded, not realizing until this moment that I had more than a good marriage. I had loved Herb totally. I had been happy, and I guess somewhere in my idealized world I thought my happiness would never end—that death, illness, and loneliness happened to other people, not me. Then Herb died and I soon learned that "perfect" isn't a permanent state, and I should have been more thankful for the years the Lord gave me—when life was roses.

"I almost got married once," Arnold confessed. "But two weeks before the ceremony I realized that I didn't love her. I liked her, respected her deeply—even admired her. But I didn't *love* her. She had asked me to write my vows, and when I sat down to write them I found I erased more than I kept, and the ones I kept were pretty insignificant when you're pledging a lifetime."

I nodded again. "She was devastated?"

"I believe she loved me with all her heart, but I couldn't give that precious gift back to her so I decided to call off the wedding. I moved shortly afterwards—haven't seen or heard from her in over twenty years."

We sat in the warm car and shared life experiences. The highs and lows. I could not believe it when I looked up and saw the living-room lamp flash. Twice. In CeeCee's high school days that was my signal for her to come in. Right now.

Guilt washed over me, and I looked at the dash clock. One-fifteen! I was horrified. "I have to go." I fumbled for the door handle.

Arnold got out and walked me to my door in silence. Seems by then we were both talked out.

The front door was unlocked. When I hobbled into the foyer, Stella met me. "Sorry," I murmured like a wayward teen. "Time got away from me . . ."

My mother-in-law didn't say anything, but her eyes spoke volumes. *What are you doing sitting in a car with a man till all hours of the morning? Have you forgotten Herb so easily?*

I wanted to deny her silent accusations. I was a grown woman. I could see whomever I wanted wherever. But I didn't. The last thing I wanted to do was hurt Stella with some insignificant incident that meant nothing more than dinner and good conversation. Two lonely people forgetting for an infantile moment that the best years of their lives were past.

"I'm really sorry, Stella. Arnold and I were talking about

Herb and me." I thought that it might help for her to know I hadn't forgotten her son. I would never forget Herb. Not ever.

"You don't need to explain."

"But you flashed the light," I accused.

"Did I? I didn't notice. I was about to turn off the lamp when I realized you were still out."

Liar, liar, I wanted to scream. A sixty-year-old woman having to explain her actions. Well, I didn't like it—and I didn't like being sixty. But being a sixty-year-old mother, I understood it.

"I hate the comb-over," I said meekly.

"Disgraceful," Stella agreed.

"And that pizza. I'll be up all night. Heartburn City." I thumped my chest convincingly.

"Yep."

"Remind me never to do this again."

This time Stella discreetly refrained from answering.

I climbed the stairs behind her, holding tightly to the rail for support. My ankle hurt and all of a sudden I felt drained and incredibly old.

Really old. Really tired. Really tapped out.

I believed, at that moment, if the Peeping Toms came tonight I'd let them look their fill.

23

It was Tuesday; Tuesday meant goulash for supper. Stella came out of the market with a loaded brown sack. She'd been about to fry hamburger when she'd noticed there wasn't a can of tomatoes in the house. No tomatoes. That meant a trip to the store on snowy roads. So she'd walked. Better to break a bone than put a dent in the Cadillac.

It got dark so early these days. By four-thirty lights began to wink in windows. She passed Helen's house and shook her head. The place was sealed up tighter than a steel drum. She didn't know what it would take to convince Helen that the Peeping Toms were harmless; leastways they had been so far. The fact that neither she nor Hargus was getting anywhere regarding the case raised her hackles. She hated to see Morning Shade locked down like a state prison.

And then there was this thing with Maude and her bothersome interest in Arnold Biggert. Disgrace to be seen with such a looker—oh, the man was easy enough on the eye. He had a good frame. She didn't like skinny men where you'd have to shake the sheets to find them. Her James had been a big man. Arnold was successful—had a good vet business going. But that hair! Her fingers itched to get ahold of that stringy thing and cut it off! *Snip!* Gone. Good riddance.

Rounding the corner, she glanced toward the outskirts of town. Streetlights were starting to blink on. She paused, shifting the groceries to the opposite arm. In the distance she saw what looked like Victor Johnson sitting at the side of the road.

Great balls of fire. Was he ill? Was his blood pressure acting up on him again? Victor had looked healthy enough when she'd seen him at Citgo earlier this morning.

She hesitated in the cold wind, debating the advisability of walking two blocks out of her way to check on him. It was cold, and the hamburger would be dry as a bone if she didn't get home soon. But Victor could be in trouble, and what kind of person would ignore a man in need of help? Course, she didn't know if he *needed* help. She didn't know what Victor was doing; neither did he half the time. But she'd recognize that straw hat anywhere.

Shifting the sack back to her right arm, she trekked off in his direction. When she approached, she could see Victor sitting on a rock, smoking.

Her blood boiled. *Smoking*. The fool man was sitting out in weather guaranteed to freeze a body solid in nothing flat.

"Victor!" she bellowed.

Victor's head snapped up. "Yes, ma'am?"

Stella came to a full halt in front of him. Her eyes zeroed in on the smoking Marlboro. "What are you doing? You know Morning Shade has a no-smoking ordinance."

Victor didn't have money to throw round. The two-hundred-fifty-dollar fine would put a real dent in his pocket.

He slowly stood up, cigarette dangling from the corner of his mouth, and assumed a defensive stance. "Now, come on, Stella.

I'm not breaking the law because—" he pointed to the city-limits sign directly above his head—"I'm not in Morning Shade."

Stella glanced up to verify his assertion. Sure enough, the city-limits sign was in plain view. Now wasn't this a pickle? She didn't recall the city limits being this close . . . on second look, her jaw firmed. The sign was nailed lopsided to the streetlight post. Someone had moved it.

"Destroying city property," Stella declared. "Land sakes, Victor, you're going to be flat broke after all the fines have been assessed."

Victor shifted his gaze to the sign. "Now hold on there." He stepped back, squinted, and took a closer look at the evidence. "I thought the city limits seemed awful close."

"You can't just *move* signs."

"I didn't *move* the sign," he argued. "Some kid must've done it."

"Yeah. Right." Some folks would make up anything to keep trouble off their doorstep.

"I didn't move the sign!" He threw the cigarette on the side of the road. "You got to believe me."

"Why should I believe you? I caught you here in broad daylight—broad twilight—smoking like a chimney. You know the fine for breaking the smoking ban? Two hundred and fifty bucks."

Victor paled. "I know the amount, but I wasn't smoking in the city limits—"

"But you *are* smoking in the city limits." Stella shifted the sack of groceries. "If those cigarettes don't kill you, your fines will."

She'd fined Mayor Throckmorton for the same offense; she could hardly overlook Victor's wrongdoing. Wouldn't be fair, not fair at all, but Thurvis could afford the fine more than Victor. She hated to make another citizen's arrest, but what was fair for the goose was fair for the gander.

She shook her head. "Afraid I'm going to have to arrest you, Victor."

"You can't do that, Stella. I don't have two hundred and fifty dollars for a fine. I gave any extra I had to the church last week for new pew Bibles."

Well, that did make her feel like a louse. But law was law, and when you let one break a law there'd be three more standing in line to do the same thing. "Wish I could overlook this, Vic, but you've got me between a rock and hard place."

"How's that?"

"I had to arrest the mayor not long ago. Caught him smoking."

"Mayor Throckmorton?"

Stella nodded. "Thurvis."

"Does Hilda know?"

"Haven't said a word to her—I could do the same for you. Nobody has to know about this except the mayor, and he's not going to tell anyone without implicating himself."

"But I didn't know I was *doing* anything wrong. Some kid must've moved the sign—bet that Joel Rigby did it so he could come out here and smoke."

"Maybe." Stella's upper plate worried her bottom lip. "Tell you what I can do; I can fine you for smoking, but I'll forget all about the sign. I'll take your word that you didn't move it."

"Why don't you take my word that I thought I was smoking *outside* the city limits?"

"Because you *weren't* smoking outside the city limits. Can't help what you thought, Victor. I could think that I'm Queen Elizabeth, but I'm not."

Victor jammed his hands in his pockets. "If this isn't a fine howdy-do; I don't have two hundred and fifty dollars. What's going to happen now? Am I going to jail?"

"No." Well, she couldn't say for certain. Had that even been discussed? She'd sure hate to see Victor in the slammer. Deep down he was good as gold—just had that nasty smoking habit.

"I can't go to jail—my blood pressure's been acting up. If I was to go to jail there's no telling what might happen to me. The excitement could bring on a stroke or something."

Stella mentally winced. She knew the dangers of high blood pressure, fought with the affliction all the time. Doctor had her on half a pill a day; she could blow any minute. But Victor was playing her like a violin and it wouldn't work.

"Well, look. Why don't I loan you the money?"

"How can you loan me the money? You're living on social security, aren't you? And trying to help Maude out?"

"We're getting by. And yes, I don't have money to burn, but I've got a little stash in my sock, enough to cover your fine."

"Well . . . I don't know. I don't like taking money from other folks. Don't like to be beholden to anyone except the good Lord."

"Well, sometimes a body has to accept help. You come on by the house later tonight and I'll give you the money."

Victor nodded. "I won't be able to pay you back until I have the cash from my vegetable stand this summer."

"That's all right." Stella knew he was honest as the day was long. Folks came from as far as Shiloh and Ash Flat to buy Victor's Arkansas Traveler tomatoes. His truck garden made a tidy profit each year. He'd be good for the money.

"How much interest you going to charge me?"

"Well . . . what's the going rate?"

"Don't know—but it's way down there."

They settled on 3 percent. Stella thought she could do better, but it was too cold to argue.

Victor reached for the sack of groceries. "Let me carry that home for you. Least I can do."

"Thank you, Victor." The two started off in the growing dusk.

"Anything new on the Peeping Toms?"

Stella hated to say there was nothing, but there was nothing. "Very little. Several people have seen two men peeking in the windows, but no one has seen them when they're not peeking. I thought they might be drifters hopping off the train, but it's always the same two men, and they've stayed around too long to be train hopping. We do have a size-fourteen sneaker and a woman's girdle in the way of clues, but that about covers it."

"Doesn't sound like much," he said. "May not be able to solve this case. If it's drifters, they're bound to tire of the game and move on."

"Hargus thinks they're playing mind games with us."

Victor nodded. "That'd be my guess."

Stella didn't mind games; fact was she was pretty good at them, but these two men had stumped her. They were careful not to leave any significant leads. It was uncanny how two men could consistently prowl the neighborhoods and not be spotted. Everybody in Morning Shade was on the lookout for the two lawbreakers.

Victor carried the sack to Maude's back door before he handed the groceries back to Stella.

"Since you're here, I'll get the money," she said.

"I can come back. You need to warm up and eat a bite."

"No use to come back. I'll get it right now. I have to make goulash, so we won't be eating for a while."

Stella left and returned carrying a white cotton sock. She rummaged until she found what she was looking for: two one-hundred-dollar bills and a fifty.

Victor still seemed uncomfortable with the loan.

"Go ahead," Stella encouraged.

He grudgingly accepted the money and stuck the bills into his wallet. Nodding, he stepped off the porch.

"Want to stay for supper?"

"No thanks. I got a can of Vienna sausage and crackers."

"Okay—oh, Victor?"

He turned to look back at her.

"Don't be smoking anymore."

He nodded.

"Neither one of us can afford it."

Closing the kitchen door, Stella sighed. This citizen's arrest stuff was for the birds. And costly. Next time, she was going to look the other way.

She looked up when CeeCee breezed into the kitchen. "There you are! Where have you been?"

"The grocery store."

"You've been gone over an hour!"

"I know—bumped into Victor Johnson and we got to talking." She wasn't going to say about what.

"You'll never believe it."

"What?" Stella went on point.

"The Peeping Toms; they've struck again. Mildred Fasco this time. She was about to take a bath when she saw the prowlers look through her window shade. Poor Mildred. Went tearing out the front door like a cat with its tail on fire."

"She's awful upset, Grandma." CeeCee frowned as she entered the kitchen. "I was typing for Mom when Mildred phoned. We had a hard time settling her down until Hargus could get there."

"Hargus is there now?"

"Not now. He was, but he checked Mildred's yard and like always, there wasn't a sign of anything unusual. Just some animal tracks in the snow."

"Mildred thinks it's the same two culprits?"

CeeCee nodded. "From her description it is." She shuddered, rubbing her bare arms. "This is getting creepy. I'm almost afraid to look out the window anymore. This is the fifth incident. What do these two guys want?" She paused. "Hey—I know this sounds nuts, but suppose the window peeper is someone like Arnold Biggert. He's got a king-size crush on Mom, and we know so little about him. He seems decent enough—around the kennel."

"Arnold Biggert?" Stella never considered the possibility, but she supposed some men would go to any lengths to pursue a woman. Arnold didn't have good sense when it came to hairstyles—but that didn't make him a window peeper. And there were two men. If Arnold was one, who was the other? Rick? Oh, brother, surely not. Stella had seen a lot in her days, but that was just too weird to contemplate. "Whoever is doing this is up to no good; that's for certain."

Five times, Stella agonized when CeeCee left the room. The peepers had struck five times and she'd yet to catch them.

Arnold Biggert. Hmm. Possibly. After supper she'd call Hargus and get the lowdown on tonight's incident. Have him run a background check on Arnold. You never knew . . .

She had to do something to crack this case. Good, bad, or wrong, she had to nab the men responsible for petrifying Morning Shade.

* * *

The phone shrilled at 7:45 A.M. Stella caught it on her way out the door to get the morning paper for her daily dose of the obituary column. Lately, she'd given up on training the snake. The reptile just lay in its cage looking rather bored.

"Good morning, House of Diamonds; which jewel do you want?" Which wasn't exactly the way Maude had instructed her to answer the phone, but probably better than her own preference: "Water Department, which drip do you want to talk to?"

Maude got a little touchy about the telephone.

"Stella?"

Hargus, as she lived and breathed. "None other. Whassup, dude?"

"We've had another incident."

"The Peeping Tom?"

"I don't want to talk about it over the phone, but I thought you'd want to know."

Of course she wanted to know, but that was beside the point. Hargus had never bothered himself before with what she wanted or didn't want. He needed her. Just too proud to admit it.

"Stella?"

"Right here. Do you need my help?"

"Well, I was just thinking . . ."

Not a good idea. Get Hargus thinking and no telling where they'd end up. "I'll be there in ten minutes."

"No, now wait, Stella—"

She hung up the receiver, shutting him off in mid-protest. What did he call her for if he didn't expect her to ride to the rescue? She scribbled a hasty note to Maude saying she'd get breakfast at the Citgo, grabbed her coat and car keys, and headed for the Cadillac.

What had she done before she'd started driving again? Maude was after her to turn in her keys and quit, but it would be after the battle. She recalled Charlton Heston's speech on television at the NRA convention. *After* the battle. From her cold, dead hand. If the declaration was good enough for "Moses," it was good enough for her. Now that she'd gotten a taste of freedom, give it up and depend on someone to take her everywhere? In your dreams.

She speeded up to beat the red light, cutting off the Frito-Lay truck on its way to the Cart Mart. The driver, Mick Evans, stuck his head out the window and yelled at her, but she ignored him. She knew Mick when he was in diapers. He didn't need to think he could flap his lips at her.

She slammed on the brakes to keep from rear-ending Pastor Brookes's car. The pastor was pulling out of the church drive. Wouldn't that be nice? Run over her pastor? She could hear the sermon he'd preach the next Sunday; probably be so hot it'd set fire to the church.

Good man, Brookes, but he had a temper. But then, if she was a preacher—which she never thought to be—and had to put up with an overbearing, bossy woman like Hilda Throckmorton, her disposition probably wouldn't be all that peachy either.

The Fleetwood screeched to a stop in front of Hargus's office. Stella got out and went inside, surprised to see Ruby Lassiter and Vinnie Trueblood perched on the wooden chairs Hargus kept for visitors. The pair looked more uncomfortable than the chairs warranted.

"That you squealing tires?" Hargus asked.

"I don't wear tires." It was none of his cotton-pickin' business if she happened to hit the brake a wee bit too hard. She gave Vinnie and Ruby the once-over. What were these two lovebirds doing here? Surely they weren't the Peeping Toms? Ruby with her determinedly blonde curls and pastel, floral-print dress, looking like something off a Victorian valentine; and Vinnie, the dapper man about town, looked out of place in the narrow confines of Hargus's office. She dragged a chair over to the desk and sat down, handbag on the floor and notepad perched on her knees.

"All right now, what happened?"

Ruby tossed her golden curls. "Why does *she* have to be here? She'll tell everyone in town about this."

Stella eyed Ruby over the rims of her glasses. "What. You got something to hide?"

Ruby turned varying shades of pink. "I *have* not—but you *know* how people talk."

Stella pursed her lips. "You're the peeper? Or are you the peepees?" She hesitated. That didn't sound quite right.

Hargus and Vinnie stared at her vacantly.

"The *what?*" Ruby demanded.

"The ones doing the peeping or the ones being peeped at?"

"Oh." Ruby's expression cleared. "Someone peeped in my window. Short, heavyset man, bald head, horribly wrinkled and with this wide, leering grin."

Stella noticed Hargus was letting her do all the interrogating. Well, fine. "Which window?" she asked. They were closing in on the perverts. She could feel it in her bones.

"The living-room window." Ruby glanced at Vinnie.

Vinnie cleared his throat. "I went outside to see if I could find him," he said.

Stella laid the pen on the desk, eyebrows raised. "You were at Ruby's?"

He nodded. "She had me over for dinner. Had salmon. Salmon croquettes."

Stella cleared her throat. "What time did this Peeping Tom incident occur?"

Vinnie muttered something, and Hargus took a swig of Chocolate Cow.

"When? Speak up?" Stella snapped. "Don't leave out vital information."

Hargus interrupted. "I believe I need to be the one asking questions."

Stella shot him a stern look. "You called me."

"I thought you might need to sit in on interrogations, not take over my office!"

"Well, pardon me, Mr. Man of the Hour. So start asking questions."

Hargus sat back, frowning. Stella thought he was reaching for something to say. "Uh, what time did the incident happen?"

Vinnie's eyes darted to Hargus—then to Ruby. "Uh . . . rather late."

Ruby picked up a Wanted poster and fanned herself.

"How late?" Stella demanded.

"Well—" Vinnie's eyes seemed to be searching for help—"maybe . . . a few minutes after twelve."

Stella automatically caught her upper plate when her jaw dropped. Recovering, she cleared her throat again and asked. "A.M. or P.M.?"

There was a scandal in the making now.

"Well . . . P.M.," Vinnie admitted.

"Midnight?" Stella asked. "*You* were at Ruby's house that late? Doing what?"

"None of your business," Ruby blurted. And fanned harder.

Stella bristled. "Is so my business. I'm helping solve this case."

"I wouldn't say that," Hargus began.

She whirled on him. "Am I or am I not helping?"

"I guess you are—in a way."

Vinnie intervened. "Now there's no need to get worked up. We were playing Monopoly, and you know how long that can take sometimes."

"Did you get a real clear look at the perp?" Hargus asked.

Ruby eyed him warily. "The what?"

"The perpetrator," Stella interpreted. "Criminal, the Peeping Tom."

"Oh." Ruby nodded. "I got a very clear look. I've already given you a description."

Stella reread her notes: "short, bald, and wrinkled" fit half the men in Morning Shade.

"Guess you had your shade pulled," Hargus surmised.

"Why no, I never pull my living-room shades. Why would I?" Ruby asked.

Well, couldn't be much hanky-panky going on with the shades up, Stella conceded, but it didn't look right for a single woman to be entertaining a man friend so late at night. What was the world coming to? Here was Ruby entertaining a man in her home after midnight, and Maude sitting out in the car talking to that Arnold Biggert till the wee hours of the morning—and Herb barely dead and in his grave. Decent women didn't act like that in her day.

Another thing, with those rose-shaded lamps in the Lassiter living room putting out such a soft, flattering light, Stella'd bet that glimpse Ruby got was anything but clear.

Ruby and Vinnie made noises about leaving, and Hargus cautioned them to report anything else they might recall about the Peeping Tom. Stella watched the couple retreat out the front door. This made how many incidents? Six? And that was six more than Stella Diamond needed.

"Hargus, we have to catch these men."

He stood up and took a half hitch in his pants. "What do you think we're trying to do? I don't see that you've got any call to act like we're sittin' on our thumbs."

Stella nodded. The boy was a mite touchy since Hilda had called him a do-nothing, sorry excuse for a lawman. All right, she'd rephrase it. "I didn't mean to say we weren't trying, but the situation is desperate. The town is getting restless. Someone is liable to take a shot at those men. We've never had a killing in Morning Shade, and we don't need one now."

Hargus swigged Chocolate Cow. Wiping his mouth, he squinted at her. "You got any new ideas?"

"Not at the moment, but the Peeping Toms are skating on thin ice. It's only a matter of time before we collar them. But they're smart—real smart. Don't leave a decent clue. They have to slip up sometime."

"Well, we got to come up with something soon; I'm tired of dodging Hilda 'The Hun' Throckmorton. She's still mad at me."

Stella grinned. She should feel sorry for him, but she kind of felt Hargus and Hilda deserved each other. She pulled on her gloves and picked up her handbag. "I need to get on home. Maude will be wondering where I am. Keep me posted on anything new."

Hargus glowered at her from behind the desk. "I catch you speeding, I'm hauling you in."

She stiffened. "You do and I'll tell Pansy about you buying those lottery tickets."

"I never!"

"Did so. I saw you. Three times last week alone."

"You're downright nosy. You know that?"

Threaten her, would he? Two could play that game. She left the office knowing that he needed her.

She sat in the Cadillac, key in hand, rehashing her parting words. It wasn't a bit Christian to talk to Hargus that way, and she wasn't nice about Hilda sometimes.

Guilt flooded her and she bent her head. "Lord, I'm sorry. I'm just old and I don't always think. Seems like I get upset and my tongue takes over and I'm smarting off, saying anything I want because I'm old enough to get away with it." The book of James in the Bible had it right: The tongue was hard to bridle.

She had a lot on her mind lately. CeeCee was so crazy about Rick Materi she couldn't think straight, and Maude was seeing that Biggert man. Maude was forgetting Herb. Her son. Her baby boy. Stella didn't want the love of her life to be forgotten, and she couldn't stand thinking about some other man taking his place.

If CeeCee married Rick and Maude took up with Arnold, who would want an eighty-seven-year-old woman hanging around? She'd go back to the residential care center. At first she hadn't wanted to leave the center, but now that she had her freedom she didn't want to go back.

Wasn't that just like life? You want what you can't have until you get it; then you don't want it anymore.

The house seemed almost too quiet this morning. I poured feed in Captain's dish and fixed my morning cup of tea. Time to settle down for my devotions. My daily quiet time spent in prayer and Bible reading was the only thing keeping me going.

The injury was healing nicely, but true to Sherm's prediction, the process was slow and exasperating. Sherm had been so busy with a town outbreak of influenza ("why can't people get their flu shots," he'd lamented over the phone) I had barely seen him in the past few weeks.

My eyes focused on the Bible. I was still reading in Psalms. They seemed to have a special message for me. My Bible lay open to the thirty-ninth psalm, and I stared in disbelief at the first verse: "I will watch what I do and not sin in what I say. I will curb my tongue when the ungodly are around me."

Well, if that wasn't a wake-up call. I'd kept my tongue well sharpened lately. Not that I'd used it all that much. Discretion kept me from taking my frustration out on Stella. She had a tongue of her own, and since she was still upset over my night out—two, if you counted pizza at Citgo—with Arnold, I was trying not to rile her any more than necessary.

My relationship with CeeCee was another situation entirely. I had promised not to say anything more about Rick, and, thank You, God, I had managed to keep quiet, although the more my daughter told me about Rick the more I recognized Jake Tamaris.

My biggest problem with my daughter right now was her lack of interest in helping with my manuscript. Every night she gulped down her dinner and drove to the kennel. She hadn't even turned on the computer this week.

I read the verse again and bowed my head, asking God to help me keep guard on my tongue. I knew God didn't cause me to fall and break an ankle, but I truly believed He could use this enforced leisure time to teach me something, though I couldn't imagine what. I was ready—even eager—to sit at the Master's feet, willing to learn, anxious to grow spiritually, but nothing was coming through. Instead of peace and knowledge, I seemed to be giving way more and more to resentment and anger.

I couldn't afford anger-management classes, so if my emotions were ever to be tamed, the transformation could only come about through God. I let my thoughts drift. *Don't let me use my tongue to sin*. I needed to needlepoint that sentiment and hang it on my office wall.

The doorbell rang and I hobbled out to answer. I opened the door to find Frances, Pansy, and Minnie Draper. All three were burdened with casserole dishes. I held the door open, and they marched past me on their way to the kitchen. All three women—good friends—had been here often enough to know their way around. By the time I caught up with them, Frances was bent over in front of the refrigerator making room for the new offerings.

"Good morning, ladies," I chirped. Stella didn't like for the women to dote on the Diamond household. She wanted to feel as if she could handle the load by herself, but in the past week the ladies of the church had quietly gone about their business, toting chicken casseroles and hot rolls to the house every other day. Frances and Pansy had even volunteered to do the laundry, but I had vetoed that. The house might not be spotless under Stella's care, but I wasn't about to open that Pandora's box.

I lifted the corner of a foil-covered casserole and sniffed appreciably. Baked chicken and dressing. A plastic container held gravy, ready to be heated. We'd eat well tonight. Frances had brought a pasta salad and a green-bean casserole, and Minnie hefted a dessert salad and a plate of brownies.

"There." Frances fitted the salads in the refrigerator and shut the door. "Now Stella and CeeCee won't have to cook tonight. Is Stella about through with that community-service thing?"

"Not much longer, I believe." I was ashamed to admit I couldn't remember; all I knew was I still had mine to face when the ankle and wrist healed. I had a hunch my mother-in-law was enjoying her assignment so much she'd extend it past the time limit if she could.

Pansy sighed. "It's going to be a miracle if the three of them get through this without Stella wrapping that Fleetwood around a tree."

Well, that was a happy thought.

She shook her head pensively. "Duella said Stella's driving has improved her prayer life by 50 percent. Duella's taken to shutting her eyes and praying all the way to Shiloh. She's convinced that's the only reason she's alive today."

"That's a blessing, I guess," Minnie said. "Simon said the community service wasn't too bad. The real punishment was riding with Stella."

"It's my fault," I confessed. "If I hadn't broken my ankle—and had this wrist taken care of—I could have taken them. I'll never forgive myself if anything happens." Listening to them lament over Stella and her driving was throwing me into a panic. Stella drove like she was going to a fire. Pansy was right: Only a miracle could keep them from waking up in the hereafter.

"Don't blame yourself, honey," Frances said. "You know Stella: stubborn as a mule refusing baptizing and just as contrary. She'd have found a way to get behind the wheel of that Cadillac sooner or later."

"Be a chore to get her to hang up her keys again," Pansy agreed. "Hargus says if he catches her speeding he's lowering the boom on her—going to give her a ticket that'll singe her hair. He'll do it too. She can rile him something awful."

I shuddered at the thought. Hargus was walking on quicksand if he ever ticketed Stella. It could very well be the last ticket he'd write this side of glory.

Minnie apparently had the same thought. "That would be the fight of the century. You could sell tickets to that one."

The women trudged to the door, brushing off my repeated thanks. Three good women determined to do what was right. I appreciated them more than I could ever express with mere words.

"We're just glad we can do something to pay you back for all the times you fed us," Frances acknowledged.

Pansy grinned. "Sort of makes up for all those Thanksgiving and Christmas dinners you've cooked."

Minnie struck a spiritual note. "Cast your bread upon the water and it will come back angel food cake or something like that."

Something like that indeed. I watched them saunter down

the walk, talking and laughing. Good friends. Good to me. That didn't change the fact that I was humiliated at having to accept help. I'd always been one to take care of myself. "Independent as a hog on ice," Herb used to say, and I guess he was right.

Now practically every woman in town had called and would have been here at least once if not for Stella's insistence that she didn't need help. Small-town generosity, church family. Thank God for people who lived their faith.

CeeCee was a different story. My daughter could put in extra hours at the kennel helping Rick Materi, but she couldn't help her own mother. I had opened my house to her when she needed me so desperately. I had stood by her, supported her, and prayed for her when she needed help and encouragement.

Now I was the needy one and she was nowhere to be found.

25

CeeCee left the post office and drove home. Melting snow glazed the street into unsuspecting sheets of black ice so the drive home was slow. Slow enough to make her think. She had promised to work on the manuscript tonight, but Rick needed her at the kennel. She felt torn between Mom and Rick. Both made demands on her time and loyalty, and there wasn't enough of CeeCee to go around.

She had promised Mom help with her typing, and she had meant it. Somehow she'd get the manuscript finished if she had to stay up into the wee hours of morning every night to finish it. But surely she deserved a chance at happiness again. Men like Rick Materi didn't come along every day. Mom couldn't expect her to ignore her feelings for Rick. She could be a little more understanding.

She parked in the driveway, leaving plenty of room for Stella. It took a lot of space for Grandma and her Caddy. She shook her head in amazement. Eighty-seven years old and driving to Shiloh three times a week. Terror of Highway 167. At least Simon and Duella were properly terrorized. She'd heard the women's guild had put their names at the top of the prayer list at Duella's request.

CeeCee carefully climbed the front steps and went inside. Mom was staring at the blaring television. Something about her expression said she wasn't watching Vanna and she wasn't in a good mood.

"I'm home."

Maude twisted around to face her. "For how long?"

Uh-oh, here it comes. "Long enough to fix dinner anyway."

"Dinner is ready. Pansy and Frances and Minnie brought enough food for two days."

"That was nice of them." And it was also the reason Mom was steamed; she didn't like accepting help. Well, tough. She was getting to be a baby since her injury. CeeCee didn't say that out loud, of course. One hint of what she was thinking and boom, World War III.

"Yes, it was." Maude's voice was so even it flatlined. "Especially since we're not their responsibility."

"You're saying it's my responsibility to cook every night?" CeeCee felt her temper ignite. "I don't do my share around here?"

"Do you feel you've been doing your share?"

CeeCee flinched from the condemnation in her mother's eyes; then anger took over. This wasn't fair. She *did* cook. It wasn't her fault if the churchwomen had taken it upon themselves to bring food. No one had asked for their help. She drew a ragged breath. "I do have a job, you know."

"Actually you have two jobs," Maude said. "You even get paid for one of them. I understand why you can't help me."

Oh, temper tantrum. She got it. "Oh, you do? Well, let me tell you something, Mother. I'm a grown woman, which I keep reminding you, and I'm tired of being treated like an irresponsible child. I'll type the whole manuscript tonight if that's what this is all about. And I'll dump out what those women brought and cook dinner if that will make you happy, but I won't stand here and be treated like an unruly brat."

"There's no need for a temper fit," Maude said.

Resentment boiled and bubbled. CeeCee's stomach felt like the rusted insides of an iron caldron. How *dare* she insinuate she wasn't doing her share! She was working two jobs *plus* trying to keep up with Mom's work. What did she want? Blood?

"Well, excuse me. I need to change clothes and get to work. After all, I am required to pay my way around here."

"Well, excuse me," Maude mumbled. "Aren't we all?"

CeeCee wheeled and stomped up the stairway, making certain she hit each carpeted step with a firm foot. Now she had to call Rick and tell him tonight was off.

The thought of not seeing him didn't bother her nearly as much as the thought of what his alternative plan would include.

I watched CeeCee stomp up the stairs, ashamed of the squabble I had provoked. Why had I taken my aggravation out on her? The exchange hadn't changed one thing, and these constant mini-battles were eroding our relationship.

Maybe I could hire someone to do the typing, although I couldn't imagine who it would be. Tanzel was the only decent typist in Morning Shade, and she worked full time for the church. If I could only get the Hamel manuscript finished by the deadline, I would have one less thing to worry about, and maybe I could keep a tighter rein on my temper.

Lord, I'm sorry. I haven't even gotten through this day and I've already sinned with my tongue. But it's so hard for me to accept help. I've always done everything for myself.

Could this be what God was teaching me? We *can't* do everything by ourselves. Was I too proud of my ability to manage my own affairs? I'd had a hard row to hoe after Herb died. I'd made it on my own. Now I'd reached a place where I couldn't get by without help from others and I hated it. I thought of the Israelites in the wilderness. God had taken care of their needs, but they had never been satisfied. Was that me, Maude Diamond?

Well, God was taking care of my needs too, and all I had done was complain. Not even grateful for what I had received. Always wanting and needing more. It seemed like an eon ago that I had thought I'd be happy if only my M. K. Diamond mysteries could make the best-seller list. Fool that I was, I thought that would be the epitome of bliss. Now typing seemed to be the real paradise I longed for.

CeeCee would come through for me; I had to believe that. Blood was thicker than water. But an apology was in order. Forget the chicken casserole warming in the oven.

Tonight I would have to eat crow.

CeeCee stared at the blinking cursor of her mom's computer. Dinner tonight had been tense. Sure, Mom had apologized and said that she was overly tired—she'd try to do better. The whole argument was so unfair.

CeeCee knew she should have done more, but sometimes, like now, she was stressed to the max. She hadn't realized what a difference it would make to have her mother immobilized with a broken ankle and a useless hand. Iva Hinkle took care of her invalid mother *and* worked a full-time job. For the first time CeeCee was starting to see how stressful parent care could be. And Ida didn't have Rick demanding she be at his beck and call.

He hadn't understood the need for her to stay home tonight. What had started out as working occasionally for free rent for the dogs and birds had turned into a full-time job. The change had been so gradual she hadn't noticed until it had reached the point she was spending more time at the kennel than she was at home. No wonder Mom was uptight.

CeeCee was stretched between the postal job, helping Grandma with work that needed to be done here, Mom's need for help on the manuscript, and Rick's increasing requests for the kennel. She needed a break.

The office door opened and Maude hobbled in. "Honey, I've been thinking—actually I can ask for a couple of weeks' extension. If Rick needs you at the kennel, you can put this off until tomorrow."

"Tomorrow will be just as busy. Better do what I can tonight. I called Rick."

"And he was unhappy."

CeeCee shrugged. "He'll get over it." Before Jake died he had expected her to be there when he wanted, to do what he needed, put her own wishes and needs on the back burner. She scrolled through the previous work, looking for errors before moving to the next page. If she worked hard, she'd get three chapters finished tonight. That would put her over two-thirds through the book.

She tried to ignore her mother's watchful eye as she typed. She was missing her time with Rick. She would finish this manuscript if it killed her. What more could the woman want?

When Maude spoke, it took her by surprise. "Look, CeeCee. I know we haven't got along the best lately, but I love you."

CeeCee bit back scalding tears. "I love you too, Mom, but I'm not your little girl anymore."

"How well I know, but I'm foolish enough to think I brought you up to know the value of keeping your word."

"Look, Mom. I'm keeping my word. I'm typing. Don't push it, okay?" She didn't look up from the monitor until her mother left the room. Unfortunately, Captain had entered as Maude left, and now he perched on top of the filing cabinet, his usual perch when he heard the clicking keyboard. "Not you too, cat. I have enough problems to deal with."

Captain stretched and yawned.

"Right. Me too. I'm going to finish three chapters and go to bed."

She felt restless and irritable, and it wasn't all because of her problems with Mom. What was Rick doing right now? Had he become so important to her she couldn't be away from him even one night without feeling unsettled? One of these days she would have to take a hard look at the real Rick Materi. *Was* he another Jake, the way her mother and grandmother claimed, or was he a careless but nice guy who meant well, just needed some understanding woman to take him in hand?

She was finishing the third chapter and ready to quit for the night when Stella entered the office. "You busy?"

"Just about done, Grandma. Need something?"

Stella sank into the overstuffed chair. "I've lost it, little girl."

"Lost what?"

"My cutting edge—the ability to solve crime. The Peeping Tom hit Ruby Lassiter's. That's the sixth incident, and me and Hargus are no closer to solving the crime than we were in the beginning."

CeeCee smiled and instantly felt ashamed of herself, but it was impossible to think of her grandmother and Hargus Conley as serious crime busters. More like the Keystone Cops. "What's really bothering you, Grandma?"

Stella sighed. "You know—my age."

Her granddaughter slowly lifted her eyes.

Stella frowned. "Well wait, little girl, until you live to be my age and see how certain you'll be about being around for sunup."

CeeCee typed a couple of sentences. "The prowler peeked in Ruby's window? Only one this time?"

"Yeah, though the other was probably somewhere around. The shysters hit again, and I can't do a thing to stop them. They've got me beat."

"Nonsense. You'll catch them. They have to be leaving some sort of clue."

"Nary a thing except the size-fourteen shoe, which we discovered belonged to Pete Gyres's grandson. We had to rule him out right away. The boy's been visiting his maternal grandparents since Christmas. There's been a few animal tracks in the fresh snow, but they lead nowhere. This town's full of dogs and cats. The men aren't riding horses—we're sure of that."

"Horses?" CeeCee laughed. "I wouldn't think so. I thought you said they were hopping off freights."

Stella lifted both shoulders. "That's one theory—but theory only. We haven't got any proof the incidents are connected with the railroad."

"Not in this one-horse town. They're too quick."

Its being a one-horse town was one of the reasons CeeCee loved Morning Shade. She'd had her fill of bright lights and fancy places. Her marriage to Jake had been public knowledge on a daily basis. How he'd managed to hide his debts and his women she would never understand. The man had reporters following him like a swarm of flies. He had been one clever guy, not only fooling the media but making a complete fool of her.

She realized Stella was still talking. "Sorry, Grandma; I didn't quite catch it."

"You weren't listening," Stella said. "I guess I'm bothering you. No one wants to talk to an eighty-seven-year-old anymore."

"Save your breath," CeeCee said. "I know you're a pro at handing out guilt trips, but not this time. I was listening. My mind just wandered a bit."

Stella grinned. "Better watch that. It might not come back home."

CeeCee laughed. "You're a case, you know that?"

Stella nodded. "It's one of the perks of old age. You can get by with a lot." She cackled.

"And you milk the perk to the last drop."

Stella got up and brushed at her skirt. "I do my best. I see you've got that cat in here."

"He's company."

"He's also calmed down a lot since the dogs aren't home. When are you going to bring them back?"

CeeCee shook her head. "I don't know. The reason for taking them to the boarding kennel was to get them out of Mom's hair. Now I'd be afraid she'd trip over them. She's not all that steady yet."

"Her temper's steady enough. Running on high most days." Stella paused with her hand on the doorknob. "How serious do you think she is about that Biggert man?"

CeeCee glanced up. "Not serious at all. She's just bored and wants to get out of the house, and Arnold's easy to talk to." Her tone softened. "What's wrong? Are you afraid she's forgotten Dad already?"

Stella nodded, eyes downcast.

"She hasn't. She loved Dad with every fiber in her. Arnold's just filling some very lonely hours—and she's doing the same for him. When she gets back to writing, she won't have time to think about a man. You know her. Nothing takes the place of her writing schedule."

"I hope you're right. The three of us have enough trouble getting along. We don't need a man stirring up more trouble."

Stella left and CeeCee stared at the monitor screen. No room for a man? Well, if things worked out with Rick she would be living elsewhere. How would Grandma and Mom get along by themselves? They had a hard enough time now, even with her contributing financially on a regular basis.

She finished for the night and shut down the computer. Tomorrow she was going to the kennel. If Mom didn't like it she could get over it. She'd have to learn that she couldn't pitch a fit when things didn't go her way. Enough was entirely enough.

* * *

Stella sat on the side of her bed, tired. Just plain bone tired. Maude and CeeCee were sniping at each other every day. The Biggert man called a lot. Oh, Maude made a few lame excuses not to do or go wherever he suggested, but Stella knew they were just that—lame excuses. Truth was, Maude liked Arnold.

And then this Peeping Tom thing. The case was slipping through her hands, and she couldn't do a thing to stop the slide. Altogether too much for a woman her age. She scratched her arm, looking closely for a red rash. If she didn't get a case of hives over this she was made of sturdier stuff than she'd thought. She glanced at the snake cage; she was going to have to do something about the reptile. Worthless. Wouldn't fetch a mouse if she'd throw one in front of its face.

Her mind returned to the Peeping Toms. Maybe she and Hargus were in over their heads this time. Sure, they'd solved a couple of penny-ante mysteries, but the perpetrators had been citizens of Morning Shade. The way the victims described this pair, they were foreigners—probably from the East—New York, Boston. One of those big crime-ridden cities.

She stared at cold rain splattering the windowpanes. Somewhere out there a couple of criminals prowled the streets while decent people went about their business behind the closed doors of their own homes. Would the peepers strike again tonight?

Lord, if You're listening, we could use some help here. I'm doing all I can with the abilities You've given me, but I'm at the end of my rope.

She guessed that when you got to the end of your rope you tied a knot and held on. If God helped her the way she expected Him to, Stella A. Diamond would solve this case. Then again, if the Almighty worked on the merit factor, she probably wouldn't warrant much help.

She sighed and reached for her Bible. God would help her. And the reason she felt renewed hope was simple: she'd just run out of options, and once a body got in that shape, that's when God stepped in.

* * *

CeeCee braked outside the kennel and switched off the ignition, sitting for a full five minutes contemplating Rick. What was it about her that made her go for the big, good-looking, women-attracting hunks? She could have had Gary Hendricks, who, oddly enough, had turned out to be a nice guy, sending flowers to his Karen and being more reliable than Rick ever thought about being. But she hadn't wanted Gary and she did want Rick.

But the relationship wasn't working out quite the way she'd hoped. Rick seemed satisfied enough, but for her there were the disturbing traces of an old pattern that reminded her of her years with Jake. Maybe it was just because Mom and Grandma had expressed obvious distrust of Rick and that's what was influencing her thinking. All of a sudden she had this uneasy feeling she couldn't pin down. She opened the car door and went inside.

Rick waved at her from his desk. He sat with his feet up, on the phone as usual. From his end of the conversation, she gathered he was telling someone how to deworm a cat. She grinned. Having had the experience, she knew a bit about the difficulty. Captain had put up a fierce battle, but she had won. He'd growled for a good thirty minutes afterward, clearly affronted at the assault on his dignity.

But then all cats weren't like Captain, for which everyone could be thankful. Rick had taken one look at him and refused to keep him at the kennel, which was why he was still at home. Without the poodles to torment, Captain had turned into a model of good behavior. She figured he was saving his strength for the day they came home.

Arnold walked out of the back room, pulling on his coat.

CeeCee glanced at her watch, realizing it was time for him to go home. "Hi. Busy day?"

"Not bad, considering the weather. Business is picking up a little every day."

Well, that was what she wanted. If Rick succeeded with the kennel he would stay in Morning Shade. "Where do I need to start?"

"I don't know. Ask Rick when he gets off the phone." Arnold stalled, and CeeCee had a feeling she knew what was coming. "How's Maude doing? Getting her revisions caught up?"

"Still working on them." She didn't want to talk about revisions. Mom's looming deadline was starting to worry her. It was hard to find time to type with Rick demanding so much of her time.

"Guess she's busy tonight then?"

"I don't know her plans; you'd have to ask her."

"You're right. I might give her a call." He adjusted the Payne

Stewart–style golf hat he wore. "I'll be running along. Have a good evening."

CeeCee walked him to the back entrance. Arnold was a great guy, but her father had been gone for less than two years. Like Grandma, she had trouble accepting someone else as a potential suitor for Mom. Suddenly, for the first time she realized Maude and Stella might see Rick as an interloper, a threat to the family composition.

Rick hung up the phone and got up to hug her. "How's my one and only tonight?"

His one and only? She wondered about that. "Doing fine now."

He pulled back until he met her eyes. "Now? What's that mean? Anyone giving you trouble? You just tell Rick and he'll take care of it for you. Is that Hendricks guy harassing you again?"

CeeCee frowned. "Of course not. Why would you think that?"

"I heard he gave you a set of new snow tires. I'm not sure I like some other guy doing favors for my woman."

CeeCee backed out of his arms. Jake used to have that halfway jealous tone in his voice whenever another man talked to her. It had been fine for him to cheat on her, but she couldn't be friendly with anyone else.

He spread his hands in an inquiring gesture. "What?"

"Gary's a friend. Don't try to read anything into what he did. I needed tires. He had a set and he let me have them. That's all there was to it."

"I'm only saying it was an expensive thing to do for someone who is 'just a friend.' No reason to rag on me, okay?"

"Gary has a girlfriend. He's not interested in me."

"Well, I hear he used to be interested, but you should know." He changed the subject. "The refrigerator's getting messy. How about cleaning it before you go home tonight?"

"Sure. Anything else?"

She thought about the way Gary treated Karen—fresh flowers every week, utmost respect for her. Evidently there were men who didn't put themselves first. Unfortunately, she hadn't found one yet.

Rick led the way to the back. "I thought we might get caught up on cleaning out the pens. We got in a new bunch of Yorkies today, and I want them close to the office until they get used to the place."

For the next thirty minutes, they worked together in companionable silence. CeeCee realized how much she enjoyed the kennel. She'd always been an animal lover. Someday she hoped to have a place of her own where she could keep every stray that no one else wanted. The Yorkie pups were adorable, and she cuddled each one before placing them in their new home.

She paused to visit with Claire and Frenchie, wondering if she was doing the right thing to board them here. She missed having the animals at home, but with Mom so unsteady on her feet right now, she couldn't risk her tripping over one of the dogs and falling again.

"You got time to help work on the books?" Rick asked when she'd cleaned the fridge.

CeeCee glanced at her watch. Ten-thirty. Mom would be in bed by now. "Sure, why not?"

She'd be tired in the morning, but she wanted Rick to make the kennel pay. She'd do anything to keep him in Morning Shade.

Listen to yourself, CeeCee. Stop and listen to what you're saying.

In time Rick would come around; she had to be patient. He'd eventually recognize how much she loved him. After all, he called her his one and only, and she desperately wanted to believe him.

They spent an hour going over the books, sending out statements, marking accounts paid. Close to midnight, Rick pushed back from the desk and yawned. "Let's call it a night. I'm bushed. We'll finish it up tomorrow."

She shut her eyes and massaged her throbbing temples. "How about skipping a night and let me get caught up with Mom's work."

He frowned. "Come on—you were off last night, weren't you? Why doesn't your mom hire someone to help? She's a published writer, isn't she?"

"She is, but I promised I'd help." She felt a little ripple of irritation. Between Mom and Rick she felt like slave labor.

He shrugged. "Sure. Take the night off. I can survive for one night, but it'll be hard." His grin warmed her heart.

"I'd rather be here with you, honest. It's just that I promised."

"I understand. That's one of the things I love about you, that down-home dependability. You help Maude. I'll get by best that I can. There's a teenage girl wanting a few hours a week—I might call her."

"There's no need to hire someone. As soon as Mom can use both hands again, she won't need me. Right now she does."

He stood and pulled her up to stand beside him, his arms circling her waist. "Don't worry honey bun. Go get your coat, and be careful driving home."

She leaned against him, enjoying the moment of intimacy. He kissed the tip of her nose. "Call me tomorrow night, all right? You can take a few minutes from typing to talk, can't you?"

"Sure. I can do that."

The phone jingled as she returned from getting her coat. She answered it, surprised to hear a female voice at this late hour. "Is Ricky there?"

"Just a moment." She handed the phone to him, careful not to let her expression give her away.

He took the receiver, spoke into it, and while she watched, he waved at her, mouthing the words, "See you later." He sat down and leaned back in his favorite position, feet on the desk, and phone at his ear. He was smiling.

CeeCee sat in her car later, waiting for the heater to warm up. Why would a woman be calling Rick at the kennel at this time of night? She doubted if it had anything to do with kennel business. His one and only? Maybe, maybe not.

I woke to my usual routine of Captain kneading his paws on my chest. Nothing like being trampled to death in my own bed. I rubbed the cat's ears playfully. "Okay, hot shot. I've had my early morning wake-up call. Let the stress begin." I longed to turn over and sleep for another ten minutes, but unfortunately there's no snooze button on a hungry cat.

Easing off the bed, I fumbled for my slippers and cane. Might as well get up and start breakfast, although about all I wanted was toast. Try cracking open an egg with one hand. I started coffee and hobbled out to get the morning paper so Stella could have her daily obit fix.

Damp morning air assailed me and I did hope it would clear up. So far neither CeeCee nor Stella had slid into a ditch or worse, but I lived in daily fear of the highway patrol showing up on my doorstep with bad news. I knew my daughter was a good driver, but Stella . . . well let's just say I would be relieved when I resumed the driving duties.

By the time I had set the table and popped a couple pieces of bread in the toaster, CeeCee wandered in, already dressed in her postal uniform. She yawned and pulled out a chair, sagging into it with an air of weary resignation. She looked like a limp dishrag this morning.

"You feel okay?" I asked.

She yawned again and nodded. "Late night. I missed my beauty sleep."

I had heard her come in close to midnight. "Kennel must be really busy."

"Cleanup and paperwork. It took more time than expected."

I heard confrontation creep into her tone and knew it was time to back off. Unless I wanted to drive a wedge further between us, I had to be very careful what I said about Rick Materi and his kennel. It had been the same with Jake Tamaris. My daughter had terrible taste in men, but she had a loyal streak a mile wide.

Except, apparently when it came to her mother. I swallowed those hurtful thoughts. CeeCee loved me; I needed to be more understanding. I was struggling over Herb's death, yet I enjoyed Arnold Biggert's company. Stella was as upset over Arnold as I was over Rick. So there you have it. Two old meddling women and a young, confused woman.

CeeCee poured milk over her cereal. "I'll be working on your manuscript tonight. I promise I'll be home shortly after work and get started."

I didn't even try to pretend that I wasn't pleased. "I'm so glad you'll be able to help. March 1 is coming right up."

"We'll make it. Did Arnold call you last night?"

I looked at her, surprised. "Why, yes he did. How did you know?"

"At work he asked if you were busy. I told him he'd have to talk to you. Are you going out with him?"

"Oh—" I sank into a chair—"that I don't know. I like him—

he's excellent company, but you know how Stella feels, and I hate to do anything that's going to upset her. This Peeping Tom thing has her fretting more than usual. And she was your father's mother, so it's normal for her to resent anyone taking his place."

"*Is* Arnold going to take Dad's place? What's wrong with Sherm?"

"Nothing's wrong with Sherm." In fact, everything about Sherman Winters was right. "But the good doctor is so busy I've barely seen him since the surgery and only talked to him on the phone once or twice."

"I'll bet he'd be upset to know you're seeing Arnold."

"I'm not *seeing* Arnold!"

"Then why are you so defensive?"

"Look. I *loved* your father, but he's gone. I get lonesome sometimes, and Arnold is someone to talk to. He's lonely too."

"A lot of relationships have been built on loneliness."

"This isn't a relationship. We're only friends." I felt like I was talking out of school, but I wanted to know if CeeCee was aware of Arnold's past. "How much do you know about Arnold?"

She rolled her eyes, spooning cereal into her mouth. "Not much, I guess. I work with him at the kennel. He's a great vet—wonderful with animals and people, but usually he's getting ready to leave when I arrive. Seems like a nice enough guy."

"He does," I agreed. "However, he told me on the first date he'd spent time in prison."

CeeCee's mouth dropped open. "You're kidding."

"I had the same reaction. I wasn't sure I had heard him correctly, but he told me the whole story. It seems he'd taken money out of a drawer and intended to replace it."

"My stars. I wonder if Rick knows."

"Don't tell him," I urged. "I don't want Arnold to lose his job. He seems so normal otherwise—and sorry for his poor judgment."

CeeCee made a snorting sound. "Rick wouldn't fire him for being an ex-con. Arnold's doing a good job, and besides, Rick's not like that." She must have seen the skepticism I tried to hide because she repeated. "He's *not*. I'll swear he's not."

I took a deep breath. "Honey, we live together; it's necessary for us to get along. Arnold's and Rick's names are bound to come up in conversation occasionally. We need to be able to discuss both men without flying into a rage. Can't we agree to keep the subject neutral without firing shots?"

My daughter caught her lower lip in her teeth and stared at the bowl of floating Oaties. "I'm sorry, Mom. I don't mean to snarl at you. Sure, let's keep it neutral. And Mom, I like Arnold. If you want to go out with him, it's all right with me."

"Thanks."

She stared back at me. "Then you *are* going to date him? Seriously."

I wondered what part she hadn't heard. Shrugging, I found I suddenly didn't have the energy to rehash the subject. "For Stella's peace of mind, I am not going to date him."

"Oh—" CeeCee brightened—"that's too bad. He seems like a nice fella."

Sighing, I buttered my toast and wondered (and not for the first time) if the hospital had sent me home with the wrong baby. I hoped Arnold would understand. I didn't want to hurt him either. I had a feeling he'd been hurt enough in his time.

When Stella left the art-therapy room Friday, she found Manuel Rodriguez leaning against the wall, hands jammed in his pocket. What's up with these kids' dress? The boy was wearing beige shorts that hung to his ankles and a striped shirt four sizes too big for him. And a Chicago Cubs ball cap wedged on his head sideways. Did he buy his clothing at a disaster shelter?

Stella sensed something was up. Was he mad about the counseling service? She'd taken the young man's problems to heart. He needed a firm hand, and the hospital staff agreed to set him up with a top youth counselor with degrees coming out the ears. She figured he'd hate the idea, but he'd go if she had to drag him screaming all the way. Manuel wasn't going to throw his life away on petty crime; he was going to get help or her name wasn't Stella Can't Solve a Simple Peeping Tom Mystery.

She paused, pretending to rummage through her purse for car keys. Duella and Simon wouldn't be through in their areas for another hour so she had plenty of time to stall. So she fumbled, giving the boy sufficient time to work up his nerve to do whatever he had on his mind. She hoped it wouldn't include violence.

He outwaited her. When she couldn't dawdle any longer she started off down the corridor.

His voice stopped her. "Sprinkles or gummy bears, Grandma?"

She turned, pretending to consider the choices. "Sprinkles."

He held out his right arm; she latched on to it, and they walked to the cafeteria.

When bowls of ice cream—with double sprinkles—were sitting in front of them, Manuel started to talk. "I got busted for drugs." With that, the dam burst and the boy opened up.

Stella thought her heart would crack wide-open. *Thank You, God. I don't deserve Your goodness.*

"Drugs, huh?" Stella licked her spoon. "Never could figure out how folks could peddle drugs when people like me can barely afford to buy what we need."

Manuel straightened his posture. "You need something, Granny? I can get—"

"I don't need anything, son." She took of bite of ice cream, wondering how she was going to explain that the *reason* he was here in his predicament might have something to do with his eagerness to oblige. "Why do you sell drugs?"

He shrugged. "Make money."

"Isn't there an easier way to make money other than looking over your shoulder every few minutes, afraid a cop's going to collar you?"

The slim shoulders lifted and fell.

"Are you supporting a family?"

"Mother—two sisters."

"No dad?"

He sneered.

"Mother work?"

He shook his head. "She's a druggie."

"I'm sorry, Manuel."

His chin rose defiantly and he met her eyes.

She wondered if anyone had ever called the kid by his given name. Maybe "hey, you!" or "worthless" but never "Manuel"—maybe short for Emanuel. "Well, I suppose you wouldn't be selling drugs if there was another way."

The chin raised another notch. "I quit school in the ninth grade; had too. There was no food in the house."

Nodding, Stella ate ice cream, listening to the boy's miserable life pour out. The kid never had a chance; didn't have much of one now.

"So you're going to have to do time."

"Year—maybe. Once I get out of here."

"You drying out?"

He laughed. "I don't use drugs—I'm not that stupid. I sell them."

"Oh. And that makes more sense."

Resentment resurfaced. "Whatever."

During the course of the conversation Stella discovered that Manuel was nineteen and in the hospital for an irregular heartbeat until Monday, at which time he'd be released to await sentencing. It broke her heart to think that a boy with so much potential—because his mind was as sharp as a tack—would experience prison life. It didn't seem right, not right at all. But drugs weren't right either, and wrongs needed to be righted.

"Anything I can do to help?" Stella bit into another sprinkle, knowing the boy had an angle or he wouldn't be here, eating ice cream with the "old woman."

"Would you . . . "

Stella could see his request came at a great price—release of pride. "Would you look in on my mom and sisters and make sure they have food and heat next winter?"

"Sure, be happy to." She was eighty-seven and shouldn't be making long-range plans, but she didn't have the heart to point that out to the youth. She'd have Maude or CeeCee do it if she couldn't. "There's all kinds of agencies—"

"I know about the agencies. I want *you* to check on them—make sure they're all right. I know you won't lie to me."

"I appreciate your trust, son. I'll make sure they have what they need."

"When I get out, I'll pay you—"

"Don't need a red cent. I've got all I need. I'll look after your family—I'm guessing they live around here?" If they lived in New York or somewhere else, her word would be worthless.

"They live here—in Shiloh." He gave the address of some low-rent housing area.

She'd seen the apartments. They weren't much. "I know where it is."

Relief flooded his youthful features. Stella witnessed a tremendous load lifted off this young man's shoulders. "One more thing," he added.

"What's that?"

"Will you . . . write me sometime? I'll buy some stamps so you won't be out anything."

"I've got enough stamps to burn a wet mule." Stamps were a small item, and Stella could certainly invest thirty-seven cents once or twice a week in a young man's future. "You send me your address, in care of the hospital, and I'll write you," she added.

A dawning smile touched the corners of his eyes. "Afraid to give me your real address?"

"Do I look addled?"

He grinned, displaying a row of even white teeth. Actually he was a handsome boy. Pity his life had gone so wrong so young.

Both bowls were empty. Manuel got up and deposited the containers in the trash receptacle.

They walked to the door together. The boy grinned, "I'm going to depend on you, old lady."

Stella didn't know why she suddenly felt tears pool in her eyes. She was getting soft. "I'm dependable, punk. I'm eighty-seven—you got to play the odds that I'm going to live another year or that I'm even going to remember the specifics of this particular conversation, but on the plus side, I'm still breathing and I haven't forgotten anything important in over a week. You'll get letters from me, and I'll look in on your family when needed. Got a great daughter-in-law and granddaughter who'll be glad to help."

Stella wasn't sure *glad* was the appropriate word, but it'd have to do. If Maude could put up with parrots, poodles, a bull snake, and Captain, she could take on a misguided youth with one hand tied behind her back.

When Stella turned and started down the corridor she heard the boy say softly, "Thanks, Stella."

She lifted a hand, not bothering to turn. Boys like Manuel spooked easily. She had to take it slowly, but the boy could depend on her.

Much as anyone could depend on an old codger.

* * *

Stella sat across the desk from Hargus later that day, notepad balanced on her knee. "All right now, what do we have?"

Hargus pursed his lips and stared at the ceiling.

Give the boy credit. He occasionally had an original thought.

Right now he sighed, toggling his gaze to the opposite wall. "We have that shoe we found at Shady Acres."

"That's nothing! The sneaker belongs to Pete Gyres's grandson Todd, and other than telling us the kid has a good-sized foot, it's worthless as a clue. The boy was fifteen hundred miles from here when the Peeping Tom incidents started."

"No—but wait. Where did Todd *leave* the shoe?"

Stella consulted her notes. "On Pete's front porch."

"But Pete never reported a Peeping Tom at his house."

"No and neither did Maury Peacock when the criminals stole his wife's corset, but Farley Birks did when the Peeping Tom left it at his house. I'm not sure if any of this has any significance. Why does the Tom steal things at one place and peek in the window at others?"

"Well, that's as clear as springwater." Hargus swigged Chocolate Cow. "Would you steal something and then look in the window to see if anyone was watching? Seems to me you'd head for higher ground before you had a posse on your tail."

Clear as mud was more like it. Hargus watched too many John Wayne reruns. Posse, indeed. "Still, what would the Tom want with one shoe and a girdle? Doesn't make sense."

"You need a mind like a lawman to understand," Hargus assured her. "He didn't want those things. He wanted to confuse the issue, make us look everywhere except in the right place."

"Which is?"

Hargus drew back. "I don't know—thought you might."

"Well, he's got us confused, all right," Stella muttered. If there was anything that made sense about this case, it was beyond her powers of observation. "Wonder why the Tom picked Helen's house to start his peeping career?"

"Now that's got me puzzled too," Hargus admitted. "If I was going to peep in anyone's window, I'd pick Ruby's. Now there's a real looker."

"Humph. Ladies don't entertain men at all hours of the night." She guessed maybe she'd better be careful with comments like that. Her daughter-in-law sat out in the car with a man until after 1 A.M. Never would have believed it if she hadn't seen it with her own eyes. Herb was probably spinning like a rotisserie at the thought. And there was CeeCee, spending half the night at the kennel with Rick. Well, like mother, like daughter. She sighed. Her family tree was full of nuts.

Hargus grinned. "Never seen the likes of the way you women put down someone like Ruby. She's pretty and ladylike, and men enjoy her company. What you got against her?"

Stella bristled. "I don't have a thing against her, and don't you say I do."

Nothing, except the way she dressed and the way she simpered and smirked around anything in trousers. You wouldn't catch Stella A. Diamond acting like that. Not that men were standing in line at *her* door. And if they *were,* they wouldn't be looking for her. Not much call for eighty-seven-year-old beauty queens.

She grinned at the idea, suddenly in a good mood. "We'll catch these men, Hargus. I've threatened to cave once or twice, but I know I've—we've still got it. Those two men will make a mistake one of these days, and we'll be there to snap the cuffs on them."

"I'll snap the cuffs."

"Whatever."

Hargus shook his head. "I hope you're right, but I'm doubtful. Seems like they would have made that mistake before now. We've been walking this town from end to end, and we've not found anything incriminating yet."

Well, she'd made a couple of citizen's arrests, but she couldn't say anything about that. That's the trouble with keeping your mouth shut: discretion was no fun.

She snapped the notepad shut. "If we just had a fingerprint or a footprint. Anything to go on."

Hargus shifted in his chair.

Stella pounced. "Do you know something you're not telling me?"

He hesitated, and she gave him "the look." He took a deep breath. "This is confidential, okay? I did find out we have an ex-con living here in Morning Shade. Moved here recently, too."

Stella sat up straighter, senses alert. "Oh, yeah? Who?"

Hargus picked up a pen and tapped it on the desk. "Well, that's why I didn't want to mention it. It's Maude's new friend, that Arnold Biggert. Did time a few years back. Happened a long time ago; he's straight as an arrow now."

Stella's breath caught. "Arnold Biggert is an ex-con, and he's dating *my* daughter-in-law? My stars! What next?" She couldn't believe this. Did Maude know about Biggert's past? She knew there was something sneaky about that man. She looked up to find Hargus watching her. "What?"

"You been taking Maude's friendship with Arnold sort of hard. You don't want to let your personal feelings get in the way of your detecting. You need to be fair."

Stella stared at him, not believing what he had just said. Hargus Conley was telling her how to behave? She'd have him know she had impeccable manners. Of course she wouldn't let her personal feelings get in the way of hanging the Peeping Tom case on that ex-con who had the nerve to sneak around her house courting her daughter-in-law.

She caught Hargus's knowing look and felt color stampede her face. *Lord, what was I thinking? There's not a smidgen of proof Arnold is the Peeping Tom, but I was ready to accuse him.*

"Stella?"

She met his eyes. "I've never railroaded anyone yet, and I won't start with Arnold. You don't have to worry."

"Just so we have that straight."

30

I was in the pantry trying to figure out how to use the can opener with one hand when Stella came home. She blew into the kitchen bringing a breath of cold air with her.

"You been out today?" she asked. "It's cold enough to freeze a brass cat."

"No, I've stayed home. I'm beginning to like it." I slapped the can opener down on the counter and would have gladly ripped the stupid thing apart if Stella hadn't intervened.

"Here, let me do that. What are you making?" She took the can of cream of mushroom soup and ran the opener around the rim the way I used to do before I became helpless.

"I hope it's a broccoli casserole, but the way I mess up everything I do anymore, I wouldn't guarantee that's what it will be when I'm finished."

Stella laughed and picked up the cutting board. "Here, let me chop that celery. Can't have you hurting your one good hand."

I dropped down in a chair, close to tears. "Oh, Stella, I feel like such a miserable failure. Do you ever just want to quit? Throw up your hands and give up?"

She cocked her head to one side, eyes twinkling with humor. "Well, I've thought about giving up latte, but then I'm no quitter."

I laughed in spite of myself. "You're good for me, Stella. I'm sorry I sound so pathetic. Pity parties aren't pleasant to watch."

Stella stirred the mushroom soup and sour cream into the chopped broccoli and celery. "You know what's wrong with you? You can't write. You're a writer, and this operation has interfered with the muse. Things will look better when you get back to that computer."

I stared at her, overcome by her wisdom. "You know, I think you're right. I do get nervous and irritable when I can't write. That's part of my problem."

Stella lavishly sprinkled shredded cheddar cheese over the top of the casserole and popped the oval dish into the oven. "And you're upset over Rick Materi."

"That too," I admitted. "I'd hate to see my daughter locked into another hurtful relationship."

Stella put the kettle on to boil. "Let's have that peach-flavored tea and some of Minnie's brownies. Seems like that would hit the spot right about now." She got out the cups and the squeeze bottle of honey.

I sat there and let her wait on me, and that was another bitter pill to swallow. I had always been the one to do for everyone else. I couldn't get used to being the one waited upon.

Stella poured boiling water over the tea bags and set the cups on the table. "Trouble is you see your daughter the way she was when she married Jake, young and inexperienced. She's older now, but she still has a little more living to do before she wises up about men. She's smart. Give her time. She'll see through Rick Materi eventually."

I lifted the tea bag out of my cup and dropped it on the

saucer. "I'd have thought she'd learned her lesson. Once burned, twice shy."

"No one gets through life without getting hurt, Maude. We all have our wilderness experiences. That's when we grow closer to the Lord."

I understood what she was saying. No matter how much I wanted to protect CeeCee, I had to let her go through her own wilderness. We couldn't spend all of our lives on the mountaintops. Sometimes we had to walk the valleys.

Stella grinned. "It's called mother love."

I smiled. "I'd fight all of her battles if I could, but that wouldn't be best for her. Since I can't, I'll lift her up in my prayers."

"There you go. Turn her over to her maker." Stella helped herself to another brownie. "When she drifted away from God, you kept praying until she worked her way back."

I wiped my eyes. "You're saying maybe I'm not a failure after all?"

"You a failure?" she scoffed. "Girlfriend, you're a success. Can't you see that?"

"I am?" Me, a success? The idea was new to me. Sure, I could sell a manuscript, but I thought true success had eluded me.

"A howling success." Stella marked them off on her fingers. "You were a good wife. You're a good mother, a good daughter-in-law, a successful author, and most important of all, a strong Christian."

I sniffled. This was my day to cry. "I'm not sure I can live up to all that."

"Sure you can. First you stop dwelling on your failures and count your wins. God didn't make junk, and that includes you. Stand tall and fluff your feathers."

I snorted tea through my nose—painful—mixed with laughter. She frowned and I gasped out the words, "I'm sorry . . . all I could picture was an old hen in a windstorm."

She stared at me for a moment then broke into laughter. I had myself under control until she gave a high cackle that set me off again. We laughed until my sides ached and tears streamed from my eyes.

When we finally calmed down, Stella put her teacup in the sink. "I bought me a new toy today. Think I'll set it up in my bedroom."

"What did you get?"

"A CB." She looked half defiant, like she expected me to be upset.

It took a minute to soak in. "A CB? You mean . . . ?"

"That's right, a citizen's band radio. I'm going to monitor police calls. That way I can keep on top of these Peeping Tom incidents."

"What about the snake?"

"I traded it for the CB, silly." She grinned. "One man's junk, another man's treasure. Stupid reptile wouldn't fetch a thing." She left the kitchen before I could faint with relief.

I had a mental picture of Stella in her Cadillac, rushing to the scene of the crime and shuddered.

But at least that bull snake was history.

Monday morning Stella pressed her lips together and glowered at Simon and Duella. "What is this, a mutiny?" Simon had called a meeting at the Citgo, apparently to discuss her driving.

"You could call it that," Duella retorted. "I'm tired of risking my life riding to Shiloh with you. We're rebelling. You get someone else to drive us."

"Who am I going to get?" Stella demanded. "Or did you want me to stand on a street corner with a sign: Will Work for Transportation to Shiloh."

"No need to get sarcastic," Simon said. "We don't want to hurt your feelings, but we really would prefer that someone else drive."

Lord, grant me patience. What am I going to do with these weenies? "I don't know what you're worried about," Stella said. "Hasn't the good Lord taken care of us so far?"

"Yes, He has," Duella agreed. "But I don't want to tax His patience. After all, He gave us enough good sense not to put ourselves into dangerous situations."

"And you think riding with me is dangerous?" Try to do

a favor for someone and see what it got you. After all, she was providing the car and the gas. And still they complained.

"I wouldn't say that," Simon said.

"I would." Duella said. "You drive like you own the road."

"Anything else?" Stella asked. "No one is forcing you to ride with me, you know. It's not like I hold a gun to your head. You can always walk."

"See—" Duella turned to Simon—"I told you she'd be upset."

"I'm not upset." Stella bared her teeth. "Why would I mind being told I'm a dangerous driver and a road hog? Why, that just made my day."

Dangerous was she? She'd show these two traitors. Never had a ticket in her life, or a wreck for that matter. She'd had a few close calls, but those didn't count.

"Now, Stella, Duella didn't mean that." Simon made an obvious attempt to pour oil on water.

"Yes I did." Duella's hair, tinted a cross between Ruby Riches and Barn Red, glowed with every word. "You can just bet I meant it. I'm tired of praying all the way to Shiloh, and all the way back, that Stella doesn't end up in the ditch, killing us all."

Simon got up and brought latte refills around the table. "Ladies, let's calm down and talk this over sensibly. Stella, you do tend to take chances, you know."

"Like what?" Let him name one time when she had taken a chance. Well, on second thought, he could probably name several. She hurried to head him off. "Let's say you might be right—not that I agree you are, you understand—but if you don't like my driving, what do you propose to do about it? You have to get to Shiloh, and it's a bit far for people your age to walk."

"We didn't propose to do anything about it, as you put it,"

Simon said. "We just thought you might be willing to listen to reason."

"I'm very reasonable," Stella said. "I have a car, and I filled the tank with gas not fifteen minutes ago. I'm driving to Shiloh in the morning. You're both welcome to ride along, or you can find alternate transportation. Whatever you think best."

"Simon could drive," Duella offered.

Stella agreed. "If he had a car."

Simon sighed. "All right, Stella, you win. We'll be ready to go with you, as usual."

Stella sipped the latte. Criticize her driving, would they? Wait until tomorrow morning. She'd give them a ride they wouldn't forget. She grinned at the thought. Duella's fiery mane would be stark white by this time tomorrow evening.

* * *

The seventh Peeping Tom incident seized it for Stella; Prudy Walker had wakened around nine-thirty in her recliner and recognized the outline of two men crouched in front of her window. "Just hunkered down," Prudy exclaimed when the paramedics strapped an oxygen mask across her nose.

"I don't see why I have to go to the hospital," the retired nurse protested, her voice thin and reedy. "I'll catch my breath in a few seconds."

"Ma'am, your heartbeat is over two hundred. You need to see a doctor."

"There were two of them," Prudy called over her shoulder when the two medics wheeled her to a waiting ambulance. "One was ugly—terribly ugly. Can't impress upon you, how *ugly*. I'll have nightmares about this the rest of my life! Someone has to catch those creeps!"

Stella hunkered deeper into her coat, pad and pencil in hand. She'd heard the call about the Peeping Toms on her new CB. Hargus had arrived fifteen minutes later. He'd jammed his pants over pajama bottoms and he looked lumpy. His hair was tousled, his eyes at half-mast. He stood in the gusty wind, crouched in his fleece-lined parka.

"Is Prudy's heart acting up?"

Stella jotted something on the pad. "Nah, it's only palpitations. The Peeping Toms scared the waddin' out of her."

Hargus yawned and ran a hand over his stubbled cheek. "Wish these perverts would pick an earlier time to cause all this commotion."

Stella jotted down the time and weather conditions, then stuck the pad in her coat pocket and listened to the ambulance siren fade into the distance.

"Guess someone ought to call Prudy's granddaughter."

Hargus nodded. "Suzy's got an apartment in Shiloh, doesn't she?"

"Yep—she works at the Waffle House." Stella checked the illuminated dial on her watch. "Don't know if she works a day or night shift. I'll call when I get home."

Nodding, Hargus yawned and tried to shake it off. "You checked the grounds for evidence?"

"Nothing." Like the previous six times, the two men left nothing. How they could come and go undetected was even more puzzling than why they chose to stick around, repeatedly breaking the law, and risk being caught. They didn't appear to have any interest in gaining entrance to the houses. There were no jimmied locks, no pried window frames. Hargus had a fingerprinting kit he'd gotten somewhere—who knew where? He'd dusted for prints at every crime scene, but nothing unusual ever showed up. Whoever was doing this was out for the thrill—and that made the offenders even more treacherous.

"Well, guess there's nothing more we can do here until daylight." Hargus arranged his collar closer around his exposed ears. "Think I'll go on back to bed."

A warm bed sounded pretty good to Stella, but she doubted that she would sleep. How could a body sleep when any minute they might look up and see two evil felons peering through the window? "You go on; Prudy will need somebody to calm her down. I think I'll go on over to the hospital and see if I can help."

Hargus threw her a guarded look. "You can't drive to Shiloh at this hour of night." He checked his watch. "It's nigh on to ten o'clock."

Stella had forgotten about the lateness of the hour. She'd been reading a mystery and had dropped off to sleep around eight o'clock, half listening to the squawking CB box. When the alarm sounded about Prudy and the window peepers, she'd sat up straight in bed, wide-awake.

Before she could ask, Hargus quashed her thought. "I can't take you; I have a seven o'clock meeting in the morning with the mayor."

"About what?"

"About none of your beeswax."

She shrugged. She knew better than to interfere with Hargus's so-called police business. He closed up like a bank vault anytime she tried to pump him for information he claimed she wasn't entitled to.

"Okay. Suppose I'll have to call the hospital and find out what's going on."

"Prudy's granddaughter will take care of her."

"If I can reach her."

They parted, Hargus returning to his house and Stella walking the block and a half back to Maude's. She'd prefer to fire up the Cadillac and see about Prudy, but contrary to belief, she wasn't senile.

Or an idiot.

A woman her age had no business on the highway this time of the night, and Stella Diamond was smart enough to know her limitations.

I was pouring a second cup of coffee when Stella came downstairs Tuesday morning. One glance at the clock and I knew something was wrong. It was close to nine o'clock; Stella never slept this late, especially on her community service days.

I reached for a second mug and poured her coffee. "Didn't you sleep well last night?"

"Slept fine last night—what there was of it." Stella sat down at the table and heavily laced her coffee with cream.

How the woman kept her trim figure amazed me. She could eat a horse and not gain a pound.

Stella tentatively sipped the hot brew, then sat back, apparently satisfied with the taste. "Prudy had a visit from the Peeping Toms last night. I went over to investigate."

"You left the house?" I was shocked. I hadn't heard a thing after nine o'clock. Those pain pills Sherm had prescribed knocked me out colder than German kraut.

"I went over as soon as I heard the call. Poor Prudy—we had to call an ambulance. Her heart was trying to hammer its way out of her chest."

"My goodness—I had no idea! You should have wakened me."

"Wakened you?" She snorted. "It'd take an earthquake to wake you after you've taken one of those pills."

That was true; I wasn't proud of my comas, but medication really affected me. I could take two Advil and be out for hours.

"I thought you had community service this morning."

She nodded. "I did—looking forward to giving Duella and Simon the ride of their lives today. She took another sip of coffee. "I called the hospital and told them I'd been up late last night and I wasn't up to coloring today. They said I could make up the time."

"What about Duella and Simon?"

"Them?" She shook her head. "They sounded relieved."

I nodded. "Probably do them good to have a day off."

Stella didn't comment.

"Is Prudy okay?"

"I called her granddaughter last night. Wasn't sure I'd get her, but she was home. She went straight to the hospital and called me back around eleven. They'd given Prudy something to calm her down. Suzy said the doctor thought she'd be okay."

"Prudy's granddaughter lives in Shiloh now, doesn't she?"

Stella nodded. "Moved there last summer. Took a job at the Waffle House."

I shook my head. "Poor child. It can't be easy being single and raising a child alone."

"Divorce is never easy, and I think young women have it the worst. They're not used to hard times like we are—"

The phone rang and Stella got up to answer. She took the cordless and wandered off into the living room, but I could hear the gist of the conversation.

"Was that Hilda?" I asked when she returned.

"That was Hilda—mad as a galled centipede. The mayor's

called a six-o'clock town meeting for tonight. Wants everybody to drop anything they're doing and be there."

"Really? What's up? The mayor hasn't called a special town meeting since the sewer lines broke and the town coffers didn't have the money for repairs."

Stella chuckled. "Didn't take folks long to come up with a boatload of money, did it?"

"Not in late July." My stomach churned at the recollection. The smell was horrific. Nobody opened a window or went anywhere they didn't have to go until the main trunk line was repaired and sealed.

"Did Hilda say what tonight's meeting is about?"

"She didn't say—just warned me and everybody else to be there."

I didn't like my time determined by someone else. Tonight a special episode of *CSI* was on and I hated to miss a single episode. I know that's what VCRs are for, but I also know that I would be sitting at that meeting resenting every moment while the VCR recorded what I should have been watching in the comfort of my recliner—with a bowl of popped kettle corn in my lap. What if the unreliable VCR misfired and didn't record? It'd happened before, and I'd been sick with remorse.

"Are you going to tape your program?" Stella asked.

I wondered if my addiction was that apparent. "I don't want to, but I guess I'll have to."

"Pesky meetings," Stella muttered. "Like we all don't have a zillion other things we'd rather be doing than sitting in a hot, overcrowded room in City Hall. Good golly, I hope Edgar wears his glasses tonight and gets that thermostat set on the right number."

I shook my head. "CeeCee promised to type for me tonight."

Stella eyed me and I knew what was coming. When would I learn to stay quiet about CeeCee and her good intentions?

"Has she helped one time this week?"

"Once," I defended. I could tell that went over like a lead balloon. I felt free to criticize my daughter, but I didn't like it when Stella did. I understood CeeCee's quandary. After all, she was trying to work two jobs—plus fit in a social life, though her social life was the crux of the problem. Her life couldn't be easy.

Sniffing, Stella got up and popped a slice of whole-wheat bread in the toaster. "You're too easy on her, Maude. She's a grown woman. When she gives her word she needs to stand by it."

"She means well," I defended.

"The road to hell is paved with good intentions."

* * *

We threaded our way into the overpacked room a few minutes before six that evening. We'd gulped down grilled-cheese sandwiches and tomato soup in order to be here on time, and now the food lay in my stomach like a heavy sponge.

By the size of the turnout, Hilda had managed to notify everyone in town about the meeting. Even Prudy—looking pale and shaken from her recent fright, sat beside her granddaughter, Suzy.

I hobbled over and bent to say hello. "I thought you'd still be in the hospital."

Prudy shook her head. "I should be, but you know insurance these days. Kick a body out the front door while they're still getting dressed."

"Isn't that the truth? I think it's awful. Why, I was telling CeeCee it won't be long before new mothers will be asked to mop up after themselves after delivery and turn off the lights when they leave."

Suzy leaned over Prudy to speak. "The doctor says Grandma's fine—just a few lingering heart palpitations. He released her late this afternoon. I wanted to take her straight home, but Hilda thought she shouldn't miss the meeting."

Squeezing Prudy's hand supportively, I eased into the row and sat down. Stella sat beside me. My eyes scanned the room for CeeCee and Rick, but I didn't locate them in the crowd.

Mayor Throckmorton stood up and banged the gavel. The loud buzz of voices dominating the room slowly faded.

"Thank you for coming, ladies and gentlemen."

I wondered what the meeting was about: possibly the no-smoking ordinance. I'd heard rumors that people were having a hard time adjusting to the ban.

"I'm going to come right to the order of business." Thurvis glanced up and motioned to Edgar. "Crank that heat down a notch or two, will you? It's hotter than a smoking pistol in here."

Edgar got up and slowly shuffled to the wall thermostat. I said a silent prayer of gratitude. Already women had whipped out hankies and scraps of paper and were starting to fan themselves.

"What's this all about?" a male voice in the crowd called.

"Peeping Toms."

A low rumble went around the room.

"What about them?" someone else shouted above the din. "Did you catch the two men?"

The noise level inflated with false hope. Women's anxious voices rose above the men's.

Thurvis threw both arms above his head. For a moment his

stance reminded me of Richard Nixon and his signature pose. "Hold on! Quiet down!"

The audience settled down.

"To answer Bob's question: we haven't caught the men—"

A chorus of boos interrupted Throckmorton. It took a full two minutes to regain crowd control.

"People! That's the purpose of tonight's meeting. We are here to take a vote and see if we want to bring in the state police!"

Stella shot to her feet. "State police! Why? Hargus and I are on the job!"

Hargus rose. "Yeah. Me and Stella, we're working day and night, trying to solve the case."

"But you haven't solved it," Hilda pointed out. She pointed to Prudy. "One more incident like last night and this thing is going to turn deadly. We need help—trained, professional assistance!"

I caught Stella by the coattail and restrained her. "Sit down. Remember your blood pressure."

"Trained professional help, my foot." Stella sank back to the aluminum folding chair, lower jaw jutting. "I'll give her trained, professional help—"

"Shhh. Listen to what the mayor is saying."

Well, it turned out that Thurvis said a lot. I kept staring at my watch, sweating bullets, wondering if the VCR had clicked on at the right time. If not, maybe I could call the TV station and purchase a tape of tonight's special episode of *CSI*—

The yee-haw and haranguing went on and on. I'd never heard so much fuss over one simple question: Did the town want Stella and Hargus to continue work on the Peeping Tom incidents, or should they turn the investigation over to state police?

I silently voted for the state police, but deep inside I wondered what ever happened to loyalty and the desire not to hurt folks. I wanted the perpetrators caught as much as anybody else, but Stella and Hargus had worked hard and it seemed a shame to throw them out now.

Hilda still had the floor at ten o'clock, raving on and on about the dangers of the evil society we lived in, and we couldn't expect God to take care of us if we didn't lift a hand to take care of ourselves. The tips of Stella's ears got redder and redder, and I wondered if she was going to get airborne a couple of times. Every sentence or two she'd jump up and rebut the charges, the main one being that she and Hargus didn't know what they were doing. To give the town credit, though, they didn't exactly phrase it that way, but that's what they were saying.

Tempers frayed the longer the discussion went on.

Hargus bounded to his feet when someone suggested they quit stalling and just take the vote. "There's not one bit of need to take a vote," he accused. "If you'll hold your horses Stella and I will break this case! Look what we did with the furniture movers and the chain-letter caper!"

"Luck—pure old luck," Hilda accused. "I say we vote and we do it now." She glanced at her diamond-encrusted watch. "Mortimer and Snerd are way past their nightly outing."

"Hilda and her dogs." Stella folded her arms and sat back in her chair. "Thinks more of them canines than she does her own neighbors."

I wasn't saying much; by ten o'clock I turned into a pumpkin. Gauging by the crowd's angry mood, we weren't going anywhere for a while.

Around eleven I think even the mayor had had it. He held

up both arms (I thought in surrender, but more likely to gain order). "All right! Settle down. It's late—we all need to be getting home. May I suggest a compromise?"

Voices silenced; heads turned back to the podium.

Clearing his throat, Thurvis proceeded. "Since there's a sizable division on whether to bring the motion before the people to turn the case of the Peeping Toms over to the state police, I offer a new motion. I propose that we give Hargus Conley and Stella Diamond thirty-six hours to bring us the culprit or culprits."

Out of the corner of my eye I could see Stella swallow. Thirty-six hours. A day and a half to solve a case they'd been working on for weeks? I hardly thought that was fair, but then I—like the rest of the town—would like to be able to sit in my house evenings and not worry about my privacy being invaded.

Voices swelled. Men and women turned in their chairs to discuss the mayor's proposal.

Victor Johnson stood up, straw hat in hand. "Has anyone given any thought to rescinding the no-smoking ordinance?"

Thurvis waved him down. "That's *completely* off the subject. We're not talking about city ordinances. Sit down."

Victor sat.

Hargus stood up. "You can't put a time limit on solving crime, Your Honor." Hargus never called Thurvis "Your Honor" unless he was peeved. And right now it wasn't hard to see that both Hargus and Stella were hinging between peeved and outraged. The tip of Stella's nose was bright red.

Pansy interjected. "You haven't given my son a chance! You can't just dismiss him like this!"

My mother-in-law bounded back to her feet. "I'm up to the challenge."

Hargus threw her an incredulous look. "Are you *nuts?* We haven't got one single lead—"

"Hush up, Hargus." Stella squared her shoulders. "Give us thirty-six hours and we'll bring you the criminals on a silver platter."

Thurvis loosened his tie. Perspiration dotted his florid features. "You'd save us all a lot of trouble if you'd just admit you don't have a clue who's doing this."

I thought the same thing but had decided an hour ago not to say anything. I had to go home with Stella. It would only upset her if I was in favor of the motion, but to me this whole meeting was senseless. I could be home watching my recorded *CSI*. *Please, Lord; let that contrary recorder have done its job.*

One or two town residents held out—wanted to vote then and there for the state police, but eventually even they gave in. Around 11:45 a vote to give Stella and Hargus thirty-six hours to solve the case was completed. Though not unanimous by a long shot, the motion carried.

By the time we got home it was after midnight and my ankle reminded me I'd been on my foot for too long. During the drive home, Stella had been lost in thought. I felt sorry for her; she'd bitten off quite a chunk tonight. Seven Peeping Tom incidents. A size-fourteen shoe belonging to Pete Gyres's grandson Todd and a whalebone corset belonging to Maury Peacock's deceased wife were the only clues she and Hargus had to solve a very obstinate case.

Lord, they could sure use Your help.

I washed my face and slipped into my wool pajamas. The bed felt good when I finally eased between cold sheets. I'd forgotten to turn on my electric blanket—but at least the VCR had recorded *CSI*. Praise God. But I was too tired to watch it.

Scrunched in a tight ball, I closed my eyes. *Lord, thank You for the day and for Your blessings. Stella and Hargus do need Your help. I don't know what You can do, but I'd deeply appreciate any help You can give those two. Tomorrow's a new day. I pray Lord that from the moment my eyes open until they close again at night everything I say will reveal You living in me.*

I don't think I finished the prayer—I can't honestly say. By now warmth seeped through my aching bones, and the pain medication began to work its magic. I started to float—weightlessly into a world free of pain and troubling decisions.

Impossible deadlines, crafty Peeping Toms.

* * *

Wednesday, Stella was out of the house all day. I puttered around the house, made a few notes for CeeCee to insert in the manuscript. She had called to say that she and Rick were going to grab a bite to eat at the new Mexican joint out on the highway. I wasn't aware there was a new Mexican joint, but then that's another tale. She said she'd be home early. Early could mean anytime between sundown and dawn.

After supper I walked into my office and nearly choked when I saw my mother-in-law sitting in front of the computer. My workstation was sacred ground. I didn't let anyone mess with my computer except CeeCee, and that was only by necessity.

"Stella? I thought you were upstairs in your room."

"Was, for a while." She peered over the rims of her glasses at the sheet of paper propped in front of her.

On closer inspection, I saw it was my handwritten manuscript insertions. "What are you doing?"

"What does it look like?"

"It looks like you're inserting my revisions."

"I am."

I mentally groaned. Stella wasn't the best typist. Now I would have to carefully read each sentence to make sure she'd inserted what I'd written and not added anything that would embarrass me. "CeeCee's going to do that when she gets home."

Stella looked up, lifting both brows.

"I know," I admitted. It was seven o'clock and CeeCee wasn't home yet. When she did get home she'd have to mess around an hour before she settled down to type. By then it would be late, and she'd be yawning, staring at the clock.

I dropped into the chintz-upholstered easy chair and watched my mother-in-law's progress. The slow *tap . . . . . tap . . . . . tap* drove me up a wall.

"Mildred said she had a free afternoon this week. She can help," I offered.

Tap . . . . tap, tap . . . . tap. Tap, tap. "No problem—working takes my mind off the case."

"Oh yes, the case." I checked the clock. Thirty-six hours was passing quickly. Shouldn't she be sleuthing instead of typing? "Anything yet?"

She shook her head. "Hargus and I have been going over notes all day. Nothing. But we're getting close."

I thought about that. Then shook my head. "Wouldn't it be easier to call in the state police and not have to worry about it? The men are causing a lot of trouble and angst."

"Easier? Yes, but there's something about these cases . . . it's like your writing, Maude." She paused and looked at me. "It'd be easier to clean toilets for a living, but writing's in your blood, just like sleuthing's in my blood. My giving up on the Peeping Toms would be like you sending off a M. K. Diamond mystery without an ending."

Technically, I couldn't do that, but I guess "technically" Stella couldn't give up on a case until it was solved. Way down deep I wanted her to crack this case. She wasn't getting any younger, and who knows—she might never have another case. It would be sad to go out with two very ugly, very crafty Peeping Toms the victors. I glanced at the clock again.

"The answer is right under our noses, Maude. I feel it. It's a matter of timing. Those men are going to make a slip, and when they do, Hargus and I will be there to nab them."

"But thirty-six hours. You're down to what? Sixteen hours?"

"It's worrisome, but Hargus and I can crack this case. Feel it in my bones."

"It's going to take a miracle," I gently reminded. Still, I thought it was nice that Stella was finally thinking of Hargus as a partner instead of a wart on the end of her nose.

"Well, I believe in miracles," she conceded. "But I'll settle for a good old case of colossal luck."

I glanced at the clock a final time. "I'd have thought CeeCee would be home by now."

"Kids," Stella murmured. Her thumb pumped the Backspace key and she erased whatever she'd typed. "When you need them, they're never around."

Resting my head on the back of the chair, I thought about all the times in the past that CeeCee hadn't been around. Then in a purely selfish mode I thought about all the times I'd come to her aid when I really didn't have the time or money to help. Times when I wanted my own life—had my own problems to deal with. But the odd thing was I always *wanted* to help her more than I wanted to do other things. Was that purely a mother's instinct, or was that the way it should be? God first, then family. Period. No exceptions. I knew in my heart of hearts that CeeCee loved me deeply, but she was young and she had yet to learn that friends and men would leave—but a parent stood by to the end.

At least this parent did.

A sigh escaped from a place so deep I couldn't isolate the spot. Maybe we expected too much from our children. We carried them tucked beneath our heart—birthed them, shed tears over them, protected them with every ounce of strength we possessed. And then one day they walked down an aisle—hopefully at the church that had sheltered them since infancy—and they pledged their love and their life to a stranger. If you were lucky they didn't forget you; they came home on holidays and deaths. Mothers of daughters had it better.

The old adage "a son's a son 'til he takes a wife, but a daughter's a daughter the rest of her life" is true. I knew many mothers and daughters who didn't share a close bond, but others enjoyed not only a close bond but a true friendship. I believed CeeCee and I shared a friendship, but right now she was so enthralled with Rick she couldn't see my needs. What I think is that she'll have to be fifty years old before she realizes the gift of close family and responsibilities, and by then I'll be old, and she'll be wiping my mouth at the dinner table.

I studied Stella, diligently typing in changes for me. I thought of how she'd tried to help with my fan mail a few months ago—she tried so hard to be of use. She'd probably shared many of my same disappointments: Herb was a son.

Had I been a caring daughter-in-law? Had I treated Stella with as much respect and honor as I'd treated my mother before she died?

Well, truthfully, I'd see more of Arnold if I could. I wasn't comfortable with the admission, and the words felt foreign to my tongue, but yes, I'd see more of Arnold if I wasn't afraid of offending and causing unnecessary hurt to Stella. So in a sense I was a caring daughter-in-law. Would CeeCee think of making an equal sacrifice for me?

A daughter's a daughter the rest of her life.

"Stella?"

"Yeah?" *Tap. Tap. Tap.*

"Have I mentioned how much I appreciate you?"

Stella chuckled. "Feeling the mother thing, are you?"

"Yeah." I opened my eyes and stared at the ceiling fan. The blades needed dusting—globs of something ugly oozed over the sides. "Why does it take us so long to realize how precious and irreplaceable family ties are—and how long before we realize it's great to have friends and lovers, but family ties are priceless?"

Stella shrugged. "By the time that sinks in we're starting to lose family and loved ones. CeeCee loves you, Maude. She's been a bit irresponsible lately but she'll come around. When she has kids of her own you'll discover a new CeeCee, one that will welcome your wisdom and experience."

"Oh, Stella, I doubt it." Right now the best I could hope for was that one day my daughter would see me as something other than Mom.

Convenient Mom.

Good old, take-it-on-the-chin Mother.

"Say." Stella shoved back from the computer, and I hurriedly looked away for fear she'd see my tears. "I think a hot cup of tea would taste good right about now."

"I don't want tea." I pushed up from the chair, wiping my eyes. I sounded like a petulant four-year-old. "I think I'll take a hot bath."

Stella caught my hand when I hobbled past. Turning me around to face her, she looked deep into my runny eyes. She didn't have to say anything; I knew she knew I was having another one of my self-inflicted, poor-me parties, but her eyes weren't condemning. I'm sure being the mother of a son—and a very good son—she'd had a few pity parties of her own.

A son's a son 'til he takes a wife.

A slow smile spread across my mother-in-law's wizened features, and tonight, at this moment, I realized I wasn't going to have her forever. The thought hurt.

"There's one whom we can depend on, always lean on, Maude. God is here; He'll never leave you or me alone. We can rest in the assurance."

I smiled, taking a swipe at unwarranted tears. When Stella said things like that I didn't think she was being preachy; I thought she was sharing her experience like any mother would with a daughter. "No one could ask for more."

"No. We can't."

Then softly, still holding my hand, Stella began to softly sing the words of a song I'd sung in church camp, "They'll Know We Are Christians by Our Love."

I joined in, hiccupping through the chorus.

"Second verse, Maudie!" Stella gently twirled me around the small office, taking care with my injured ankle.

Our voices lifted in unison, both of us laughing now. Captain sprang to his feet and marched across the file cabinet and out of the room, tail high and twitching.

With each verse I felt my cares lightening and my spirit soar. Words poured out of my mouth in blissful therapy.

"Be there in a sec, honey." Rick pulled on his coat, flashing CeeCee a contagious grin. "I'll lock up and we'll be on our way."

"I need to be home early," she reminded. "Mom's expecting me tonight."

"Hasn't she hired anybody yet?" Rick's voice came from the back of the kennel. CeeCee could hear him switching off lights, talking to pups. "What's she waiting for?"

"She could, but there's no need to spend the money." Guilt assuaged CeeCee. Mom had always been there for her, and she didn't feel good about the past few weeks. She'd had great intentions, but something always seemed to come up every night that prevented her from getting home early enough to type.

But she had a life too, and Mom had to understand. She didn't know Rick; she wouldn't take the time to get to know him. If she did, she'd see that he had his faults—who didn't?—but he was a caring person. He was in constant demand with local charities, and he'd cart puppies and kittens to the children's pediatrics ward in Shiloh every Thursday night, weather permitting. Children took to Rick like ducks to water.

Just like Jake.

CeeCee shook the grating thought away. She picked up a file and moved to the cabinet. Rick was not Jake.

He isn't?

No, she argued. Rick loved football—most men did or were equally engrossed in baseball or golf. That was the only similarity other than his outgoing and friendly nature.

Jake loved women.

Rick *respected* women—and women were drawn to him. Why not? He was good-looking, successful, single, and the only boy in a family of four girls, who had spoiled him shamelessly.

He lies.

He . . . *stretched the truth* occasionally—but only to avoid hurt feelings. She had to admit she didn't like it when she heard Rick telling some cock-and-bull story to a female customer, but she figured business was business, and though she wouldn't lie about a delivery date or a contract term, Rick seemed to think the customer expected it.

"Be right with you, doll baby!"

CeeCee closed the file. "Ready anytime you are!"

Actually, tonight's dinner invitation had caught her by surprise. Rick had a meeting with a rep tonight, but at the last minute the rep had canceled. Rick hadn't seemed concerned, but CeeCee knew the account was important and contributed greatly to the kennel's cash flow.

"I'll meet with him the next time he's through Morning Shade," Rick had said.

CeeCee slipped into her heavy jacket and fished in her pockets for mittens. Rick's voice drifted to the front. He was talking baby talk to the new litter of dachshunds. CeeCee grinned, thinking what a great father he'd make once he settled down and started a family. And he would settle down; just give him time. Rick was made of good stuff; he'd just never been tested.

The phone shrilled. CeeCee glanced at the instrument, wondering if she should answer. Officially the kennel closed half an hour ago. Maybe Rick would pick up in the back room.

On the third ring, she relented, thinking the call might be Mom needing something.

The woman's voice on the other end was looking for something all right. "Is Rick there?"

"Yes—hold on." CeeCee laid the receiver down on the desk and walked through the door leading to the back of the kennel. A cold blast of fresh air met her, and she realized Rick had taken the trash to the outside receptacle.

Returning to the phone, she said, "Sorry, he stepped out for a moment. May I take a message?"

Hesitation. Then, "Tell him Maria called. I'll be through here around eleven. Tell him to meet me at the house."

"Maria?" CeeCee wrote the name on a pad. "I'll give him the message." The business account—but Rick said *he*. He would catch *him* the next time *he* was through Morning Shade, and what was this about a house? As a rule you didn't meet clients at a house.

The woman hung up.

Moments later Rick breezed back in the office. "Did I hear the phone?"

"Yes." CeeCee tore the note off the pad and handed it to him. "Maria called. She said she'd be through around eleven, and for you to meet her at the house."

A shadow briefly crossed Rick's face. "Maria . . . oh. Maria Johnson—the rep who handles the Sportmix account." He shook his head and circled his temple with a forefinger. "Nutty as a peach-orchard borer."

"Eleven o'clock is pretty late for a business meeting." CeeCee wanted to ask about the he/she contradiction but instead found herself being ushered out the front door. Rick switched off the light and locked the door behind them.

"That's Maria. Eccentric as they come."

The offhand way he dismissed Ms. Johnson eased some of CeeCee's suspicions, but the drive to the restaurant was quieter than usual. The place was crowded, but Rick had a reservation so they had only a short wait before being seated. The waitress took their order, and CeeCee started to relax over a diet Coke, chips, and salsa. So maybe the he/she thing was a slip of the tongue. They had a lot of men reps come in the kennel—maybe that's where Rick's mind was—on reps in general.

The Hacienda had opened last week to great fanfare, and tonight the restaurant was hopping. A live mariachi band made it almost impossible to talk, but Rick didn't need conversation to make a woman feel special. He held CeeCee's hand, looked deep into her eyes, leaned close to whisper in her ear.

When CeeCee finally noted the time, she was appalled: past nine o'clock! Mom would think she had forgotten again. Or worse yet, deliberately lied to her. She panicked. "I really have to be going."

Rick seemed in no hurry to leave, though she had noticed he had consulted the time more than once. Undoubtedly he was dreading the eleven-o'clock appointment with the dog-food rep.

She leaned over and gave his hand an affectionate squeeze. "You work too hard; I worry about you."

His eyes softened, and he bent closer. "I work for the future—my future wife and children."

CeeCee's heart hammered. *Too soon,* the inner voice screamed. As much as she thought she was ready for the relationship to take a deeper turn, something inside her coiled and rejected the idea. She smiled, pulling back. "I need to go, Rick."

"Spoilsport." He affected a pout, trying to feed her another chip loaded with salsa.

She gently moved the temptation aside. "I really have to go. I promised Mom I would be home early."

He leaned closer and kissed her, stealing her breath away. The band played on and they lingered, exchanging brief moments of affection. CeeCee knew she was falling for this man—hook, line, and sinker. When Jake died, she'd vowed to never remarry, but then Rick came along and he reminded her so much of her deceased husband. . . . And then a moment ago he'd sounded so . . . positive about the relationship.

This time the niggling thought stuck. Rick *did* remind her of Jake. He didn't have Jake's wandering eye, but he did have many of the same mannerisms. The way he held his fork—how he'd sometimes stop in the middle of a conversation and draw her to him and kiss her. The expression in his eyes when he was telling her that she was his one and only.

She shook her head, trying to clear away the similarities.

Rick bent closer. "Something wrong?"

Stop it! When she was with him, life was perfect. "Nothing, just a little tired. Can we go now?"

He kissed her lightly behind the right ear, his breath warm against her flushed skin. "I don't want you to ever leave. Honest, CeeCee—why don't I hire someone to type for your mom? I need you, sweetheart."

She smiled, leaning into his embrace. "I don't want to go, but . . . Mom."

"It's almost ten o'clock—too late for work." His mouth made little shivery forays up and down her neck.

Oh, he could be so persuasive . . . "Really—I should go. We still have to go by the kennel and get my car."

"All right." He conceded shortly, signaling the waitress for the check. "Be ruthless. Send me off to a lonely bed and a bowl of popcorn." A teasing light danced in his eyes.

"You have a business appointment at eleven," she reminded.

He made a face. "I think I'll call Ms. Johnson and inform her we'll have to make it another time. I'm a little bushed myself."

CeeCee grinned, pressing closer. Why was she so relieved? It was only a business meeting, but she was glad he'd rather go home to a lonely house and a bowl of Orville Redenbacher's than spend time with another woman, albeit it was only business. "This Ms. Johnson. Is she pretty?"

"Pretty? I've never noticed."

She wasn't sure whether to believe him or not. A good-looking woman was hard not to notice, and she'd seen the way he looked at pretty customers. Most men would notice. This smacked of evasion. Well, she supposed any man window-shopped as long as he kept his hands off the merchandise.

During the drive to the kennel, CeeCee snuggled close to Rick's warmth. In some ways it seemed she'd known him a lifetime, yet at other times he felt like a stranger.

The intimacy of the car favored the former; she rested her head on his broad shoulder and listened to Enya drifting softly from the CD player. Everything was so right she couldn't help but wonder if this was the man God had chosen for her all along.

I know I didn't . . . didn't even think about asking the first time, Lord, but I am asking this time. Is Rick the life mate You have chosen for me? If not, dear Lord, please open my eyes because I think I'm head over heels in love with this man.

I had lingered with a long soak in a hot tub until nine-thirty, trying to wash away disappointment. CeeCee still wasn't home. Should I confront her, start an argument, or should I let this incident slip by like I'd let all the others? Where was the fine line between a mother's concern and meddling?

I honestly didn't know.

I'd finally climbed out of the tub and single-handedly lathered almond-cherry-scented lotion all over my body. The small pampering took the edge off my irritation. I suppose I could argue that CeeCee was still in mourning; I had to allow her some space. If the kennel was the only thing occupying her spare time, I wouldn't be so upset, but I knew where the real danger lay: Rick.

I slipped on a fresh gown and a warm robe. Simple pleasures—a long, leisurely bath and scented lotion. Funny how we often overlook the smaller treats, while waiting for that once-in-a-lifetime, super-sized blessing that will knock our socks off. God must get very impatient with our lack of appreciation. I felt restless, not ready to settle down yet.

I knew I shouldn't be bothering Arnold at this time of night, but he'd said once that he was a night owl. Calling at 9:38 wasn't exactly breaking an etiquette rule, and maybe he'd welcome a quick call. I picked up the small notepad I kept beside the bed and searched for his number; it was written across the top: Arnold Biggert: 366-3962.

I punched in the digits before I lost my nerve. When Arnold's voice came on the line I suddenly felt lighter. Why, I couldn't say, other than I had someone to talk to—someone who'd listen like Herb used to after we'd gotten into bed. We'd talk about the day or whatever was on our minds until sleep overtook us . . . another simple pleasure and one I missed desperately.

"Hi, Arnold—it's Maude. I hope you don't mind my calling this late."

"Maude! Good to hear from you. I don't mind at all. I'd just come into the kitchen to get some cheese and crackers."

"Late-night snacking," I teased. "Supposed to be the worst thing you can do. Your body makes cholesterol at night—did you know that?"

"I know it, and I'm the world's worst rule breaker."

My mood sobered. "I . . . know I shouldn't be bothering you with this, but there's something I'd like to ask—and please, be candid."

"You know me. I'm honest as a mirror." I could hear the *clink* of a plate hit the countertop. "What's up?"

"It's Rick."

"Uh-huh. What about him?"

"I guess you've noticed that CeeCee is spending a lot of time with him."

"I have noticed—they have dinner together frequently."

I slipped under the sheets and wiggled my toes. My, that felt heavenly. "She's out with him again tonight."

"You don't say. Well, they're young. They can stand the nightlife."

We both laughed.

"What kind of man is Rick?" I held my breath, hoping I wasn't too transparent. The last thing CeeCee needed was a mother who refused to cut the apron strings.

The long pause on the other end of the line concerned me. *Candid, Arnold. I need for you to level with me.*

"You want my observation?"

"Please." I knew I could depend on him—why I wasn't certain, but I knew.

"I think he's got a heart of gold. I think he's a shrewd businessman, loves kids and animals."

"What about women?" I asked softly. "How much does he love women?"

"Women are his weakness."

I closed my eyes, biting my lip until tears formed in my eyes. Hurting for my daughter, who was so blind at the moment she couldn't see the train wreck about to happen.

"I was afraid of that."

"Many a great man has missed out on the joys of life because of that one weakness. It all started in the Garden of Eden, Maude."

"Why—" I choked back hot tears—"*why* can't CeeCee see the similarities between her late husband and Rick?" Between bouts of tears, I managed to fill Arnold in on CeeCee and Jake and their rocky relationship.

When I finished, Arnold said softly, "When we're in the grip of attraction it's hard for any of us to recognize reality."

"I can't bear to see CeeCee go through another hurtful loss. She's barely survived the first one."

"Has Rick and CeeCee's relationship deepened to that extent?"

I nodded, although I knew he couldn't see me, wiping my nose on a tissue. "I know the signs; my daughter is in love with Rick."

Another long, meaningful pause before Arnold spoke. "CeeCee doesn't notice the various women who come in and out of the kennel? Women who phone Rick regularly during work hours?"

"She thinks the calls are all business related."

I could practically hear Arnold silently shaking his head.

I sighed. "She isn't stupid—she's just sold on this idea of forever love."

"Well, can't fault her for that, although forever love is difficult to find."

"Would—would you talk to her?"

"Me? Why she barely knows me other than through our work at the kennel."

"I know that she respects you, Arnold. She needs a fatherlike figure to talk to right now. I've tried to make her see—well, my words go in one ear and out the other."

"I'm flattered that you'd ask, Maude, but I'm not sure what I can do or say that she'd listen to me any more than she'd listen to you. But if it's important to you, I'll try to broach the subject with her."

"Would you?" Relief escaped me like a leaky valve. "I know it isn't your problem, but I'd be so relieved if you'd speak to her—try and open her eyes."

"I'll do what I can. Now you try to get some rest. Tomorrow CeeCee's future will look brighter to you."

"Thank you. You're . . . very kind."

I hung up and to my surprise I dropped off to sleep like a baby. Every bone in my body released, and involuntarily—moments before I went under—I reached over and touched Herb's pillow.

"Arnold's a good guy, honey. I think you'd like him."

I knew I sure did.

My momma's hands.

Stella sat in the dark staring at her hands. Streetlight illuminated the living room enough for her to make out the prominent blue veins and age spots. She had her momma's hands.

Overhead the floor creaked. Maude was getting ready for bed. Her steps were more certain these days; the injuries were healing. But Stella knew Maude kept her private emotions locked up until they festered and burst. Always fretting about money and writing. Thought the whole world was on her shoulders. She worried about circumstances beyond her control. Stella had tried to tell her, but since Herb's death Maude had taken an even heavier load on her shoulders.

Nobody could control her own life; Maude was old enough to know that. Whether one agreed or not, God had a plan for each life and He kept to it.

Lately Stella had seen a hint of softening—some mute resignation in Maude's eyes that said, "I've tried to carry these problems alone and failed." Ah, if only the sweet woman could keep the thought, maybe she wouldn't be so determined to resist any offers of help. Or be so resentful when she had to accept said help.

When the unexpected royalty check arrived at Christmas, it had seemed like Maude had finally discovered something about herself: she was strong through God's strength. Stella sighed, unfolding her hands. Even God's foolishness is wiser that man's intelligence.

But Arnold was another story. Stella knew that Maude had held a special place in her heart for Sherman Winters for a long time, and oddly enough, Maude's feelings about Sherm didn't bother her.

Sherm was sort of like family—had taken care of the Diamond household for over thirty years. Saw to all the details after Herb's death.

But Arnold Biggert. Now what was Maude thinking? Here she was, running around with a man who couldn't find a decent hairstyle. Stella sniffed. The shame of it; what must the neighbors be thinking? Maude had never been given to flights of fancy other than in her work. And loneliness? Well, Stella could tell her a thing or two about loneliness. When James passed she thought the world had come to an end. Hers had, but she'd pulled herself up by the bootstraps and gone on. Why? Because she wasn't given a choice.

She sat for a moment reliving those dark awful days. She wouldn't wish that sort of grief on her worst enemy. Long nights and even longer days to fill with what? Nominal chores that no longer meant a hill of beans. But she'd decided—or maybe God had reminded her—that her days were not fulfilled. And until the Lord took her home she still had a purpose, though she'd looked for it now some twenty-three years and hadn't found it yet.

It wasn't that Stella didn't want Maude to be happy; she did. She loved that girl as much as she'd loved her own flesh and blood. In time, Maude would start to date and build a new life. But not now. It was too soon.

Leaning back in the recliner, Stella drummed her fingers on her Bible. The house was so quiet tonight. She glanced at the clock and mentally calculated the remaining hours left to solve the mystery.

Twenty-four hours ago the town was about to take a vote. Twenty-four hours had gone, and neither she nor Hargus had produced the Peeping Toms. Stakeouts had failed, the shoe caper at church had been a washout, and the so-called clues they'd discovered—the size-fourteen sneaker and the corset—were dead ends. The only description they had of the Peeping Toms was . . . ugly. Even J. Edgar Hoover couldn't have done much with that. Now they were down to twelve hours. If the Peeping Toms didn't hit tonight, she and Hargus would be off the case.

Sighing, she got up and slipped through the darkened living room to the hall coatrack. She wouldn't be able to sleep a wink thinking about the state police doing her job. Maybe a quick hop around the block would clear her head. Instinct said she and Hargus had missed something. Some infinitesimal clue that held the key to the mystery, but how did she unearth it?

Slipping on her heavy coat, she was reaching for a warm scarf when she heard CeeCee's key turn the lock. Her granddaughter came in, rosy cheeked, nose stung bright red from the wind.

Stella barely glanced her way. "You just get home?" Her tone effectively registered censure. CeeCee had promised to help Maude tonight and she was just now getting here?

"Hi, Grandma . . ." CeeCee's smile faded.

Stella brushed past her coolly. "Your mother needed your help tonight, child."

"I know—Rick and I got to talking." CeeCee glanced up the stairway. "Mom still up?"

"No, she was tired. She turned in early."

CeeCee's eyes skimmed Stella's attire. "Are you going out this late? It's after ten o'clock."

"Need a breath of fresh air; I'll be back shortly." Stella grabbed a flashlight, stepped onto the porch, and listened for the lock to catch. She was in no mood for CeeCee's rambling excuses. Maude needed her, and CeeCee had let her down.

Winding the scarf around her head, she started off at a brisk stride. Overhead a crescent moon mirrored weakly off deep snow. Stars twinkled like cut diamonds against a backdrop of black velvet. Woodsmoke lazily curled from chimney tops and the smell hung in the air. Nothing like a cheery fire on a cold winter night.

She turned the corner on Main, and suddenly a new scent dominated the crisp clean air. Lifting her nose, she sniffed.

And sniffed again.

Cigar smoke.

Thurvis Throckmorton.

Or was it Victor Johnson breaking the no-smoking ordinance? Stella fumed. Of all the *nerve*—after she'd leant him the money for the first fine, here he was doing it again!

Straight ahead she could make out the wooden park bench. The streetlight was still out—odd since city maintenance rarely let a bulb go unattended.

Pausing, Stella whipped off her glasses and cleaned them on the hem of her coat. She hooked the rims back over her ears and peered intently.

Nada. She couldn't see a blame thing.

"Turn around and walk the other way," she told herself. "You can't afford another two-hundred-and-fifty-dollar hit."

* * *

CeeCee showered and donned pajamas, her mind on the previous hours. Basically Rick was nowhere near Jake in the ways that counted. When he called her his one and only, he meant it.

She switched off the lamp and sat down near the window. Grandma hadn't come back in yet, unless she had slipped upstairs while the shower was running. She was too old to be wandering around by herself at night. Not that she'd listen to anyone who tried to tell her that.

CeeCee had voted to go with Grandma and Hargus at the town meeting last night, but she really didn't have any faith in their sleuthing. If something didn't break soon, they'd have no choice except to call in the police. After all, Thurvis had thrown down the gauntlet and Grandma had picked it up. Trust her not to run from a challenge.

She shivered, feeling the cold through her thin pajamas. Why hadn't she insisted on going out with Grandma? She wasn't very high on Grandma's and Mom's helpful list these days.

She left her post by the window and crawled into bed, feeling like a harried mother waiting for the last teenager to check in for the night.

Rick Materi. She blinked, rubbing her eyes. She didn't want to go through another bad marriage.

Been there, done that, didn't plan on being suckered again.

* * *

Stella hadn't walked very far before her conscience smote her. She was an upstanding citizen of Morning Shade. How could she walk away when someone was breaking the law? If Victor was deliberately smoking inside the city limits again, he could pay his own fine or go to jail. After all, he was a grown man and in full possession of his mental powers, not like poor Maury Peacock, who didn't know his behind from wild-apple honey.

She marched toward the park bench, which was empty now. But she still smelled cigar smoke. So all right, the culprit had flown the coop. She'd scour this town, up one street and down the other, until she found him. No one was going to break the law under Stella Diamond's nose and laugh about it.

Twenty minutes later she caught the sweet aroma of a good Cuban cigar. Ah-hah! Thurvis Throckmorton. Surely not. She'd thoroughly humiliated the mayor, and he wouldn't be silly enough to pull another foolish smoking stunt. Victor Johnson? Thought he could outsmart her, did he? She'd show him.

Stella cautiously moved from shrub to shrub, house to house, pausing to sniff the air. She tailed the culprit along a circuitous route, which brought her back to the park bench, the bench under the streetlight with the conveniently burned-out bulb. Maybe there was a reason no illuminating rays shone on that bench.

When her eyes adjusted to the lack of light, she could make out a black shape and the round, red glow of the end of a cigar. The smell of smoke was so strong on the winter air she felt almost heady with the rich scent. James used to smoke cigars. The memory made her feel very much alone. Her husband wouldn't have wanted her to be alone out here at night, tracking a criminal. The thought came and went—as many tended to do these days. James was gone and life had gone on without him. She wasn't a wife any longer. Solving crimes substituted for a lot of things she'd had to give up.

She crept along the edge of the grass until she reached the back of the bench. The man sitting there lifted his cigar and took a leisurely puff. As far as he knew there wasn't a soul around to catch him. Little did he know; he was about to learn that crime didn't pay in Morning Shade. His sins had just found him out.

She tapped the man on the shoulder. "Hey, bub. What do you think you're doing?"

The reaction was like a minor explosion. He jumped as if he had been shot. One arm flew up straight over his head, and the cigar took wing, flying into the bushes where it continued to glow. "Uh . . . uh . . . uh . . ."

Stella slapped him on the back. "You all right?" She shone her flashlight on the bent figure, figuring she had scared him into a heart attack. Maybe she should have been a trifle less covert—kind of advertised her presence, so to speak. She wouldn't want a near death on her conscience.

The light illuminated the startled features of Thurvis Throckmorton, his eyes bulging out like a pair of headlamps. He blinked in the sudden glare. "Turn that thing somewhere else!"

The beam went out. "Just making sure you weren't having a fit."

"I nearly had a stroke! What do you mean sneaking up on a body like that?" His voice trembled and he slumped back against the bench. "I thought you were Hilda."

"Oh?" Well, Hilda was a terror all right, but surely she didn't inspire that kind of fear in her husband. But then you never knew what went on behind closed doors. Some of the most prominent community leaders had the best-kept secrets.

"It's not that I'm afraid of her, you know," Thurvis began.

"Oh, certainly not." Stella sat down on the bench beside him. "I caught you smoking again."

Thurvis brushed the obvious aside. "So you did. That's a minor problem."

Stella stiffened. Minor? Was that the way the mayor of Morning Shade felt about breaking the law? Seemed to her they needed a recall election and soon. "I wouldn't exactly look at it that way. The law is the law."

"Well, yes, but you don't understand. I wasn't smoking for fun."

"You weren't?" Stella pushed out her lower lip. Here it came. An excuse meant to confuse an idiot. What sort of lamebrain did he take her for? "I suppose it was punishment for something."

"Not exactly." Thurvis's tone turned more serious than she'd expected. "Smoking helps me think, and I got some serious thinking to do."

She nodded. "The weight of the office and all that bunk."

"No, it's not that," Thurvis protested. "There's no need to take that tone of voice. I got me a real problem, and I needed to think it through. I was just sitting here thinking when you came along and almost scared me into a fast freight to glory."

"You were smoking too," she reminded him. "A clear violation of the no-smoking ordinance."

"I wish I'd never heard of that contrary ordinance. It's got me into more trouble than I know how to deal with. Just one thing after another."

The man sounded troubled. "What kind of problems?" She guessed she owed him a chance to talk after the way she'd scared him into the middle of next week. He might need time to recover from that nasty shock. She'd never heard of Thurvis having heart trouble, but she didn't want to discover his health problem the hard way. If it helped him to sit and talk, then they'd sit and talk. Then she'd arrest him.

"It's those dogs of Hilda's. Her 'babies,' she calls them." His tone dripped sarcasm.

Stella figured he didn't share the same parental feelings. "What do Mortimer and Snerd have to do with you smoking?"

"They're the reason I'm thinking! I come out here every night to walk those mutts because Hilda thinks they need exercise. Well, I'm not about to stumble all over town being drug by those refugees from Hades, so I turn them loose and let them run; then when they come back I take them home."

"You mean you lied to Hilda?" Talk about living on the edge. The man had nerves of steel.

"I guess you could say that—but my sinful ways have caught up with me."

"How so?"

"Tonight they didn't come back, and I can't go home without them. How do you think Hilda's going to take it if I come home without the dogs?"

"Not too well." Now the truth was out. Hadn't Stella caught him smoking once before on this very same bench? The man had been breaking his own ordinance every night. He was lower than a polecat.

"Not too well? That's an understatement." Thurvis slumped lower on the bench. "I'm between a rock and a hard place. Don't know whether to leave the bench and go looking for them, or sit here waiting for the dogs to return or for the light of a new day, whichever comes first." He leaned forward, propping his elbows on his knees, the picture of desolation.

Stella's heart stirred with compassion. Poor mayor—he did have his foot caught in a crack; however, the law was the law, and he'd broken this law all to pieces. She slapped a hand on his shoulder. "Thurvis, my friend . . ."

He turned to look at her—least that's what it seemed like. It was so dark you couldn't see your hand in front of your face.

She took a deep breath. "I'm making a citizen's arrest."

He flapped a hand in her direction. "Don't bother me right now."

"Say what? You're resisting arrest?"

"No, I'll pay the fine. Can you help me look for those dogs?"

"Me?" She'd seen the way they jerked him around. She was eighty-seven years old and in deep trouble if Maude discovered she'd been out this late at night.

"Yes, you. I've got to find those dogs, Stella. My life won't be worth living if something happens to Mortimer and Snerd. Please," he added when she hesitated, "I really need your help."

Oh, for goodness' sake. The man was a quivering bowl of jelly. Well, she'd ride to the rescue again. "Okay. I'll help." She got to her feet, peering into the darkness. "Which direction did they go?"

Thurvis stood up and pointed to the right. "You go that way; I'll go left and we'll meet back here in thirty minutes. Okay?"

"Ten-four." Stella took off down the street, thinking maybe she was too old for this sort of crime busting.

It was a sure shot Hargus was sitting at home warm and comfortable, munching on popcorn and drinking Chocolate Cow while she scoured the wintry streets of Morning Shade looking for two wandering dogs. She glanced up at the cold light of the crescent moon. Miniature clouds in frosty drifts now laced the sky.

Lord, You listening? I could use some help here. I'm cold and I haven't felt my feet in fifteen minutes.

I opened my eyes and looked around the dark room. Something had jerked me out of a sound sleep. What? Not the Peeping Toms, not on the second floor. Unless the two men now carried a ladder. Captain's eyes glowed from the folds of the quilt on my bed. I spoke in a half tone, not wanting to rouse Stella and CeeCee. "What's going on, cat? You hear anything?"

He watched me for a moment before jumping off the bed and stalking toward the door. I stared after him, wondering what he was doing. He never left my bedroom at night. Now he waited patiently for me to follow. I got up, pulled a robe around my shoulders, and stumped across the floor, wondering what I would find outside that door?

Captain marched down the hall, pausing at Stella's room. I followed, a prickle of apprehension stinging my spine. Captain never went to Stella's room. He would have been facing mortal peril if he had entered that hallowed space. Now he sat in front of the closed door, as though demanding entrance.

I reached out and took hold of the doorknob, turning it slowly so I wouldn't wake Stella if she happened to be asleep. Light from the streetlamp in front of the house washed over the bed—the bed that had not been slept in tonight. The bedspread was still pulled tight, the pillows undisturbed. Stella was AWOL.

I whirled and hobbled as fast as I could down the hall to CeeCee's room. I rapped on the door to alert her before entering. I hit the light switch.

My daughter sat up in bed, her hair strongly suggesting that she'd been in a recent windstorm. "Wha—"

"Wake up! Stella's gone."

"Gone? Gone where?" CeeCee asked in a sleepy stupor.

"I don't know. Her bed hasn't been slept in tonight."

CeeCee threw back the covers and swung her feet over to hit the floor. "This is my fault. She was going out when I came in, but I didn't try to stop her. I should have."

"What time was that?"

"A little after ten."

Fear stopped me in my tracks. "That late?"

"I'm sorry, Mom. Rick and I got to talking, and time slipped away."

I pulled my thoughts back to the problem at hand. "Well, something else has slipped away—your grandmother. I hope she's all right." I knew her absence had something to do with the Peeping Toms. Tomorrow morning the state police would be summoned. Was she making one last desperate attempt to apprehend the culprits?

CeeCee reached for her discarded jeans, all business now. "I'll go look for her."

"I'm going with you. Should we call Hargus?"

"I'll bet he's with her somewhere, doing some harebrained stakeout or something like that."

I stopped, one hand on the door frame. "You may be right, but I think I'll call just to be sure. Wait for me, okay?"

"Sure. I'll warm the car."

I hurried to my room and threw on sweatpants and an oversized sweatshirt. A glance in the mirror made me grab a sock cap and tug it down over my hair. I didn't have time to fuss with my appearance, and I probably wouldn't see anyone I knew anyway. I reached for my cell phone and dialed Hargus's number, letting it ring eight times with no answer. CeeCee was probably right, but just in case, I called Pansy, who answered almost immediately.

"Hargus? No, I haven't talked to him tonight. Why, is something wrong?"

"No—just wondered if he'd had any luck solving this Peeping Tom thing." No need to get Pansy worked up. There was nothing she could do.

"I don't think so. I'm downright upset with Thurvis, setting that time limit. He didn't give Hargie and Stella a chance to solve the case—not a proper one."

"Look, Pansy, I have to go. If you do hear from Hargus, tell him to call me." I hung up the phone before she could ask why.

CeeCee was waiting in the car when I came out of the house. I climbed into the front seat, about as graceful as an elephant on roller skates. If I ever got this cast off my foot, I'd make sure I never did anything as foolish as falling on ice again.

I buckled my seat belt. "Where do we look first?"

"I don't know. Morning Shade isn't all that big, but it does sprawl out a bit. Maybe down by the railroad tracks?"

"It's as good a place as any to start. Stella keeps saying she thinks the Peeping Toms are vagrants. If she's doing a stakeout, it's probably in that vicinity."

CeeCee shifted into reverse and backed the car out of the drive, then wheeled and drove over the curb and headed for the railroad tracks. If Maury Peacock was watching, he'd think we were both drunk. I felt so helpless; I had to find Stella. Herb would expect me to take care of her, and here she was out somewhere, alone at . . . I checked the time: 12:30! My stars, was it that late? Pansy must think I've lost my mind calling her at this hour.

I watched through the windshield, willing myself to see her. "I'm afraid she's fallen somewhere and can't get up." She'd freeze to death tonight. I couldn't bear the thought.

"Don't borrow trouble," CeeCee said. "You know Grandma. She's as feisty as all get out. No telling what she's up to."

"If she's all right, I'm going to hang her."

CeeCee stifled a snort of laughter. "Well, that should take care of the problem, permanently."

"I didn't mean literally," I protested. "How could she do this to us? She should have known we would be worried. She could have told us she planned to be out."

"In which case, you'd have moved heaven and earth to stop her."

I thought about that, knowing she was right. That still didn't excuse Stella, but I had known she wouldn't let the deadline go past without making one more stab at solving the case. This was my fault. I should have been more vigilant.

"Don't blame yourself," CeeCee said. "With that deadline looming, Grandma would have found a way to get out of the house. I bumped into her coming in, and I wasn't quick enough to catch on. She's up to something; we can only hope it's something simple. Maybe she's given up on the case and she's playing dominoes with Renee Stanton. They play late sometimes, you know."

Well, the truth is, we were both remiss. But Stella was a tough cat to corner. Like CeeCee said, she would have found a way to outfox us. This apparently wasn't all that difficult.

Stella walked the street for nearly half an hour. She was about worn-out, and not one sign of those dogs. Once more around the block and it would be time to meet up with Thurvis.

She rounded the corner of the street where Helen lived. If she didn't find anything soon, she was going to go home and let Thurvis Throckmorton get himself out of his hole.

Something moved at the side of Helen's house. Stella stopped, her heart thumping like a bass drum.

There. Right there, on Helen's front porch was Hilda's poodle. The mastiff bounded from around the side of the house and lumbered up the steps to join his buddy. Both of those blamed dogs—and they had to be on Helen's porch, the most edgy woman in Morning Shade.

Now if only Stella could catch them and get away without waking Helen. She crept up the porch steps, whispering, "Here, boy, come here."

The dogs ignored her. They pressed their noses against the pane of the front picture window, although the interior of the house was as black as soot. Helen had the shades drawn, of course. The rest of the house was probably locked up tighter than a fortress too.

Stella made her way across the porch, moving lightly. She reached out, grabbing hold of the collar on each dog. Now that she had the animals, what did she plan to do? The mastiff was as big as a freight train.

She tugged, trying to pull them down the concrete steps when a sound like a steam whistle split the air.

Helen. Screaming. Oh, boy, was she screaming.

Lights flicked on up and down the block.

Stella tried to yell above the din. "Helen! It's me, Stella. Shut up!"

Silence.

Stella tried again. "Helen? Stella here. Open the door."

She waited for a full minute before the door slowly edged open a crack and one eye peered out. "Stella?"

"Right. You okay?"

"The Peeping Toms are out there, both of them," Helen whispered. "They just looked in my window—you were standing right behind them. Are you in cahoots with those criminals?"

Stella whirled to check her back. Her eyes skimmed the deserted front lawn. She turned back to Helen. "There's no one out here except me and Hilda Throckmorton's dogs."

The door opened wider. "What are you doing with Hilda's dogs? She's going to be real upset."

"You don't know the half of it, Helen." Hilda was going to pitch a hissy fit that would make an Arkansas tornado look like a spring zephyr. Poor Thurvis. He'd never hear the last of this, and thanks to Helen's imitation of an air-raid siren, there was no way they could hide the fact that Thurvis had let the dogs run loose.

The mayor puffed up the porch steps. "You found them. Good. I'll take them home before Hilda comes looking for me."

"Not so fast." Stella pursed her lips, staring thoughtfully at the window. "I can't believe I've been so stupid."

"What? What?" Thurvis sputtered. "You know I have to get those dogs home before Hilda discovers what I've done."

"Now, Hargus—I can believe he'd be that stupid, but where was my common sense?" Stella shook her head, feeling like a complete idiot. She'd been bested by a couple of *canines*.

"Come on, Stella—"

"Hush up, and let me think." Stella continued to size up the situation. She stared at the windows, then back at the dogs. "I may find a way to get you out of this mess after all."

She handed the dogs off to him. "Let's do a little experimenting. You lead the dogs up close to the window, like so. Now, Helen, let's you and me go inside and see what we can see."

As soon as they hit the living room, Helen started screaming. "That's them! The Peeping Toms. See how ugly they are? Real mean-looking."

"Oh, hush up, Helen," Stella admonished. "Can't you see? That's Hilda's *dogs*. There never were any Peeping Toms. Just two curious hounds, and they've been terrorizing this town long enough." She marched back to the open front door. "You hear that, Thurvis?"

"I heard, Stella." He sighed. "I'm a walking dead man. Wait until Hilda hears that her dogs are the Peeping Toms. This is the last time I'll ever get out of the house at night . . . alone."

"And there go your Cuban cigars."

He sighed heavily.

"About time the mayor of Morning Shade started obeying the law, don't you think?" Stella demanded.

"Don't rub it in, Stella."

She cackled. She'd never seen a man so crestfallen. Maybe she could think of something to buck him up. "I'll tell Hilda we were conducting an experiment tonight. Saved my best for the last hour. You turned the dogs loose so we could check out my theory. This was police work."

The look in the mayor's face was a little less suicidal. "You think she'll buy that?"

Stella shrugged. "I don't know; it's worth a shot. I'll back you up. After all, we *did* solve the case."

"That's right, we did." Thurvis straightened. "Police work. She'll buy that."

Stella decided not to point out that while this might let him off the hook tonight, it wasn't going to hold water for all the other nights he'd turned the dogs loose to roam. She cackled with delight. Mortimer and Snerd. Well, they *were* ugly; the victims had that right. Hilda was going to pin the mayor's ears back big time, but that was Thurvis's problem. She was glad the case had been solved and they still had ten hours left! Hot dog—she still had it!

Thank You, God. I knew You'd come through for me.

Suddenly Maude's car careened around the corner and jerked to a stop. CeeCee bounded out, and Maude followed a little more slowly, but moving fast for a woman wearing a cast.

The crowd of neighbors who had gathered parted to let the women through. CeeCee threw her arms around Stella's neck. "Grandma! We've been so worried about you!"

Maude thumped up the steps. "Stella Diamond! Where on earth have you been?"

"Working," Stella said with as much dignity as she could muster with CeeCee hanging on to her, and Mortimer and Snerd sniffing her at her feet. "For your information, ladies, I've just solved the Peeping Tom case."

"You have?" CeeCee released her, mouth agape. "By yourself?"

"Well—" Stella paused for emphasis—"I had a bit of help. The mayor graciously allowed me to use his dogs tonight." She should have known when they found that shoe and the corset. Just the thing a dog would do, drag stuff all over town. She couldn't wait to tell Hargus.

"Mortimer and Snerd tracked down the culprits?" Maude turned to gawk at the dogs.

"Well, no, they *are* the culprits. We've all been scared to death of Hilda's mutts!"

Hargus's truck careened around the corner, lights flashing and siren squealing. He leaped from the vehicle as soon as it stopped, sprinting toward the front porch. "Okay, ladies—I'm here. What's going on? Got a call there was a lot of commotion going on—" He stopped midsentence and stared at the mayor. "Hilda's been looking everywhere for you."

Throckmorton nodded. "Figures."

Stella eyed Hargus over her glasses. "About time you showed up. I've just solved the Peeping Tom case."

Hargus stared at her, eyes flashing. "Without me? How could you do such a thing?"

Stella bristled. "Easy. Where have you been?"

Hargus shifted awkwardly. "Well . . ."

"Out with it."

"I was on a stakeout over by the railroad tracks. I saw Maude and CeeCee coming through, and when I stopped and asked what's going on they said you had disappeared. About that time I got the call there was a ruckus going on at Helen's place. And here you've done gone and solved the case. If that doesn't beat all."

Stella preened. "Well, some of us have got it, and—"

"Stella!" Maude admonished.

The sleuth's lower lip quivered. "Oh, all right. Hargus, allow me to introduce you to the town perverts: Mortimer and Snerd."

"Get outta here," Hargus scoffed.

"Tell him, Helen."

"I'd never have believed it, but Stella saw it right away. Those two dogs—through the closed window shade—look exactly like two men silhouetted there. Scared the dickens out of me, I'll tell you. I think I'm going to move. Crocodiles crawling around in my backyard, dogs staring at me through the windows. It's enough to give anyone the willies."

Hargus took a hitch in his pants. "Does Hilda know that her dogs have been causing the stink?"

Thurvis came to life in a hurry. "No, and I've got to get home and break the news. She'll be fit to be tied." He snapped the leashes on the dogs' collars. "We can hash this out in the morning."

"Now hold on . . . ," Hargus began.

But Stella stopped him. "Wait, Mayor—maybe Hargus wants to tell Hilda."

Hargus gave her a look guaranteed to blister paint, but he visibly calmed down. "No, Thurvis, you go right ahead. I'll see you in the morning."

Mayor Throckmorton led the dogs away, and Hargus broke up the crowd. Stella turned to Maude and CeeCee. "I'm ready to go home. It's a little past my bedtime."

"Oh, Stella." Maude bit her lip, tears glistening in her eyes. "I'm so glad you're all right."

"Fine as frog hair," Stella said. "Just another night in the life of a professional crime buster."

She walked tall on her way to the car. Maybe she could get some business cards printed.

Stella A. Diamond, Private Investigator
No crime too big or too small

Had a nice ring to it—but a waste of money. After all, she was eighty-seven years old.

38

Life in the Diamond household had a holiday air the next morning. CeeCee treated us to homemade Dutch babies—puffy rounds of baked batter slathered with strawberry jam and frosted with powdered sugar. I ate my slice, eyeing the three left on the plate. Life was looking up. If I could get the Hamel manuscript finished on time, by some miracle, I could relax.

Stella was apologetic, which was a good sign too. "I'm sorry I worried you last night. I wasn't thinking of anything except that deadline. It was looming over me like a dark cloud. I knew time was running out and I had to solve the case."

"That's the way with deadlines," I agreed, thinking about mine. March 1 was next Monday.

CeeCee poured more coffee. "I'll finish the manuscripts tonight."

"That's all right—," I began, but she interrupted me.

"I know I've not followed through on my promise, Mom. Last night, searching for Grandma, made me realize how important family is to me. The two of you have been there for me every time I needed help. But helping family should be a two-way street. I have to do my share too. I mean it. I'll finish the revisions tonight."

Would wonders never cease? Apologies from *both* CeeCee and Stella—and on the same morning. I drank my coffee, feeling guilty.

"Well, if we're into confessions, I guess I have one too. I've been so proud of carrying my own load, it's been difficult for me to accept help. I guess I've been a thorough pain in the neck since the accident, but I do believe God has been teaching me that no one can stand alone. I need His help first and foremost, but I also need family and friends." I crossed my heart. "Maude Diamond will never try to do it all by herself again."

Stella sighed. "God is good."

"He surely is." I agreed. "How do folks get through life without Him?"

CeeCee got up and stacked the dishes in the sink. "I've got to run. I'm due at the post office in ten minutes. Mom, I'm going to stop by the kennel for about half an hour, and then I'll be straight home."

I could feel my expression sour, my bubble burst. My cork pop. My daughter held up a hand. "Scout's honor."

I relaxed. "All right, honey. I'll be waiting."

She left and Stella winked at me. "She'll be here. The girl's made of good stuff. Don't worry."

I smiled. "You know, I think you're right. I believe we're going to make it after all."

* * *

I was running the vacuum—my first sortie into the real world since my surgery, when I thought I heard something. Switching the machine off, I discovered the phone was ringing.

Rummaging through the sofa pillows, I found the receiver.

Jean Sterling, my agent, was calling from New York. "How's the healing process?"

"Very well, thank you. Sherm says the cast can come off in another couple of weeks."

"That's wonderful. Maude, I've had another call from Birkhead."

The publisher who'd last month expressed interest in speaking with me. I hadn't forgotten the offer, had even given it considerable thought the past few weeks.

"And the call was about . . . ?"

"Setting up a meeting with you. They're willing to fly you to the publishing house, take you to dinner, and let you meet the staff." When I didn't immediately answer Jean continued. "They're openly courting you—you realize that."

"I know publishers aren't in the habit of flying writers halfway across the United States just to say hello."

Jean laughed. "Well? They're talking big, Maude. If you'll go with them exclusively, they're willing to pay. And the proposed marketing is exactly what you want; they'll position your books storewide, and you're sure to make the best-seller list—at least for a week or two."

The tantalizing dangling carrot was like offering fudge to a chocoholic. "Choices," I said. "I hate them."

"Change is often good—then other times loyalty, in the long run, is rewarded."

I had remained loyal to my publisher, Bethlehem, for over ten years, and so far I was still struggling to get the support Birkhead was offering. I let the idea of the best-seller list and larger presences in bookstores settle over me like warm milk chocolate. Here Birkhead—through Jean—was offering me my dream. . . .

"Well? I know they earlier indicated that they wanted to wait until the convention to talk, but it's still six months away. They want the meeting as soon as your health permits. Sounds to me like you're in the driver's seat. What say ye?"

What say I? The deal would afford Jean a tidy 15 percent of the royalties. It would afford me the self-validation that I'd searched for years to achieve. Did I leave the publishing house that had become like family to me and begin anew with Birkhead?

Or was this a clear case of better the devil you know than the devil you don't?

39

CeeCee parked in the back of the kennel, relieved to see Arnold's car gone. He must have left early today.

How was Rick going to take her departure? He'd gotten so used to her being there every night; he expected it. Well, he'd have to be patient. For once she was putting Mom's needs first.

He was coming out of the back room when she entered through the back door. "Hi, babe. About time you were getting here."

She stepped into his waiting arms and gave him a brief hug. "I can only stay a few minutes. I didn't get anything done on Mom's manuscript last night, so I promised I'd finish the whole manuscript tonight. I'll be up until the wee hours."

She felt his terse withdrawal even though he smiled. "We have a couple of sick pups, and there's a pile of invoices you need to file." His tone was agreeable enough, but she sensed underlying resentment.

"Sorry—I'll stay late tomorrow night." She tensed when she saw a frown shadow his handsome features. "It's just until we meet the March 1 deadline. I promise." She waited for understanding to dawn. It didn't.

He absently dropped a benign kiss on her forehead. "I hope you're not like this once that book goes into the mail."

The remark struck her wrong. Mom was Mom, and if she needed help CeeCee planned to be there. She stepped back and reached for the pile of invoices.

"After all," Rick added, "you're my one and only, and I can't get by without you." He brushed past her and walked to the charred coffeepot. "If you're cutting out early, I'd better get the back-room work done while you're here to answer the phone. And would you mind cleaning this pot—it hasn't been washed in days."

"Your hands broken?"

He turned to stare at her.

She shut the file drawer.

When he walked away she knew he wasn't happy with her, but then she wasn't exactly ecstatic about his attitude.

A brown delivery truck pulled up in front of the kennel, and a young man bounded out of the cab, carrying a large package. He opened the door and came into the office. "CeeCee Tamaris?"

"That's me." CeeCee eyed the box, wondering who'd be sending something to her at the kennel. The young man radically scribbled on his clipboard, then handed her the box. Seconds later he was back out the door. She watched as the truck turned around and sped off.

Turning the box, she slit the tape and took out a beautifully wrapped package. After tearing into the Victorian-patterned paper, she pawed through cotton-candy-colored tissue and grasped the filmy underwear, holding the minuscule scraps of iris blue material up to the light. She suddenly crammed the lingerie back into the box, flushing a bright crimson. Why . . . who'd send her such a thing?

Her eyes fell on the enclosed card. Lifting the note, she read:

When I saw this I thought of you and KC. What a night!
You're my one and only. Rick

Kansas City? CeeCee tried to recall the last time she'd been in Kansas City. It had been years. She reached for the card and reread it. This time she saw the name. *Jill.*

Before she could reconstruct her thoughts, the front door opened, and a sheepish-looking delivery boy, toting a smaller box, walked in. Clearing his throat, his eyes focused on the mangled package lying on the desk. "Sorry . . . I delivered the wrong package. The package in your hand belongs to Jill Baxter—a couple blocks down. This one is yours."

Speechless, CeeCee took the second box. "But I opened—"

"Don't worry. I'll take it back to the office; they'll figure out what to do." He thrust the clipboard at her. "Sign here."

CeeCee signed. The moment the door closed she tore into the small box. In it she found a tin of assorted barbeque sauces from Kansas City, shipped from the Westin Crown Center—where Rick had stayed two weeks ago during a breeder's conference. The card read: "CeeCee—my one and only. Rick."

A slow burn started at the base of CeeCee's neck and spread to her cheeks.

Rick sauntered in a moment later, his eyes going to the box. "Was that a delivery truck?"

CeeCee struggled to remain coherent. Lifting the tin of sauces, she said. "It's from you."

He grinned. "I knew you'd like it—it's great sauce, and I know how you like to eat."

CeeCee stared at him. *Eat!*

She snatched her purse off the file cabinet. "I'll be taking Frenchie and Claire and my birds home with me tonight. I quit."

"Quit!" He glanced at the tin, then at her. "What? You don't like the sauces?"

"I like it better than the underwear!" She stalked out the room and collected Frenchie and Claire, leading the excited poodles to the car. Securing the animals in the backseat, she went back for the birds.

Rick stood in the doorway, wearing a baffled look. "Have you lost your mind? Can't we discuss this like two adults?"

"Sorry, I don't feel very adult at the moment." He didn't know about the first package yet. She'd been fool enough. Thank God for confused delivery boys.

"Come on—if you don't like the sauces we'll send them back, babe." He lifted both arms. "You're my one and only—"

"Don't waste your breath, Rick."

"I can't believe you're being so hard-nosed about a few bottles of barbeque sauce. Come on; have a heart. It's a gift."

He still didn't get it.

"Does the name Jill Baxter ring a bell?"

"Jill . . . ?" His features turned hard and impassive. "What about her?"

"I got her gift earlier—by mistake."

Color drained from his face.

CeeCee lugged the birdcage to the car, stowed the squawking birds in the backseat, and then slid behind the wheel. Seconds later she gunned out of the kennel parking lot trailing a blue stream of smoke.

Well, great, CeeCee. Another relationship down the tubes. It looked as if the Diamond women were right back where they'd started. No, that wasn't fair. Her fury started to ebb. God had brought them through the last few weeks, and He'd be with them in the future. She'd learned a lot since Jake's death, and it wasn't God's fault if learning hurt sometimes.

She turned the corner, swiping at tears swimming in her eyes. Mom and Grandma would be glad to know that her eyes were fully open now, and they weren't the type to gloat. They'd do their best to help her heal. Thank God for family.

Frenchie and Claire reared up on the headrest, swiping wet tongues across her cheek. She reached back and scratched Frenchie's ears. "Thanks, guys. I can always count on you."

She was learning that's what families were for. And right now she was doing just what she wanted to do: taking her dogs and birds and going home.

I have good news and bad news: CeeCee came home earlier, dropped off the birds and poodles, and left, saying she had to buy a crate of tissues. She'd be home shortly. I took that to mean bad news. And I have those worrisome birds and dogs again.

But the good news (good for Stella) is that Morning Shade had a new mystery, immediately on the heels of the Peeping Toms. What did Hilda Throckmorton threaten the mayor with to make him swear off his Cuban cigars? Whatever she'd said—or done—Thurvis had publicly declared he'd never touch another cigar as long as he lived.

Some speculated that was the reason for his drastic declaration: He wanted to live. Under Hilda's roof. What was the old adage? There's no fool like an old fool?

Anyway, the no-smoking ordinance wouldn't go away. Ironically, a new study had been published vis-à-vis the link between heart attacks and smoking. There were all kinds of studies concerning cigarettes and secondhand smoke, and admittedly a dedicated smoker could challenge about every finding with some credibility, but then most everybody agreed that smoking is a bad habit. I hate the smell of smoke in my hair and clothing after I've spent an hour in a blue haze, but then that's me, and if the whole world was vanilla it'd be a pretty dull place to live.

All in all, I'd take dog poopie and bird droppings any day in exchange for CeeCee's future happiness, which wasn't going to be found in Rick. And I hoped by the sudden reappearance of her menagerie, she'd come to her senses.

Stella was on cloud nine tonight. She'd gone out to celebrate solving the crime—if you could call the recent escapade *crime.* Peeping Toms.

Dogs.

I shook my head, thinking how Morning Shade's so-called mysteries would never make *The Police Gazette.* Sherlock Holmes would be downright appalled at our crime sprees.

I scribbled in the last of the Hamel revisions and relaxed, resting my back against my chair. Jack Hamel's book was complete, and I had to say it had great ministerial value—as I'd prayed it would. Oh, I know, I'd sure done a lot of whining in the process: about money, writer's block, no help, stress.

Guilty as charged. The Lord and I had been having a few private consultations since my accident and surgery. I'd come to accept that because I'm human I want things, such as being on the best-seller list, that sometimes God doesn't want for me. But my *desires* have nothing to do with serving.

I took a moment to explore my rationale.

I would argue that God couldn't have chosen a more imperfect soul to serve Him: I'm stubborn, emotional, and much too self-centered. I often think if only I could smother—strangle—this need for visual proof of success (high sales, better marketing enthusiasm, etc.), I'd be a whole lot happier.

Well, listen up, Maude. Having a servant's heart (for which I pray unceasingly) ain't easy. It isn't—truly. I was slowly coming to realize that I was here, doing what I do, because it's what I'm supposed to do. If God used only perfect people, nothing would ever get done.

I've traveled a long and rocky road the last couple of years, and if God so wills, I still have a few good books in me. And my stories—my contributions to the writing world—will reach the ones God intends, and maybe not be so meager in His eyes.

One soul at a time.

I'm finally okay with that.

I opened my eyes when I heard the front door shut. I knew it was too early for CeeCee to be home—but then she said she would . . .

"Mom!"

My heart shot to my throat. CeeCee was back. And exactly when she said she'd be. Was she sick? There'd been a really vicious bug going around . . .

"In here, sweetie."

CeeCee poked her head through the office doorway. "Hey."

"Hey, yourself. Are you sick?"

"Never felt better—why?"

I glanced at the wall clock. "Forget something?"

"Nope." She peeled out of her coat and tossed it over the high-backed chair. "What are you doing in here?"

"Just finished penciling in the last of the revisions."

"Good."

I smiled. "I think God has used me."

"Ah, Mom—you know God always uses your work to further His kingdom. When are you going to finally believe that?"

"Now," I said. "Right now—until I have a relapse, which will be tomorrow and I'll have to start working on the problem again. But I guess what's important is that I will work on it—and keep working on it until I get it right or the Lord comes to take me home."

"So? What's the big news? Are you going to fly up and be wined and courted by Birkhead?"

"Nope." I shook my head. "Someone's actually offering to support my work and I said no. I'm staying with Bethlehem."

"Aw, Mom. I'm sorry."

"Sorry?" I laughed. "It was my choice." Just being able to say that took the sting out of my conscience.

"But why? They're offering what you've fought so hard to get for the last few years."

"Yes, they are, and I am flattered beyond words. But I've turned my career over to God. When it's time to move, He'll let me know. Right now it isn't right. I'm going to hang on and see how wild the ride gets."

CeeCee leaned over and gave me a hug. "You're precious, you know that?"

I didn't. Of all the things I'd been called, *precious* was not one of them. But I'd take the compliment. "Want a bowl of soup before you go to the kennel? Stella made a pot of steak soup this morning before she left the house."

"Nope, have too much work to do. I'll grab some cheese and crackers later." She sat down in front of the computer and dramatically flexed all ten fingers. "I have to get the rest of those revisions typed in tonight."

"You're actually going to finish the revisions tonight?" I knew I sounded as shocked as if she'd proclaimed that she was about to turn water into wine.

"Not leaving this chair unless nature makes me." She turned

to look at me, eyes shining with regret. "Sorry I flaked out on you, Mom. I'll make it up to you."

"What about Rick?" I was still reeling from the sudden change.

"Rick who?" She flipped on the monitor.

I took the statement to be a declaration: My daughter had finally come to her senses. *Dear God! Only You could have accomplished this transformation. Thank You. Thank You for answered prayer.*

"I'm sorry, hon." I was the one who hugged her this time, welling emotion painfully tightening my throat.

She nodded wordlessly. I knew the breakup hurt; CeeCee was the kind who fell hard and didn't get up easily.

I tightened my hold on my daughter. I was so proud of this young woman. Loved her so very much. "You know, I think being off a few weeks has given me time to rethink my priorities."

CeeCee's nimble fingers were already flying over the keys. The revisions would be entered and forgotten about by the end of the day.

"What about?"

"About everything. One of the best things to come out of my surgery and injury is that I'm back in my morning devotions and loving it." Stretching my back, I smiled. "I can't tell you how liberating it feels to know that I'm not in charge of anything."

Eyes on the monitor, CeeCee grinned. "You mean you've finally decided to rely on the Lord, and not yourself, for help. Lift up your eyes to the hills from where your help cometh."

I grinned, realizing she'd just slaughtered Scripture. "Took me long enough to reach the conclusion, huh." When you were self-sufficient at heart, lessons sometimes came hard.

"Well, at least you've reached your goal. I'm afraid I'm still staggering around, looking to everyone but God for deliverance," CeeCee stated.

"That's not true." I gently massaged the tight tendons in her shoulders. She'd changed so much in the brief time she'd been home. She was going to be all right. Someday she'd meet Mr. Right, they'd marry and have darling rug rats, and all would be right with my world. "You've taught me a lot about faith."

CeeCee laughed. "I'm afraid I belong to the Church of Fickle Fools. I pick the wrong man every time."

"Then I guess we'll have to be more diligent about asking God to send the right man next time."

CeeCee nodded and turned a manuscript page. "Call me an optimistic fool, but I believe he is out there, Mom."

"Of course he is, dear." I thought of Herb and our wonderful years together. And Arnold—how that tenuous relationship might be different if only Stella would . . . and then there was Sherm. What a wonderful man . . .

I shook the thoughts away.

"Think I'll fix a bowl of that soup. Sure you won't join me?"

CeeCee mutely shook her head as the computer keys clicked rhythmically. "Got work to do."

The office door shut. CeeCee's fingers paused. She hurt. She hurt inside. Sitting back in the chair, she wrapped her arms around her stomach. She'd been so certain Rick was the one. . . .

But then she'd thought the same about Jake.

Was she judging Rick unfairly? No man or woman was perfect; they all had faults. But infidelity—even without the bonds of marriage was unacceptable. She couldn't go through life always wondering where her husband was and who he was with.

Closing her eyes, she bit her lip, reinforcing her decision. Rick was no good for her. She wanted more—she *deserved* more—and if it took a lifetime for God to send her the right man, she was willing to wait. No matter how many mistakes she made.

She sat in the silence for long moments, blinking cursor before her. She needed to talk to someone—someone on impartial ground. Mom would listen—so would Iva, but they would be on her side. She needed an unbiased ear. Reaching for the phone book, she turned to the *H*s and ran her finger down the long column. Hendricks, Gary.

She picked up the phone and punched in the number. It rang

six times and she braced herself. He wasn't home. Of course he wouldn't be home; he'd be with Karen.

With the receiver halfway between her ear and the phone cradle, she heard a male voice answer. She whipped the headset back to her ear. "Gary?"

"Yeah?" He sounded out of breath. "Who's this?"

"CeeCee. CeeCee Tamaris."

"Hey!" Caution turned to friendliness. "CeeCee Tamaris. What's the occasion?"

"Occasion?"

"My postman—postlady—calling me personally. Did my mail blow up in your face?"

CeeCee laughed. "Maybe I'm afraid to go near your house. There's always a pop bomb about to go off."

"Aren't those a scream!"

That they were. She'd heard neighbors screaming from as far away as three blocks when the dry ice swelled a sixty-four-ounce plastic bottle and detonated.

"I thought maybe you weren't home—I was about to hang up."

"I was in the garage gluing a model airplane together. Suppose I should take a cordless out there with me when I work."

Suddenly CeeCee felt tongue-tied and flustered. What did she say now? And why did she pick this particular man's shoulder to cry on?

"Karen working tonight?"

"Yeah, she closes on Tuesdays. What's up? Is it time for church raffle tickets again?"

"No—just thought I'd call." A pregnant pause followed. "You know—thank you again for the snow tires. They're really nice."

"Glad I could help."

CeeCee cleared her throat.

"Weatherman's calling for more snow over the weekend," he offered.

"Yes—that's what I heard. Been a bad winter."

"Yes—real bad."

Silence stretched. She scratched the back of her head with the tip of a ballpoint pen. "You and Karen getting along okay?"

"Sure—fine." His tone turned guarded. "Why? Did someone say something—"

"No—no," she denied. "I was just wondering. You two make a great couple."

"Well, thanks. You and Rick do too."

She sighed, thanking God for the opening. "Rick and I broke up tonight."

Concern entered his voice now. "No kidding. I'm sorry—maybe tomorrow you'll both have a chance to reconsider—"

"No—no. It's permanent."

After a bit he said, "Well, I always thought you were too good for him."

"Really?" CeeCee sat up straighter. "Did everyone in town but me know the kind of guy Rick is?"

"No. I'm good with first impressions. They usually prove to be right."

CeeCee closed her eyes, gripping the receiver. "I've been such a blind fool."

The torrent broke. Words, bitterness, disappointment rolled out of her mouth like hot lava. She couldn't dam the deluge.

Gary listened attentively. When she'd told her side—and that's all she'd really wanted, to tell her side and be heard—he said quietly, "There's an old saying: 'If you love it, set it free. If it loves you, it will come back.'"

"If it doesn't, hunt it down and kill it," she finished, blowing her nose on a soggy tissue.

"Well, I don't think that applies—"

For the briefest of moments, hope returned to CeeCee. "Do you believe that? Is it possible for a man to change—I mean really change?"

"It's possible." The unlikely assumption "but not probable" hung heavy between them. "At least now you know," Gary said.

At least now I know, she thought, and for some crazy reason the knowledge made her feel better.

They talked for over an hour. When CeeCee looked up and saw the time and the blinking cursor, she freaked. "I have to go."

"Okay. It was great talking to you."

"Thanks—it has been nice. And Gary?"

"Yes?"

"Thanks," she said again, because she couldn't think of anything but gratitude at the moment.

"Anytime. Always happy to talk to you."

She leaned over the desk, reluctant to hang up yet empty of anything more to say.

"Hey, CeeCee?"

She lifted the phone back to her ear. "Yes?"

"Don't be so hard on yourself. I'd hate to think how many times I've thought 'this is the one' and it wasn't."

"Thanks, Gary." She felt almost guilty about talking to him—about such a personal matter. Karen might object. . . .

"You've helped me—a lot."

When she hung up, she sat, chin propped in hand, staring at the cursor, wondering when Gary Hendricks had ceased being a certifiable dufus and turned into a kind, compassionate human being.

* * *

Stella slapped a six-pack down on Hargus's desk. "Drink up, sonny boy. Make that three for me—naught for you."

Hargus eyed the bottles of Chocolate Cow dispassionately. "Wondered how long it would take you to gloat."

"Not long." Stella pulled out the chair and sat down. "Come on—I'm in such a good mood I'll even drink one of those revolting things with you."

Hargus reached for a bottle and uncapped the lid. Handing her the drink, he glowered. "You didn't solve anything. If it wasn't for Thurvis breaking the smoking ban you'd never have figured out the Peeping Toms were Mortimer and Snerd."

"Maybe." Stella took a swig, held the bottle up for closer inspection, and took another swig. "Not bad."

"Not bad?" Hargus tipped his bottle and swallowed. Wiping his mouth, he smiled. "Put hair on your chest!"

"I don't want hair on my chest, but it's good to see you in better spirits." Stella bent forward. "Thought you were going to be a spoilsport—you know. That's three for three."

"Pure luck." He tipped the bottle again. "I knew it was something like dogs all along—that's why I didn't get overly upset."

"Oh, bull."

"Yes, bull," he argued.

The two sat in silence, swigging Chocolate Cow.

"Next time," Hargus said, "we'll see who comes out on top."

"May not be a next time." Stella finished and set the bottle on the desk. "I'm eighty-seven, you know. Can't live forever."

"Read of a woman over in Shiloh who just celebrated her one-hundred-and-first birthday this week."

"Well, that won't be me. I can practically hear the chariot coming."

Hargus sneered. "You'll be around to haunt me until I'm cold in my grave."

She grinned. "Maybe—maybe not."

"You keep driving that Cadillac and you're not going to live another month."

"I'm a good driver."

"You're an accident waiting to happen."

Stella leaned back, contentment washing over her. God had given her eighty-seven good years; lot of folks didn't get half as much. "You know, Hargus, our cases keep me going. And though Maude doesn't say much, I think her writing improves when we're working a case, so I guess, in a way, I do still have some purpose here on earth."

Hargus nodded. "You got purpose or you wouldn't still be here. You'd be up there in heaven, driving St. Peter nuts."

Stella beamed. "That's the nicest thing you've ever said to me, Hargus."

Red crept into his babyish features. "You've been good help to Maude."

"I've tried to be—I've read some of her new material—even typed in a few changes because CeeCee's been so tied up with that Rick louse."

"You shouldn't call him a louse."

"That's what he is."

"I know that's what he is, but you just shouldn't openly call a man a louse. CeeCee might end up marrying the guy."

Stella scoffed. "Never. She's got more brains than to marry a man like Rick Materi."

Twilight lengthened. Muted rays filtered through the dirty office window. Stella watched the fading winter light and hoped—no, she silently prayed that the good Lord would grant her a few more years. Not that she wasn't looking forward to heaven; she just wasn't ready to board the bus yet.

She reached into her coat pocket and took out a piece of paper. "You ever get any of those 'dear friend' e-mail things?"

"Yeah," Hargus said. "Nuisance, but I pass on a few things. How about you?"

"Get them all the time. You know how those things are—you never know where they originate from, but I think the one I got this morning pretty well sums up my feelings about my life."

"What's that?"

"Well it starts out 'Dear Stella'—though I don't know the person who wrote it. I'm just supposed to pass it on. Anyway, here's what it says:

"Dear Stella,

"I'm reading more and dusting less. Today I'm sitting in the yard and admiring the view without fussing about the weeds in the garden. I'm spending more time with my family and friends and less time working. Whenever possible, life should be a pattern of experiences to savor, not to endure. I'm trying to recognize these moments now and cherish them.

"I'm not "saving" anything; we use our good china and crystal for every special event such as losing a pound, getting the sink unstopped, or the first amaryllis blossom. I wear my good blazer to the market. My theory is that if I look prosperous, I can shell out $28.49 for one small bag of groceries. I'm not saving my good perfume for special parties, but wearing it for clerks in the hardware store and tellers at the bank.

"Words like someday and one of these days are losing their grip on my vocabulary. If it's worth seeing or hearing or doing, I want to see and hear and do it now.

"I'm not sure what others would've done had they known they wouldn't be here for the tomorrow that we all take for granted. I think they would have called family members and a few close friends. They might have called a few former friends to apologize and mend fences for past squabbles. I like to think they would have gone out for a Chinese dinner or for whatever their favorite food was. I'm guessing; I'll never know.

"It's those little things left undone that would make me angry if I knew my hours were limited. Angry because I hadn't written certain letters that I intended to write one of these days. Angry and sorry that I didn't tell my husband and parents often enough how much I love them. I'm trying very hard not to put off, hold back, or save anything that would add laughter and luster to our lives. And every morning when I open my eyes, I tell myself that it is special. Every day, every minute, every breath truly are gifts from God.

"Life may not be the party we hoped for, but while we are here we might as well dance."

Stella refolded the paper and sighed. Life was good here in Morning Shade. Not exciting like New York City; why she was tickled pink to encounter *any* mystery in this one-horse town, even if the case turned out to be dogs causing the ruckus. But life was really good.

Maude was feeling better both spiritually and physically. CeeCee was about to come to her senses and leave Materi to his dogs. Stella felt it in her bones, and her bones rarely lied to her.

Yep. Couldn't beat Morning Shade with a stick.

Peaceful. Folks with warts who chose to love each other anyway. That's living victoriously through Christ. That's what it's all about.

Stella would live her last days out right here and praise the Lord with every breath for loyal friends and first-rate neighbors. Even Hargus.

And for a woman eighty-seven years young, that wasn't a bad goal.

Lori Copeland has published more than eighty novels and has won numerous awards for her books, most recently the Career Achievement Award from *Romantic Times* magazine. Her recent novel *Stranded in Paradise* marks her debut as a Women of Faith fiction author. Publishing with HeartQuest allows her the freedom to write stories that express her love of God and her personal convictions.

Lori lives with her husband, Lance, in Springfield, Missouri. She has three incredibly handsome grown sons, three absolutely gorgeous daughters-in-law, and five exceptionally bright grandchildren—but then, she freely admits to being partial when it comes to her family. Lori enjoys reading biographies, attending book discussion groups, participating in morning water-aerobic exercises at the local YMCA. She loves to travel and is always thrilled to meet her readers.

When asked what one thing Lori would like others to know about her, she readily says, "I'm not perfect—just forgiven by the grace of God." Christianity to Lori means peace, joy, and the knowledge that she has a friend, a Savior, who never leaves her side. Through her books, she hopes to share this wondrous assurance with others.

Lori welcomes letters written to her in care of Tyndale House Author Relations, P.O. Box 80, Wheaton, IL 60189-0080.

Turn the page for a preview of the first book in Lori Copeland's exciting new series,

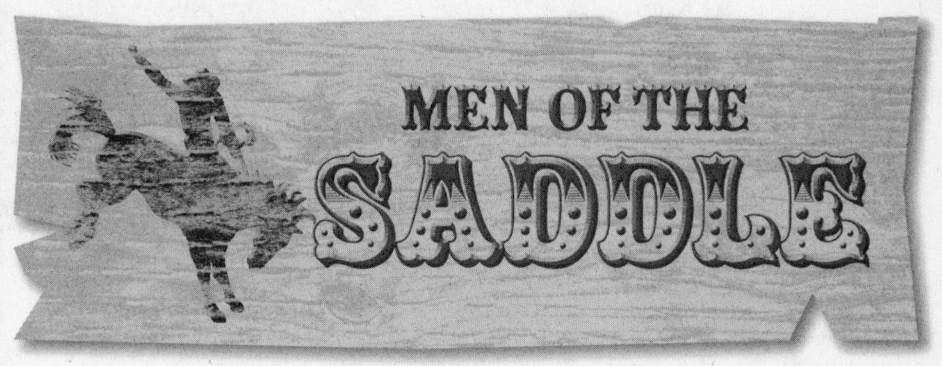

Available winter 2004 from Tyndale House Publishers

ISBN 0-8423-6930-9

MEN OF THE SADDLE

BOOK ONE

July 1865

WYNNE ELLIOTT coughed and daintily lifted a handkerchief to her nose as clouds of choking dust swept through the open stagecoach window. She flashed a weak smile at the gentlemen who sat across from her for what seemed like the hundredth time and fervently wished the tiresome trip were over. She'd never dreamed it would take so long to travel from Georgia to Missouri.

Turning back to the scenery, she compared the harsh countryside to her own beloved Georgia. July, a time when flowers were blooming, when breezes were moist and balmy, and moss draped through the trees like a bride's spidery veil.

Here the ground was hard, the grass dry from lack of moisture. While there was little evidence of the death and destruction that her dear South had endured, there were still visible scars. Burned homesteads. Barren fields. The war had taken its toll here too, but not with the terrible devastation she had witnessed farther south.

The farther the coach traveled the more rugged the contour of the land became. Ozark mountain country, she'd been told, was a place where people either survived or didn't, and given the landscape, she could well imagine why.

Low mountains with virtually untouched forests dotted the landscape, and the road they traveled twisted and snaked through gaps and valleys with endless walls of shale and limestone. On at least two occasions the coach had stopped, and the driver and guard had removed fallen rocks from the way. Wynne had taken to watching the hillsides for rolling boulders, although, if she saw any moving in their direction, it would already be too late to avoid impact.

She feared that at any turn in the road a band of outlaws would gallop from behind those massive boulders to waylay the coach. During the last rest stop, she'd heard mention of the name Alf Bolin and his men, an unsavory faction that waylaid unsuspecting travelers. And there was talk about the Baldknobbers—Ozark vigilantes meting out their own bloody brand of justice. The men's casual conversation had given Wynne the willies.

It wasn't the first time she'd heard such shocking tales. Stage hands at the way stations delighted in relating such stories to shock and distress lady passengers.

But she had to admit nothing she had been told had prepared her for Missouri's rugged beauty. And the land was beautiful. Great oaks and maples. By the trees' size alone she guessed them to be hundreds of years old. Colonies of ferns spread a lacy carpet across the forest floor. Branches as big around as her waist reached out to form a canopy over the trail. Sturdy tree trunks sank deep roots into soil, which was alternatively black loam and rich red clay, but so stony that no smaller plants could hope to survive.

Still, natives of the area appeared to eke out an adequate living, and apparently in Springfield, a regular metropolis she'd heard, businesses were thriving. Just yesterday she'd overheard that the railroad and more stores and hotels would locate there soon. If this were true, then Missouri would come out of the great conflict in better shape than her own beloved Georgia.

Wynne sighed as the stagecoach tossed its passengers about. How much farther to River Run? Traveling by coach had not been easy—the jostling about, the dust, and the insufferable heat. How she longed for a bath, a long, hot bath, with scented soap and shampoo. She sighed longingly. Revenge could indeed be tedious at times.

She absently rubbed the smooth, odd-colored stone she'd carried for over a year. He had given the token to her. Strange that she hadn't rid herself of this last painful reminder of him. She didn't need anything to remind her of Cass Claxton. His image was burned into her mind.

That *man.*

The worthless trinket worn smooth by the continual wash of river water had become a worry stone. Her thumb fitted perfectly in the tiny hollow, which looked as though it could have been formed for such a purpose—but then Wynne knew worrying was not of God. Nor was revenge, for that matter. She couldn't expect the Almighty to look with approval on the purpose of her journey, but her blood ran too hot, her anger too deep to forgive and forget.

Her fingers endlessly smoothed the rock in silent litany: *I'll get him . . . I'll get him if it's the last thing I do . . . I'll get that man. . . .*

The journey to Missouri had been long and tiresome, and it

wasn't over yet. She tried to bolster her wilting spirits by reminding herself that it wouldn't be much longer. As soon as she caught that deceiver . . . she would go home. Home to baths and warm food, comfortable beds and people who loved her. Home to Moss Oak, the plantation where she had been born and raised. The only home she'd ever known.

Wynne wiped ineffectually at the small trickle of perspiration that escaped from beneath her hairline, and then adjusted her hat. It was hard to stay presentable, but she wanted to look her best. When she finally ran Cass to the ground, she wanted him to see what he had walked away from.

Her attention settled on the flamboyant young woman dressed in red sitting next to her. Now here was a fascinating example of womanhood. One that Wynne had never expected to find in her circle of acquaintances.

Miss Penelope Pettibone was on her way to a new job at Hattie's Place. According to Penelope, Hattie's Place was a drinking establishment where a man could go for a hand of cards, and "other gentlemanly pursuits." At the mention of "other gentlemanly pursuits," Wynne's eyes had widened knowingly, and she had felt her cheeks burn. She had never met one of . . . "those" women before, and she found she had a certain averse fascination with Miss Pettibone.

Penelope smiled and winked at the man sitting opposite them, and Wynne fanned herself quickly and turned back to the Missouri countryside. A lady never winked, or if she did, she should have something in her eye.

Only that scoundrel, that disgraceful, deplorable, unforgivable Cass Claxton, occupied her thoughts now. The mere thought of that rogue left her breathless with anger. Not only had he left her standing at the altar in complete disgrace, but he'd also managed to walk away with every penny she had except the small pittance she kept in a tin box under her mattress for extreme emergencies.

True, she'd been foolish to fall in love with a man she knew so little about, and even more imprudent to offer financial assistance to a business venture he was about to embark upon, but she had always been one to put her whole heart into everything—especially in matters of love. Of course, she'd not had all that much experience with matters of love, but after studying at Miss Marelda Fielding's Finishing School for Young Ladies, Wynne considered herself a sophisticated woman of the world. That's why it hurt so much that she had let Cass Claxton take advantage of her.

If it hadn't been for the war and her suspicion that Cass had enlisted the day they were meant to marry, she would have tracked him down like a rabid skunk and put a hunk of lead straight through his thieving heart for sullying her trust—not to mention her character. But surely it would have been considered treason to shoot a Confederate soldier, a defender of the homeland, no matter how much he had it coming. However, the fighting had ended and now she felt free to wreak her vengeance on the lout who had taken advantage of her in such a shameful way.

Her temper still boiled when she thought how gullible she'd been. Well, she was no longer gullible, and the war was over. Quite by chance she'd been told by a close acquaintance of Cass's that he had indeed enlisted and survived and had been seen in Kansas City a few weeks ago. The friend had said Cass was en route to his home in River Run and should arrive any day now. She intended to be there to meet him.

Wynne clenched her fan in her hand; her eyes narrowed pensively. It had been a long time coming, but Mr. Cass Claxton would soon pay for his sins. She smiled in satisfaction. Very soon Cass would rue the day he'd ever heard of Wynne Elliott.

BOOKS BY BEST-SELLING AUTHOR LORI COPELAND

Roses Will Bloom Again . . . . ISBN 0-8423-1936-0

Brides of the West Series

- *Faith* . . . . ISBN 0-8423-0267-0
- *June* . . . . ISBN 0-8423-0268-9
- *Hope* . . . . ISBN 0-8423-0269-7
- *Glory* . . . . ISBN 0-8423-3749-0
- *Ruth* . . . . ISBN 0-8423-1937-9
- *Patience* . . . . ISBN 0-8423-1938-7

TYNDALE FICTION

Child of Grace . . . . ISBN 0-8423-4260-5
Christmas Vows: $5.00 Extra . . . . ISBN 0-8423-5326-7

Morning Shade Mystery Series

- *A Case of Bad Taste* . . . . ISBN 0-8423-7115-X
- *A Case of Crooked Letters* . . . . ISBN 0-8423-7116-8
- *A Case of Nosy Neighbors* . . . . ISBN 0-8423-7117-6